SHATTERED MEMORIES

By:

Susan Harris

CLEAN TEEN PUBLISHING

SHATTERED MEMORIES

Cover Design by: Marya Heiman
Typography by: Courtney Nuckels

ISBN: 978-1-63422-060-6

For more information about our content disclosure, please utilize the QR code above with your smart phone or visit us at

www.cleanteenpublishing.com.

Michelle,
"Friendship isn't a big thing—it's a million little things"
Thank you for all the little things.

> "What a shame we all became such fragile broken things."
> (PARAMORE: LET THE FLAMES BEGIN)

ONCE I HEARD A SAYING... THAT MEMORIES ARE WHAT YOU NO longer want to remember. I can't help but wonder if that happened to me. Even though I can speak, write, and recall lyrics to songs, I don't know some things about my past. At one time I was training to be a retrieval marshal. Reciting the now redundant Bunreacht na hÉireann is easy and every word in the new United Constitution comes to me without effort. But for all the silly things I remember, other memories of the past year elude me.

They say that I did terrible things and would never wash their blood from my hands. I was labelled a murderer and sentenced to death. My psychologist holds out hope that I will remember... that my mind has blocked out those recollections for self-preservation. They are memories that may prove me innocent or simply tighten the noose around my neck.

But time is running out for me. In only two and a half months, I will turn eighteen, the legal age for execution. According to the coalition, whether I remember or not, the date is set. If you had less than six months to live, what would you do?

Me? I'm stuck... will never see the outside of the prison walls again. I have been found guilty of murdering my family and am going to pay for that crime.

My name is Alana McCarthy and I'm seventeen years old.

> "I remember it now; it takes me back to when it all
> first started."
> (KODALINE: HIGH HOPES)

IRISH HISTORY HAS ALWAYS BEEN STEEPED IN THE BLOODSHED of our ancestors and our constant struggle for complete independence. We believed that when Ireland had been declared a Republic that it had finally happened. But we were wrong. Foolish decisions by a delusional government paved the way for a future where Ireland ceased to exist and our heritage merely became chapters in a history book.

In 2023, after years of unemployment, corruption in our banking systems, and complete unrest amongst the Irish people, the government claimed that the country had turned a corner. Ireland had begun to work its way out of economic crisis. But it was all a lie, a false hope so the government could hide the true extent of their debt.

Behind closed doors, Ireland had begun to haemorrhage money. Repayments of our national debt to the European Union were not being paid in full, and a faction of the government began skimming a percentage off the top. The promise of more jobs, less emigration, and better living conditions for all, not just the entitled, fell flat. The combination culminated in a devastating revelation that began Ireland's complete destruction.

When it was revealed, in 2025, that The European Central Bank wanted Ireland to pay back its debt immediately, Ireland was unable to do so and suggestions started to pour in about how to ensure the debt would not cripple the global economy. In an effort to save as much money as possible, the government put a cap on national expenditure. Legislators passed a motion eliminating free public schools. Social welfare benefits for the unemployed were scrapped, as were medical cards, old age pensions, and children's allowance. Unless citizens could afford thousands for schooling, they simply did not attend.

Our health service had always been lacklustre, but cuts to try to keep the country afloat resulted in hospital closures, along with decline in those who could afford to attend college to study medicine. Unlicensed doctors and clinics began popping up, leading to more deaths and infection.

The government passed an Emergency Powers Act, giving power to the Taoiseach to make choices in the name of maintaining Ireland as a country. During his time in charge, the Taoiseach introduced water taxes and increased tax brackets. He revoked the traditional allotment per child and levied a new tax for couples who had more than two children... to stabilize population numbers.

With the increasing lack of educational growth, investors withdrew hundreds of companies from the country, abandoning the fast-sinking ship. Even though the rest of the country was struggling, it seemed as if the government still lived beyond the country's means.

After years of unrest, rioting, and degradation of a once vibrant and hardworking society, Ireland got the unification it dreamed of... but not in any way that was ever wanted. Political parties came together as one with secret meetings and planning under clandestine circumstances. Supporting a political party became outlawed and citizens were urged to follow a newly formed, united government.

The policing system disintegrated. Corruption within the Garda Shíocána and the government's secret 'hit squad' sought out those who wished to speak out against the ruling government. Many former political ministers were murdered during darkened nights, and any citizen found possessing anti-government propaganda would meet an untimely death. Despite all that, the Irish people held strong and defiant against a government that refused to look after its own people causing a siege that united the Republic and its northern counterparts.

When thousands of Irish people marched on the government buildings in Dublin in 2030, the so-called men and women in power had nowhere to run. Each member of the current seats of government was slain. Public hangings showed a barbaric side to a now-ruined country. The massacre known forevermore as Baile Átha Cliath Lá an Bháis, or The Dublin Day of Death, left more problems in its wake. Ireland had no direction, no purpose, no clear person or group in charge. The Emergency Powers Act had given the government all the authority it needed to turn Ireland over to the US in order to maintain global financial security.

Ireland was not the only country to change during that time, but it was the one most likely to be influenced by outsiders. The United States grew in power, amassing large numbers of countries to control. Germany and France signed a treaty with the US, promising their backing of any vote for a reduction in France's national debt. Germany would maintain representatives from the Bundestag in place to help sustain the currency, no matter what. Turkey backed the newly established power of Russia, finally gaining acceptance into an EU that would change forever. Once that situation was in place, Russia claimed it was willing to withdraw all energy resources from those who dared to compete against them. The US had no choice but to agree to Russia's terms, leading to a volatile partnership.

All of the former foes of the US were defeated, so by 2032, the world at large was run by China, Russia, and the US. A new treaty was signed, forging a new parliament and a coalition to enforce the law. The document ensured the world turned in their favour and that all military control was now in the hands of the powerful alliance.

Public figures, royal families, and dignitaries were assassinated using a special covert operations branch of the new United Parliament.

One aspect of life in the new world did not suffer... technology. Teams of experts, sanctioned by the United Parliament, found new ways to grow the high tech industry, and ways to control those who dared to defy the new Parliament were conceived.

Currency had long since been forgotten when the Parliament introduced a single exchange into circulation. The United Dollar became the global currency and was distributed throughout the world, increasing financial control of the Big Three.

No matter what, some parts of society could not be changed. Crime became rampant across the globe for many obvious reasons: hunger, shortage of medicine, gang activity, lack of education, boredom, and a general desire to fight back against a biased, controlling, power hungry parliament.

The United Parliament met on a historic day in 2036, and an ambitious member of the American counsel presented the leaders with a solution to the issues. He suggested they use the vastness of the Irish country and build a prison which would reach from the top of Derry down to the tips of Cork and Kerry.

The debt Ireland owed had not been repaid, and in a country full to the brim with anger and hostility, a prison state would be used to pay off Ireland's debt. It seemed like a good idea. The need for workers to build and maintain the prison would bring jobs and prosperity to the country. Most of the population seemed appeased.

Ireland was essentially wiped from the world map and renamed as a prison island. A new International Court of Justice was slated to review every crime committed, and a new proclamation of punishment would be established. Sectors of the technology and science communities that had grown in secret were slated to police the prisons.

This new prison was designed to incarcerate murderers, rapists, terrorists, and minor offenders. A section for underage criminals was planned and the new International Court of Justice deemed it necessary to reintroduce the death penalty in order to preserve the world's stability. Any offender over the legal age of eighteen was subject to execution.

Once the proposal was passed by a unanimous vote, the Grand Masters of Justice were given approval to begin construction on the prison. The United Parliament increased jobs in Ireland, using the local Irish people to create their new, state of the art facility. Recruitment officers also held enlistment days much like the ones used when emigration had been rampant. These job fairs promised careers and education in exchange for serving the new government. Those who signed on to became marshals, technicians, wardens, and other staff positions in the new prison, were offered housing, wages, and food. Those who declined offers to work vanished. Their disappearances were officially listed as escapes to the Free Islands of Australia and New Zealand, where they refused to conform to The United Parliament rules.

In 2038, the prison opened to much grandeur and posturing. Ceremonies were performed by the man whose concept changed the face of justice in the world, Grand Master of Justice, William Johnson. The first execution of a prisoner occurred mere hours later. The elderly man had helped his wife die before her cancer got any worse. Under new law, juries didn't exist. Grand Masters and Masters of Justice handed down their own version of fairness. Prisoners from all over the world started arriving by ships and planes, lowering crime rates throughout the world.

And so, future generations of the Emerald Isle, in villages where the sole purpose was to house those who worked and maintained the prisons and training facility, did not know of its rich heritage. They were born members of the United Parliament. Should they step out of line, they would die as prisoners of the Department of Corrections. Life on the once lovely island had become so horrific that some began calling it, in a language now banned, Oileán Ifreann or Hell Island.

This future, where science and technology were worth more than gold or currency, was more corrupt and power hungry than any past in our history books. Those reference materials had long been destroyed… another indication that Ireland was no more… and politics was very much alive.

ALANA

"My secrets are burning a hole through my heart and my bones catch a fever."
(Bring me the Horizon: Sleepwalking)

I READ DETAILED ACCOUNTS OF A PRISONER ONCE SAYING that, even after he was released, the sound that haunted him throughout the years was the harsh bang of the metal lock sliding into place, keys clanging together as the cell door locked for the night, sealing him inside with the darkness. He claimed that having time to dwell on his crimes nearly drove him mad.

Prison life in my time was very different, so I can only imagine.

You see, during recent days, technology did wonders for the world and especially this prison. The state of the art facility no longer required metal doors, keys or a vast amount of prison guards to patrol. Our cell doors were electronic sliding ones that closed by a key panel outside. Once our inmate number was keyed in, the guards chose to open or close it, or in case of emergency, the control room had the option to open all cell doors at once.

Privacy remained non-existent. Doors were actually see-through, shatterproof glass panels. If someone were looking for privacy, this wasn't where they'd want to be. In the section of the jail where I was housed, that wing contained about 500 cells, with most having at least two occupants. Prisoners perceived as dangerous or high risk didn't share a space. *Guess who has her own room?*

My cell consisted of a hard, metal bed with a thin mattress and an even thinner pillow. It wasn't as if I spent much time asleep because most nights I ended up sitting on the cold floor, knees hugged to my chest, resting my head on my knees, eyes closed. During that time, I hoped and wished that each night would be the one when my memory returned. Plain beige painted walls surrounded me; the only inconsistency from the blandness of the room was the entrance to the toilet. It too had a sliding door that opened when a buzzer was pressed whenever I needed it. That area, also beige, had only a toilet and sink. You might think there would be some privacy there, but if the red blinking light in the corner of the room was any indication, I think not.

Prisoners weren't divided up by gender either, except with cell sharing. Prison officials never worried that we might couple up and sneak off and do what teenagers do because the behaviour chip embedded in our shoulders kept us under control. The chip, when activated, sent a series of electrical currents throughout the inmate's body, causing immense pain. Eventually, the brain would shut down, rendering the victim unconscious. *I am fortunate not to have first-hand experience of the effects but have seen it used on others.*

You might have wondered how a prisoner would know so much about the inner workings of the prison. Firstly, at one time my dad was actually the warden of this unit, the Underage Department of Corrections Unit or UDCU. Well, that was before I supposedly killed him. Also, I was training to be a retrieval officer, someone who goes to different countries and takes prisoners into custody and transports them back to Hell Island. *I know it's not the official name, but if the shoe fits, I suppose it works.*

How can I talk so flippantly about my father's murder? I have no memories of the last year. I remembered going off to the training facility north of the country—and then nothing—until I was arrested, covered in blood. They said I had slaughtered my entire family, my mother, my father, and my baby sister, all dead by my hands.

So where that man dreaded the nights locked in a claustrophobic cell, I welcome it. Left alone in the darkness with nothing but the faint gleam of moonlight that slips in through the electricity fuelled windows, I have time and space to try and force myself to remember.

It's been almost five months since I was arrested and sentenced to death for my crimes. The United Parliament states that if there is irrefutable evidence to prove me guilty, then a trial can be forgone and a sentence handed down.

Here I sit, until I turn eighteen in two months.

A few in here think I've faked the memory loss, in order to stave off an execution, but believe me… I wish I could remember. If I don't, then I will go to my grave believing that for some unknown reason I took my father's gun, shot him between the eyes and then turned to my mother and shot her in the back of the head as she tried to run away.

For me, the worst is the accusation that I dragged my baby sister, Sophia, from her bed and while she tried to scramble away from me, I wrapped my arms around her, placed the gun to her chest and shot her. Then I supposedly brought her downstairs and turned the gun on myself. Before I had a chance to pull the trigger, the door burst open and the United Parliament Army stopped me. All the details lined up to paint a horrific picture of my unthinkable crimes. But why would I kill everyone I dearly loved? The pain in my chest, when I think about it is sometimes so bad that I wish the army had been a few seconds late so I could have done them a favour and killed myself.

By now, I'm resigned to the fact that unless I have a miraculous memory recall, once I turn eighteen, that wonderful execution chair and I have a date.

Things haven't run smoothly around this place since I got here. Inmates were well aware that when I arrived, I was barely shy of becoming a retrieval officer. They turned their hatred for the warden and her officers on me. Guards assigned me a single room when my cellmate tried to strangle me during the night, and I got my first glimpse of how the behaviour chip works. One second my cellmate had me locked in a headlock, and I could not breathe. Instantly, she was writhing in agony, a bloodcurdling scream ringing in my ears and her body flailing around—then nothing—she just lay there. One of the guards lifted her into his arms, walked out and locked me in. I've been on my own ever since.

Depending on your crime, UPDC has specific schedules and activities lined up for inmates. If prisoners are to be reintegrated back into the world as functioning members of society, they are provided all the tools needed to do so. Some courses of study offered range from learning construction and woodwork to cooking, first aid and more. *Since I'm going to die in two months, I guess I just don't qualify to learn any of those things.*

Growing up, I watched my father leave for work every day and travel the short distance from our little village on the outskirts of the Underage Unit. I was privileged enough to have had a great education and knew from early on that I would follow in his footsteps and become a serving member of the UPDC. Always the observant child, I absorbed information from an early age and was eager to please. When I turned sixteen, they gave me the entrance test to see where I would fit in the program. I was delighted to be assigned to the Retrieval Team.

Being a member of that elite team meant that I got to travel the world on behalf of the Grand Masters of Justice and bring criminals back to the Island. I learned all about weapons, retrieval techniques, and how to disarm or subdue a reluctant prisoner. One of the officers told me that I had finished top of my class at the academy, a full year ahead of schedule. I had a promising future ahead of me… well, I used to. *It's strange that I remember all of those early events but nothing that happened during the last year.*

I forced my eyes to open as the cell door slid with a familiar whirl as the guard barely paused to check on me before he toddled off to the next cell. Pushing away from the wall, I stood and stretched out my tired limbs while slipping bare feet into plain black shoes and pulling the round neck sweater over my head. Black attire from head to toe was standard for death row prisoners. Inmates who wore red were dangerous offenders, in for rape, assault, and mental health issues. Those wearing blue were light offenders, in for robbery and weapons charges. Green jumpsuits indicated drug offences, either for distribution or using.

Wrapping my arms around myself, I stepped out of the cell and watched from the landing. From the outside of the cell, the mess hall was visible below where we all converged for meal times. Since I arrived at the prison a few months ago, I liked to watch as a sea of green, red, orange, and the occasional black outfits merged on the stairs. Five levels, each containing one hundred cells made for an array of colours blended as one unique painting of the hopeless.

Authorities weren't afraid to blend every type of offender together in the general population because of their ability to control inmates with the electronic chips. My stomach rumbled slightly so I shuffled along the floor and became one with the crowd. Normally, I tended to keep to myself around that area for obvious reasons, but I always sensed eyes watching me, wondering, and asking the same old questions: *"How could that little girl have done something so horrific? She's so small;—could she have ever become an officer? I bet I could take her. She barely looks old enough to be out of school, no less training camp."*

It was my goal, and I worked damn hard to prove that my five-foot height and slight build would not deter me from being good at my job. *I barely looked like I could fight my way out of a paper bag, but appearances are really deceptive.*

Sensing eyes watching me from above, I cast my gaze upwards towards the control room. Sure enough, the warden was perched high, watching her empire below. Dressed in a navy skirt suit, her hair was pulled back in a bun to reveal the harshness of her cheekbones. A scowl hardening her face, Warden Theresa Lane's eyes met mine as I continued down the stairs.

Her frown deepened as I held eye contact, refusing to break her iron stare. I'd known the warden for years, remembered her in my house for dinner as she and my father discussed matters at the prison. She had been my father's friend and his second in command. I'd always had a gut feeling about her... something I couldn't quite put my finger on but never could figure it out. Now she had my dad's job and from the looks of it, enjoyed the power far too much.

Finally, she tore her eyes from mine as a guard tapped her shoulder and she had to engage him. A small smile crept over my face. *Hooray for small victories, right?* I slipped in front of a greener in line for breakfast. She immediately cast her eyes at her feet... a fringe benefit to being on death row.

You might think that with state of the art technologic advances, the food would be a delightful cuisine. Think again. I held out my hands and a bowl of porridge was slapped down. Servers barely spared us a glance, their faces the epitome of boredom. They obviously couldn't have cared less if we were fed or not.

Taking my bowl of cold porridge, grabbing a spoon and moving out of the conveyer belt, I sat as far from anyone else as possible. I deliberately propped my feet up on the bench to prevent any brave souls from climbing in next to me. Luckily, in the last few months, our section experienced a decline in the amount of inmates. I dug my spoon into the porridge and shoved it into my hungry mouth. It tasted foul, and I struggled to digest the cold, sticky lumps as it made its way to the back of my throat. What I wouldn't have done for a slice of bread and butter. Instead, I forced down a few more bites before my stomach rebelled, and I could no longer suffer the bleak meal. Shoving the bowl out of reach, I rested my chin in my hand and watched the others around me.

Sometimes inmates kept to themselves, dividing up into country groups or forming alliances, singling out the weak from the strong. The Russians tended to keep to themselves, and the overwhelming sense of righteousness was too much for some people. Their country was one of the power three and the rest of us were just bugs to be stepped on. Veronika Petrov, their ringleader, had been my cellmate when I first came there. When she found out that I had been training to become part of the Retrieval Team and that my dad had been the warden, she lost it. The girl, barely sixteen at the time, had the most kills under her belt, slaughtering six of her roommates in a prestigious Russian boarding school. Apparently, she murdered people simply because they had laughed at something she wore. She used a kitchen knife to slit their throats, and a teacher found her talking to herself about what a nice colour it was while painting the walls with her victims' blood.

Yup, she's the psycho who has it in for me. The prison held a group of about twenty Russians in for various crimes, but the black Veronika wore meant she and I shared the same fate, although I was more isolated than her. She caught me watching her, and sneered, running her finger across her neck. I hated to tell Veronika that her continuous threats would be more effective if I weren't already slated to die in two months.

So I waited with everyone else for the bell to chime for us to go about out daily activities. I longed to stretch out my body fully but wasn't allowed to spend any time in the gym, or outside, for that matter. It seemed like forever since I had breathed in fresh air, felt the cold wind lash against my face or shivered as the rain drenched me to the skin. Such luxuries were not mine to have.

All in all, there were barely ten of us on death row, but according to hushed whispers and gossip, Veronika and I were the ones everyone feared. Veronika, I could understand… but me? I just went about my days as quiet as possible, avoiding everyone and praying I got my memory back. Most of the time, I tried not to listen to what others had done but was more curious about those on death row than the other offenders. At least one of the boys was in for manslaughter, but it was the terrified little Muslim girl who made me think of Sophia's death. The girl was about thirteen and had a frightened rabbit look. Her dark eyes constantly darted from side to side as if someone was going to come tell her it was all a mistake, that she was not a terrorist, and her family had arrived to take her home.

Unfortunately, that was not going to happen. I had spent my first few weeks in tears begging them to tell me it was all a nightmare, and I would wake up soon. It didn't happen. I was glad when I saw the girl being taken under the wing of some of the older inmates, their array of colours ranging from small-timers to one or two like me. As far as I knew, mine was the next scheduled execution, making me even more of a celebrity than I already was, and certainly more of one than I wanted to be.

A bell chimed, signalling the end of breakfast, and I sat still, waiting for the scramble as people hurried to their respective doors. Each one led off into corridors where their lessons and such would take place. I'd never get to see past those doors. After ten minutes of endless waiting, the doors closed and the rest of us exited the mess hall and headed back to our cells. Prisoners on kitchen detail began to clear the tables, probably only getting cleaned up in time for the next meal to begin.

Making my way up the stairs, I watched as Veronika bumped into the defenceless Muslim girl. The young one muttered an apology, but Veronika blocked her path. I stopped on the steps and cleared my throat. The few others glanced in my direction but quickly turned away. I raised my eyes to see if the guards were watching, but they made no move to intervene, which was typical because they only did so if situations got physical. The poor girl looked as if she were about to piss herself. Having sworn never to get involved in prison politics, I put my fingers between my lips and whistled.

The shrill sound cut through the silence and dragged Veronika's focus to me. I tilted my head slightly to the left, and we held each other's gaze, giving the girl enough time to scamper away from her bully and up the stairs to me.

In heavily accented English, the girl spoke, "I thank you."

My eyes never left Veronika's cold stare as I simply replied, "Don't thank me. Just stay out of the bitch's way. Got it?"

The girl nodded and rushed off, disappearing into her cell at the far end of the landing. Not wanting to look away first, but conscious of the audience gathering from the control room to watch us, I turned and headed back up the stairs. There was no getting around feeling the heat of Veronika's glare on the back of my head.

I escaped into my cell and waited to be escorted to my daily therapy session. Apparently, the sessions were to help me try to come to terms with my impending death. Dr Costello really did try and convince me that he wanted me to remember the last year more than anything in this world. I suppose all shrinks would say the same thing, trying to assure their patient they're on your side, not the Parliament's.

Lying back on the bed, I let my eyes drift shut, the familiar sights of blood-soaked carpet and lifeless bodies rushing to the forefront. The only memory I clung to was a vision of me on my knees in front of my dead family… my hands and face covered in blood… my father's gun on the floor at my left. My own blood pounded in my head as the front door was smashed open. Guards, my future colleagues, swarmed in. Dragged to my feet as tears stained my bloody face, I heard a familiar voice and snapped my head up and stared into eyes that condemned me from the get-go. Theresa Lane, in her then pristine UPDC uniform, took one look at the scene and demanded that I be arrested for the murder of my entire family. And as I screamed hysterically that they got it wrong, a sharp pain radiated my skin and everything went to black.

A polite knock on the wall caused my eyes to dart open, and I sprang to my feet. Standing in the uniform I would have worn was an officer who had always been nice to me, despite my situation. About twenty years old, he must have been in the field for over two years. His ginger hair and freckles indicated that he probably had been born on the Island, like me. Although the term *Irish* no longer existed, since Ireland had been erased from the new world map, Connors most definitely had Irish

17

heritage.

He flashed a grin and nodded his head as if to say *come on*. "Rise and shine, McCarthy. Time to see the doc."

"Oh joy, how will I contain myself?" I drolled, rolling my eyes, but Chris Connors just laughed. Instead of walking ahead of me like most guards, he strolled beside me, keeping me company in the quiet. His boots squeaked, clean shoes on a clean floor as we walked in a comfortable silence to the end of the landing. Connors scanned his wristband and the door slid open, revealing a corridor.

"You know, McCarthy, I always look forward to our daily conversations. I thought by now you'd feel comfortable enough to tell me some gossip."

"And what makes you think I have any, Connors? I'm just simply passing time here."

His smile widened, and his dimples deepened as he ran fingers through his curly hair. "You take more notice of things than we do. You woulda made one hell of an officer."

Our journey ended as we came to a halt next to a door with an engraved plaque with *Doctor Daniel Costello* embossed on it. I looked up at the smiling officer and found myself smiling back. He knocked at the door, and we stood in silence, waiting for a reply. A voice beckoned me to come in and I chuckled as Connors took a bow.

"McCarthy, I look forward to our continued conversation for the next couple of hours. For how else will I get through the day if not for your wit and enthusiasm?"

If we were anywhere else, I could have enjoyed Connors' obvious flirtation, but deep down inside, I couldn't let myself relax in his presence. He was a member of the UPDC; he took an oath to serve those in power and rule on the side of justice. I was just another criminal. Sighing to myself as I watched Connors walk back down the long corridor, humming a tune, I keyed in the proper inmate code and the door slid open.

I watched from the doorway as Dr Costello pushed his glasses up on the bridge of his nose. His brown hair dipped into his eyes, but he seemed oblivious. He chewed on the end of his pen and chose that moment to glance up at me, those sky-blue eyes brightening as he first spotted me.

If I had been a normal girl and he was a normal boy, then the feelings in the pit of my stomach would have been a welcome distraction. I could imagine that he looked at me as though I were the only girl in the room for him. It wasn't a problem he could fix.

But real life wasn't as clear cut as that anymore, and it hurt more than ever that I wished it was. I stepped out of the doorway and made my way to one of his comfy armchairs.

DANIEL

"There's nowhere left to hide, in no one to confide.
The truth burns deep inside and will never die."
(MUSE: SING FOR ABSOLUTION)

I SENSED HER WATCHING ME, THOSE DEEP CHOCOLATE EYES studying me before she dragged her feet across the floor, approached her favourite chair and tucked her legs underneath herself. She turned her head to stare out my window. This routine happened every day, taking in the scene from outside my window, the lazy sun heating her face. I allowed her this small luxury. Hell, I would have tried to break through the shatterproof glass if only I could, for one minute, if it would erase the haunted look from her face.

And I hated to admit that I enjoyed observing her. I loved how her nose crinkled when the sun hit her face as if she were surprised by it. When she was anxious, she twirled her hair and tended to chew on her bottom lip, especially when discussing her parents and sister. Even though she didn't remember me, by God, I remembered her and I, for one, was not convinced that my Alana could have killed her family. She didn't have it in her.

When I first saw her all those months ago, I was captivated by her strength and beauty. Barely five foot tall with hazel eyes and a wavy mass of brown curls, Alana stood in the sparring arena of our training centre, poised to strike a boy twice her size. But damn, she was fast. She ducked and dodged his blows, masterfully avoiding his strikes until frustration got the better of him and she got

20

the advantage, kicking him in the back of his knees until they hit the floor.

Unlike other opponents, she didn't celebrate her victory; she simply nodded acknowledgment to her trainer and stepped off the mat and back in line. Alana had a lot to prove for being a warden's daughter, but that never stopped her.

Back then, I was a lowly academic, not physically strong enough to be an officer, but smart enough to be the youngest in my class to ever have qualified as a psychologist. I had returned to the training centre to undergo classes for profiling and assessment of prisoners when I had met Alana. Our futures would never be the same again.

As I leaned back in my chair, I closed my eyes, thinking back to when we first met. Officially, anyway.

The bell chimed to give the signal for lunch and soon the halls were crowded with hungry trainees eager to spend an hour away from the torments of training. Once or twice I was bumped as overly muscled youths cleared a path obviously necessary for their inflated egos. Of course, nobody took any notice of the tall, geeky guy with glasses. No one except her.

Preferring to turn my back to the wall while waiting for the throngs to pass, I finally achieved space to breathe. I never went to the centre's cafeteria. Having seen enough old movies on how cliques merged and tended to pick on the weakest among them to prove superiority, I tended to hide out in the library. Even with technology easily available, I found it calming to sieve through old, dusty books in search of answers to questions I had about various subjects. There was something to be said for the sense of accomplishment after hours of research and ending up learning something new. Now, you can see why I avoided the cafeteria.

As I pushed away from the wall and continued to the library, I caught sight of her again. She was alone in the training room, punching a bag. Her hands were covered in tape and her feet were bare. I couldn't help myself; I was entranced by the sheer beauty and fluidity of her movements. Quietly sitting down on one of the viewing seats by myself, I had a full view of the magnificent training room. It was reminiscent of a Roman coliseum, a circular arena adorned with seats and steps leading down to the wooden floor where Alana stood.

She must have sensed someone watching her, she paused and daggered her stare in my direction. I braved a smile, but that only caused her brow to crease more. My hand raised in apology. Her face softened, but the gaze still held mine. She started to undo the tape from around her hands, but not once did she take her eyes from mine.

"Did you need to use the room?" Alana inquired as she cautiously climbed the steps.

I laughed; I couldn't help it because one look at me would tell just about anyone I was not built for physical activity. She looked at me as if I had gone mad. Then, after raking her eyes from head to toes, she studied me again and smiled.

"I'm sorry to interrupt your workout. I just couldn't help myself."

She raised a quizzical eyebrow, her lips quirked up into a half smile. "So do you find yourself staring at young girls due to your lack of impulse control a lot? Because there is a law against that, dontcha know?"

I smiled and replied, holding up a battered text of Gross: The Science of Mind and Behaviour. *"Would you believe me if I said it was all for research?"*

Alana reached out and took the worn textbook in her hands. She examined it, reading the back cover in full; I watched her eyes darting from side to side as she read. Handing the book back to me, her face changed and the tough exterior seemed to drop, if only an inch.

"So does that mean you weren't checking me out? 'Cause I hate to admit it, but I'd be a bit disappointed."

22

I must have looked completely shocked as she laughed… the sound a symphony in my ears. Damn. She was beautiful but was she pulling my leg?

"It's okay Romeo. It was a joke… I know I'm a social pariah considering who my dad is."

I cleared my throat. "I don't even know your name, so how can I know who your father is? And I'm certain that you were messing with me—I mean what beautiful girl wants to go out with the geek?"

She studied me again, and something crossed her mind because she leaned in. With her fingertip, she pushed my glasses up my nose. Alana pulled back and smiled. "Did anyone ever tell you some girls find geeks sexy?"

"I haven't met any yet."

Her smile grew, and she brushed an unruly curl from her face. Holding out her unbandaged left hand, she tilted her head and said, "Hi, I'm Alana McCarthy."

I took her hand and shook it. "Daniel Costello."

"Well, Daniel, are you going to ask me to get a coffee or what, so I don't think you're stalking me?"

"Are you always this forward?" I grinned.

"Take me out for coffee and you'll see." She bounced back down the stairs before turning around to look up at me. "Meet me outside campus at five, okay?"

I dumbly nodded and turned to go, the shock of it leaving me lost for words. Gathering my books, without another word, I started out of the room.

"And Daniel…"

Spinning around one more time, I saw her re-wrap tape around her wrist. She wasn't looking at me, but her voice carried across the room. "Keep the glasses. I like the glasses. Makes your eyes look bluer."

My answering smile was involuntary as Alana went back to punching the bag, and I walked to the library unable to think of anything but our date. At the time, I was certain she wouldn't show up, and it was all a joke. So you can imagine my amazement when she did come. Beautiful, even dressed in ripped jeans and a teal blouse, she linked herself to my arm and bombarded me with a hundred and one questions about my life.

It made no difference to me that she was seventeen and I was almost twenty-one. From day one, I knew this firecracker was the one for me and no one would ever compare.

Sometimes life isn't fair, but the girl I was head over heels in love with didn't remember me... and that cut down to the bone. It had taken me four months to convince the Grand Masters at the training centre that I had changed my mind. I told them I wanted to do some research on memory loss and trauma before I took my place in the behavioural science department. Who could disagree with a student who had more qualifications than all of them combined? So I had arrived at the facility two months ago and was assigned Alana's case. It took every bit of self-control not to shake Theresa when she laid out Alana's crimes and told me how dangerous she was.

All lies. I was certain of that, at least. One theory was that Alana was pretending not to remember in order to use that as part of her defence. But in a judicial system so flawed that she would have no trial, no chance to tell her story, what would be the point?

"You fall asleep on me, Doc?" Her voice slammed me back to reality, a reality I'd rather ignore.

"Of course not, Alana. I am just, as usual, giving you the space to open up."

"It's hard to open up, Doc, when you lost a year of your life."

"And how does that make you feel?"

"How do you think it feels?"

"Why do you always deflect from talking about your feelings?"

Alana blew out a frustrated breath, her jaw ticking

24

slightly as she tried to rein in her short temper. I bit the inside of my mouth to stop from smiling as Alana pursed her lips.

"Why do you always answer a question with a question?"

"Does that make you angry?"

"No. It makes me think you get some sick, perverted pleasure out of trying to piss me off."

"And does that annoy you?" Inside I was trying my hardest not to laugh as she daggered me with her stare.

"Nope. Just messing with you, Doc." She sighed, a deep sound as if she has just remembered where she was.

"You can call me Daniel, Alana."

She snorted and tilted her head to the side.

"And how does that make you feel, Doc?" A faint hint of amusement lightened her tone.

"Touché," I said as she placed her feet on the ground and strolled around my office. Every time I broached the subject of the night our lives changed forever, she balked, using her wit to disguise whatever she was feeling. Most days it took every ounce of strength not to go to her, take her in my arms and reassure her that everything would be okay.

"So how are you feeling today, Alana?"

At first, she didn't answer as she continued to walk around my office, touching the framed diplomas, taking her time to examine each title on my bookcase. When she came full circle, returning to the armchair, she sat and folded her legs underneath, sitting on her feet again.

"I still haven't remembered anything, if that's your roundabout way of asking."

I shook my head side to side. "That was not my question, Alana."

Shrugging, she turned her face away from me while I used what little time we had left in the session to take in her profile. Her long lashes cloaked her eyes as she let them drift shut. Alana's nose crinkled and her brow narrowed. I could see she was thinking hard, concentrating, as if by doing so her memories would miraculously reappear. We'd worked together for two months to build up our trust, and I planned to work to save her until she took her very last breath.

"I try and get a sharper picture of that night but can't. It's as though the edges are foggy, and I can't piece together what's real and what isn't. There is so much blood but no noise apart from my sobs. Why would I be crying if I killed them? See? This just doesn't make sense."

Removing my glasses, I folded them and set them on the desk in front of me, rubbing my tired eyes. "When someone is affected by a traumatic incident, sometimes the mind, in order to protect the host, blocks out certain memories that could be traumatic if returned all at once."

"No offence meant, Doc, but it's not as if I have time to waste."

Her sharp, clipped and defensive tone proved that she wanted and needed to remember. It also made my stomach summersault while I was yet again reminded of the deadline. I could not continue being gentle about things if I expected her to get her memories back. Part of me was still uncertain if those recollections hadn't been somehow *taken* from her. Who knew what scientific programs were available in this society? Behaviour chips were a perfect example.

I didn't reply to her comment, simply out of fear that if I tried, my voice would crack, betraying emotions a stranger should not have towards his patient. The weather outside darkened to match our moods, the clouds greying as rain began to dance on the window.

"Do you think I'll get to go outside before I die? Is there some sort of dying wish thing or something? I mean… if I don't get to live… that's the least they could do, right?"

A note of sadness tainted her voice and even though she focused on me, I saw a fleeting look of hope in her eyes before it disappeared. I couldn't answer, simply waited for her to open up.

"Can you see if that's possible? Would you mind asking if I can go outside once before I die? Please, Daniel. It's all I will ever ask for."

On any other day, the sound of my name on her lips would have created imaginary symphonies in my ears. But the desperation in her voice opened a way to delve deeper into our therapy, and I had to take it.

"I will try my hardest, Alana, but you have to give me something to show them that you are responding to our sessions. They require me to file reports, and if I do not show them your willingness to remember, I cannot guarantee you outside time, even for a few minutes."

"Then tell me how to remember."

I shook my head. "If it were that easy, Alana, I would have told you weeks ago. What I want you to do tonight, just before you go to sleep, is lie down on your bed, close your eyes and clear your mind. Do not try and force yourself to remember, just let your eyes remain shut and count down from one hundred until you fall asleep. Once your mind is clear and you are somewhat relaxed, it may trigger your subconscious into dreaming."

Alana contemplated my suggestion for a moment before nodding. "I'll give it a try."

"That's my girl." I tried not revealing how horrified I was as those words slipped past my lips, but the little blunder seemed to float over her head.

Almost instantly, she returned to staring out the window, watching as the rain got heavier, concentrating as thunder rumbled in the distance. We remained in the comfortable silence until a light rap sounded on the glass panel door. Two hours was not enough time to spend with her, and I craved more. But asking for more time with one patient would only put eyes on me that I needed to keep looking in other directions.

The door slid open and Alana's escort, Connors, stood in the doorway. Exhaling sharply, she straightened herself and headed for the door. I exchanged a brief nod with Connors, who winked at me over Alana's head. I trusted him to watch out for her as we had done for each other as children. He knew my secret.

My friend disappeared from view as Alana hesitated in the doorway. I pretended not to notice, returning the glasses to the bridge of my nose and chewing my pen as if mulling over today's session. Connors' voice rang out in the quiet.

"Come on, McCarthy. And here I was hoping you would keep me amused on the way back."

She tried to stifle a grin, but Connors could drag a smile from the most downtrodden person. I opened my notebook, scrutinizing the blank page as Alana crossed the threshold.

"Daniel?"

"Yes, Alana," I said without looking up from the page.

"Don't ever get rid of your glasses, they make your eyes seem bluer."

As my breath hitched in my chest, I stared at her as she disappeared from view, listening while she bantered softly with Connors until their voices were nothing more than an echo in the hallway. A million different questions raced through my mind, hoping, praying even, that this was it—the start of her memories coming back. But hope was a commodity, a luxury I couldn't count on having for long.

Dropping the pen on the notebook, I leaned my head

back into the chair. A headache was brewing, the weight of carrying this secret heavy in my heart, the pressure of trying to find a way out of this mess evading me.

Startled out of my personal thoughts, the office door slid open again and Connors entered the room. After closing it behind him, he slumped down on the couch and draped his limbs out over the arms of the chair. Flashing me a mega-watt grin, he folded his arms behind his head and leaned back.

"Your girl is safe and sound back in her room."

"Thanks. I appreciate you looking after her, but do you have to flirt so much with her?"

"Gotta keep you on your toes, Danny-boy." He chuckled, always easy to laugh when I was so serious. "You know I'm only trying to be her friend, give her someone to go to."

I chose not to answer him because he knew I understood, even if their banter irked me. My silence forced him to become more serious. Still in his relaxed position, he asked me the question I couldn't answer... not yet.

"What if she doesn't remember, Danny-boy? What we going to do then?"

I contemplated that question for a long time, well into the evening after Connors had returned to his duties. The situation was frustrating because I really didn't have a plan if Alana didn't start to remember. All I could do was count the hours until I saw her again. Each meeting allowed me to breathe in the very essence of her, those eyes, her smile, that inner strength. It made me a better man. I would do everything in my power to set her free. That was an undisputed fact.

Before I left my office for the night, I pulled a key from around my neck and unlocked the desk drawer. Removing a wooden frame, I set it on top of the desk and stared at the photo of Alana and me. We were smiling, happy, my arms wrapped around her waist as I kissed her neck. She had turned and laughed up at the photographer. It was the last photo we had taken together before she had left the centre to return home to see her family.

We appeared so happy, so in love. It seemed beyond strange that the couple in the photo could be the girl who didn't remember me and the boy who had manipulated his way into a position here to be with her. I focused on the picture for the longest time before grudgingly returning it to the drawer where I closed it and turned the key, locking away my happiness until next time.

The key was safely back around my neck, the cold of the metal stinging my bare skin beneath my shirt. I turned out the desk light and rolled my chair away from the desk. At that moment, I wished that I could take the photo back to my room. Of course, it wasn't possible in this place with eyes everywhere. The locked drawer was the safest place for it. Instead, I pressed the button to turn off the main light and let the darkness engulf the room.

Outside, I keyed in my personal code, sealing the room so only I could enter. Another day might lead to fresh hope, but as I trudged away from my office and that photo, all hope faded. My happiness was locked in a drawer next to a velveteen box that I couldn't force myself to look at.

ALANA

"And these walls surround us, always black and
grey I see
And we found this time, on our weakness it will
feed."
(YOU ME AT SIX: THE SWARM)

THE AIR WAS CRISP, ALMOST CUTTING WITH EVERY BREATH I TOOK,
the wind whipping against my skin, but I didn't care. The smell
of freshly cut grass tickled my nostrils as I blinked and put a hand
on my forehead to protect myself from the sun as it peeked out from
behind the clouds. Squeals of pure childish pleasure pulled me back
to myself while I turned and held out my arms towards my baby
sister. Sophia ran full speed and almost jumped into my outstretched
arms.

Light where I was dark, Sophia's dirty blonde hair was gath-
ered in one plaited mess that bobbed from side to side as she ran.
Her blue eyes took in everything as she gripped me into a tight hug.
Despite the age gap, seven years, we were as close as sisters could be.
It was my last week at home before I left to take up my place on the
course to become a retrieval officer, and I would miss my little ray
of sunshine every day.

Kissing the top of her forehead, I put her back down on her feet.
She danced away from me with a reckless abandonment that only
a child could have. Sophia twisted and twirled in our back garden.
I admired the way she took everything on the chin, from the teasing
because of our father's position… to her sadness at having her sister
leave for a six-month period for training. She was truly the light to
my dark. Where I was always a glass half empty type of girl, my
beautiful sister did not share that pessimism.

I drank in the sight of her as she skipped over to the swing set.

It was one I had helped my father restore on a rare weekend when he did not get interrupted by a phone call requiring his immediate attention at the prison. My dad and I had spent that wonderful sun-soaked weekend, sanding the frame in the early morning. Later, we treated the metal and repainted it before fixing brand-new chains and attaching hand-carved wooden seats. I remember my fingers had bled and my bones were weary after the weekend, but it had been the most uninterrupted time I had spent with my father in a long time. It was bliss.

"Push me on the swing, Na-Na!" Sophia called as I laughed at my nickname. It stemmed back to when Sophia first learned to talk and couldn't get her tongue around Alana. From then on, I became Na-Na.

Rolling up the sleeves of my jumper, I wrapped my fingers around the cold, metal chains and pushed. Sophia burst into fits of childish giggles. With gentle pushes to the small of her back, Sophia asked to go higher and higher but only laughed harder when I denied her wishes. Even at that age, I was conscious of the fact that she had inherited my lack of height and even though she was almost nine, she appeared much younger.

As I listened to Sophia's laughter cut through the air, neither of us cared that the sun had disappeared behind the clouds, and the wind had kicked up harsher as it bit the skin on our faces. I caught my mother watching us from the kitchen window, wiping a stray tear from her eye. Sophia was her double. From her looks to her mannerisms, my mother had remarked more than once that I was too much like my father and she could not decide if that was a good or a bad thing. When she caught me staring at her, she waved me off but not before tapping her antique watch and disappearing from view.

Feeling the tip of my nose going numb from the cold, I pulled Sophia to a stop. She puckered her lip in a mock pout, and I laughed, inclining my head towards the back door of our house. Sophia bounced forward before halting on the back steps and plonking her butt down on the cold ground. Joining her, I hugged my knees to my chest, partially from the cold and partially from the sadness at having to leave her for so long.

"You know I have to go, don't you, Soph? I mean, you won't even know I'm gone. I'll be back before you know it." Unsure whether the words were meant to reassure her or me, I sighed.

Leaning her head against my shoulder, she replied, "I know Na-Na. I am sad you will miss my recital, but I can tell everyone at school my big sister is an officer of the UPDC and they can leave me alone 'cause you can kick their ass."

"Sophia Millicent McCarthy. Wash out your mouth before I tell Dad what you said." I struggled not to giggle, but when Sophia looked at me with mock sternness, easy laughter fell from my lips.

"No, you won't because I learned all my best words from you." Little minx had me there.

I dangled my arm around her shoulders, and we remained sitting on the back steps awhile, me enjoying the stillness and the warmth of my sister's hug. Hopefully, Sophia took comfort in it too. As the inevitable rain began to trickle down our foreheads, I suggested we go inside. I stood, pulling Sophia up by both hands and she wrapped her arms around my waist, her tears mimicked the raindrops as they slipped from her eyes and down her pale cheeks.

"Don't forget me when you're gone, Na-Na. Please don't forget me."

Her quiet sobs shook her shoulders, and I detangled myself from her arms and crouched down in front of her. Looking at her dead in the eyes, I held her gaze as I spoke. "I will never, ever forget you, Soph. I promise. I will be back before you know it, and you'll be begging me to go away again. Got it?"

She nodded slowly, and I ruffled her hair before she ducked out of my grasp and climbed the steps, turning the door handle and going inside. I struggled but held my emotions in check. The rain became a downpour, and I stood still in the torrent, closing my eyes and letting Sophia's words ring in my head. "Don't forget me when you're gone, Na-Na. Please don't forget me."

I bolted up in bed as a scream pierced the silence. Sweat beads dotted my forehead, dripping down my face as hair clung to my sweaty skin. My heart pounded against my chest as I struggled to gulp in air. When the door to my cell opened, I realized that the screams were my own. Clasping a hand over my mouth as two of the night guards stepped inside my room, Sophia's voice continued racing through my mind.

"You okay there, McCarthy?" One of the uniformed officers asked. The female officer was a few years older than me, with masculine features and hair cut tight to her skin.

Taking in a few more cleansing breaths, I pulled the sheet up over myself, allowing time to recuperate from the dream. I returned her gaze, but when I opened my mouth to speak, nothing came out, so I tried again. Shouts came from other cells, but I needed to answer the guards before they reported me to the warden. Giving her reason for watching me more closely wasn't high on my to-do list.

"I'm sorry... Bad dream." The guards shared a knowing look and I recognized what remained unspoken between them. Dr Costello had warned me that my memories might come back in dreams at first. I had done what he asked by clearing my mind and concentrating on Sophia. When I had fallen asleep, one of the last memories I had came racing to the forefront of my mind.

"You sure that's all it was, McCarthy? Do you need to go to medical?"

What I needed was to speak to Dr Costello, but asking the guards to see my shrink would only cause more questions. At the moment, any indication that I might be suffering from some sort of Stockholm syndrome would surely get me sent to a room with rubber walls.

"No, no. I'm fine... just some weird dream about a

fire and being trapped inside. Suppose it's to be expected, right?" Carefully trying to brush it off as flippantly as possible, the female guard, Wilkinson, I think her name was, nodded. She eyed me suspiciously before turning and marching out of the cell, her colleague following on her heels.

As soon as the cell door closed, I couldn't hold back the tears. In an effort to keep quiet, I stuffed the hem of the sheet into my mouth as a scream inched its way from my gut to my throat. What was the purpose of that particular memory? Why would my subconscious remind me of something that I already knew and remembered? Was I going to gradually remember everything I had forgotten only to run out of time before becoming just another executed murderer?

I dared not close my eyes again for fear of what I might see. In the darkness of my cell, I heard Sophia's voice begging me not to forget her. Dear God, how could I have killed someone so defenceless, so warm and kind... one who loved me unconditionally? As I hugged my knees and rocked in bed, I couldn't help but believe that I was wrongly accused of committing the terrible acts against my family. I loved them all. None of it made sense. And why was I still alive?

Time passed without notice. I must have sat there staring at the blank walls for a quite a while because before I knew it, light filtered through the skylights brightening the gloomy mood of the cell. It must have been around five o'clock in the morning, still another couple of hours before breakfast. The thoughts of stomaching another bowl of stone-cold porridge made bile poison my throat, but I swallowed it back.

With the sun barely filtering onto my darkened walls, I slipped out of bed and went to the area of the cell where the sun had actually reached. Facing the rays, I slid down the wall and thought back over the dream, trying to make sense of it. I just couldn't. Maybe Dr Costello would have a clue now that I had more details. But could I trust him?

At some stage of my turbulent thoughts, I must have drifted off again, this time into a dreamless sleep because I was startled awake when someone crouched in front of me. I sprang up, taking a defensive position and shoving the person away, then relaxing slightly at the sight of Connors slumped against the bed.

"Oh god, I'm sorry!" I exclaimed, rushing forward to help him up. Connors just grinned, dusting off his uniform and holding his hands up in mock surrender. "I come in peace. I just stopped by to see if you were okay? I heard about the disturbance last night and when you didn't come down for breakfast, I wanted to make sure you were good. Next time I'll knock harder."

"Christ, Connors, I could have killed you. I'm all right, just had a bad dream is all. Did you say I missed breakfast? Damn, how will I survive without my scrumptious porridge?"

Connors chuckled, a low rumbling sound from deep in his chest. He peeked outside the cell and spun back around to me. Carefully pulling out a slice of folded bread from his jacket, my mouth watered. I couldn't help but think the bread would be in better condition if I had not just knocked Connors on his ass. Plus, if it had been any other guard, I'd have been hauled to solitary for the rest of my days. Connors held the bread out in front of him, and sensing my hesitation, placed it in my hand.

"Hurry up and eat that before I get caught. Can't have 'em saying I'm giving certain prisoners special privileges, now can I?"

I didn't hear a word he said as I devoured the bread, taking a large bite out of the gift. The taste of real butter burst to life in my mouth and it took all my concentration not to groan in pleasure. *When you have spent the last few months eating nothing but bland porridge and even blander meals, it might surprise you at how wonderful a simple treat of freshly baked bread and butter could make you feel.*

Wiping the crumbs from my mouth, I smiled at Connors, who waited for me to finish. "Why are you so nice to me?"

"Because I happen to believe it when you say that you can't remember. I worked for your Da, and he always spoke of you with pride and love. He helped me out of a few jams, and I'm returning the favour."

My chest instantly tightened as Connors spoke about my dad and I thanked him, even though the words couldn't truly convey how much his gesture meant. As if sensing my mood, Connors slipped back into his usual flirtatious self.

"Well, don't go all girly on me, McCarthy. Come on, it's time to get showered and stuff before your session with the doc."

Gathering up some fresh clothes, I let Connors lead the way as we went in the opposite direction to the door that led to Dr Costello. Trying to take my mind off the nightmares, I listened to Connors mumble on about some football game the guards were having after work. Feigning interest seemed rude after he had given me such a nice gift, but my mind was preoccupied with my upcoming therapy session.

As we scanned through one door, leaving the cells behind us and walking the short distance to the shower room, Connors stood outside. He scanned me in and said, "I'll be out here when you're finished."

A blush quickly coloured his freckled cheeks, and I couldn't help but tease. "And here I thought you'd jump at the chance to see me naked."

With the most serious face I had ever seen on him, he sputtered. "Hell no... Dan... I mean... the warden would have my nuts. I'm quite fond of them, you know."

Shaking my head and chuckling under my breath, I ducked into the room. At this hour, I should have been alone with the exception of maybe one or two stragglers. Each colour designation had a scheduled day for shower room use twice a week. I suppose it was entirely girly of me to admit that I couldn't wait to wash my hair. Similar to a high school locker room, rows of benches lined the walls in front of a couple dozen showers. Even though male and female prisoners shared most things, showers were thankfully one place the prison officials separated.

I stripped off my clothes, having lost all modesty during the first month of incarceration. Walking over to one of the cubicles, I turned on the water. While checking the water temperature with my fingertips, I waited until it was a blissful lukewarm and stepped in. Attached to the walls were bottles of shampoo and conditioner, one of the few luxuries allowed. Running my fingers through my mess of hair, I tried to separate the knots before lathering in the citrus smelling liquid, rinsing it through before repeating again. Finally, I used fingertips to apply conditioner to the ends. I had stayed under the stream for a few more minutes before the water turned ice cold, and I quickly turned it off.

Yanking a towel from the top of the pile on a bench, I had started patting myself dry when I heard the door open. The small Muslim girl entered. Her eyes were hidden behind unruly dark hair that flowed down in front of her face, and she appeared startled at seeing me there. I acknowledged her and went back to drying off as she scurried over to a bench as far from me as possible. Charming.

I dressed in my black uniform and wished I had

some perfume or something so I at least smelled nice for Daniel. The thought surprised me. Damned Stockholm syndrome again, latching on to the one smart, attractive guy in this place. Plus, he was the only one trying to help me, besides Connors.

While still towel drying my hair, I slipped into my shoes and heard a sharp intake of breath and a cry of agony. Abandoning my damp hair to frizz, I spun around in my seat, shocked at the sight of Veronika holding the tiny mouse of a Muslim girl up, off the ground by her neck. Her feet dangling as she wiggled in Veronika's grasp.

Don't get involved, Alana... It's not your problem to fix. You have enough of your own problems.

But did I listen to my thoughts? Nope. Against my better judgment, I stood and closed the space between me and Veronika. She snarled and spoke in a heavy Russian accent.

"Mind your business. It does not concern you."

"Well, when you pick on someone weaker than you, then I will make it my business. Let her go."

"Stupid girl. Do you not know who I am?" Her grip tightened around the girl's neck and the small one's face turned red under the strain.

"Yeah, I know who you are, Veronika. I just don't care. Let her go." Something told me that, in the long run, I was going to regret my words and actions. Sometimes bullies need to be taken down a peg or two.

Veronika all but tossed the girl aside, the poor thing hitting the ground with a vicious thump, her eyes falling closed. I made my way over to see if she was alive, but Veronika grabbed a fistful of my hair as I passed her, and she yanked me backwards. Pain lanced my skull, but I fought through it, ducking under her arm as she tried punching me in the stomach.

Unfortunately, she seemed to anticipate my move

and her clenched fist connected with my eye sending me reeling, darkness blurring my vision. Another fist met my chin and I stumbled back, the back of my knees hit a bench. I sat down hard.

I'm not proud of it, but I saw red. I should have been able to take her down; it's what I had learned in training, using my speed and height difference to my advantage. Prior to learning those lessons, I'd seen it as a disability. But when you have a hulking, Russian, murdering bitch breathing down your neck, sometimes logical thinking flies out the window.

I lunged forward almost rugby tackling her, my elbow digging into her stomach. We both crashed to the ground, Veronika digging her fingernails into my cheek as we lumbered to the ground. Veronika's back collided hard with the tile floor. I dug my knee into her side and bitch-slapped her so hard, my tiny hands left a red imprint on the side of her face.

She screamed out in fury, and I tried to keep her other arm pinned down with my knee, but she had the tenacity of a rabid pit bull. Frustration and adrenaline kicked in and Veronika struck back with her teeth, biting down hard on my skin. I yelped in pain. Lifting up a hand, I clenched my fist and slammed it into her stomach, and she rolled on the floor in agony. As I jumped off her, the Russian kicked out her right leg, her long limbs able to reach my shorter one. While her foot connected and cracked my knee, a firestorm of pain roared throughout my body.

Veronika recovered quickly, pinning me in the same manner she had the mousy girl except her nails dug into my skin, and I felt the blood trickle down my neck. I tried to scream out, but her vice-like grip restricted any sound other than a weak cry.

"Now, you will see what happens when something is

not to my liking." She sneered. Her concentration was so fully on me that she never noticed her first victim crawl to the door and pound on it... hard. My vision became unfocused, and I kicked out helplessly, thinking that I mightn't even have two minutes of life left... never mind two months.

As my eyes drifted halfway shut, my lungs screamed for relief. That's when the door slammed open and bounced off the wall, and I made out Connors' red hair. I barely heard the guards, their pleas for Veronika to let me go sounded like hearing voices when your head is under water. Soon I would be unconscious, a willing captive of the darkness, the shadows long ago becoming friends.

Suddenly the pressure on my neck vanished, and I heard a cracking sound as my skull hit solid ground. I opened my eyes for a mere second and watched as Veronika twitched and screamed, her body writhing with the electric shocks of her behaviour chip. Eventually, her eyes rolled back in her head and she was still.

Take that, you Russian bitch.

All I wanted or needed was to go to sleep. I offered Connors a weak smile when he knelt in front of me and pulled me into his arms. I felt all floaty and my head pounded in pain. I really just needed to sleep.

"Stay with me, McCarthy. C'mon doll. Don't go to sleep on me. You look like shit, by the way."

"You should see the other guy." The words came out in a slur. If I closed my eyes and slept, it would all be over. He knew I probably had a bad concussion, but all I wanted was to sleep off the pain. My lids were heavy and I couldn't hold them open any longer. I welcomed in the darkness as it wrapped its arms around me in a protective blanket. The last thing I heard was Connors shouting, "Where the fuck is the medic?"

ALANA

"So I bare my skin and I count my sins and I close
my eyes and I take it in."
(IMAGINE DRAGONS: BLEEDING OUT)

WAKING UP WAS ALMOST AS PAINFUL AS GETTING MY HEAD
smashed against the wall. Every inch of my body
protested at the slightest move. Groaning, I forced my
eyes open, the intolerable light blinding me for a second
before I could focus on my surroundings. I suspected
I wasn't dead because the smell of disinfectant and
cleanliness smothered the already thick air.

So this was the infirmary. I lay still on the bed, my
head propped against a firm pillow and staring up at the
sterile white ceiling. The need to inhale existed, but my
ribs protested, obviously unaware of the requirement to
fill my lungs to keep me alive. My head pounded a dull
ache that reminded me why I ended up here. Slowly, I
turned on my side. Spying a glass of water on the table,
I reached for it, ignoring my screaming limbs. When I
grasped it loosely in shaking fingers and raised the glass
to my lips, I gulped down the ice cold liquid as if I had
not had a drink in days.

"I would suggest you drink slower, my dear, or it
might make you sick."

The voice frightened the life out of me, so much so
that I almost dropped the glass and spat out the water
simultaneously. I knew that voice; I dreaded hearing that
voice because it meant I had gotten too much attention.
Instant regret over helping out the Muslim girl washed

over me before I realized it. Looking back, I would have done the same thing again. *Me and my stupid moral compass.*

Taking in another rough breath, I returned the glass to the stand and angled my body in the bed so I had a clear view of my unwelcome guest. Standing just under six foot tall, Theresa Lane seemed every bit as imposing as she did keeping watch over her inmates. Even before my memory blackout, I didn't like my dad's number two. She looked every bit as surly and hard now as she had back then, and my gut clenched as I fought the urge to puke.

She was dressed in navy blue again, a pantsuit this time, her hair dragged back into a grip. Her navy blazer displayed the badge of the United Parliament, the UPDC, and the mark of the International Court of Justice. My dad's uniform had been the same; had I graduated, my own uniform would have been pretty much identical. She sat cross-legged on a plastic chair, her hands neatly folded in her lap. Behind her, through the window, I watched two guards manning the doors. Were they protecting her or guarding me? I raised my gaze to meet hers and bit the inside of my lip hard to keep my mouth from acting without my consent.

"How are you feeling, Alana?" The warden spoke, her words full of concern but her tone of voice betrayed those words, giving me the impression that she was here out of obligation, not concerned about my welfare.

I had pondered my thoughts carefully before answering, "Like I got beat up by a psychotic Russian, who can't play nicely with others."

The warden laughed, a harsh bark of a sound that hurt my ears. "Indeed my dear, indeed. Unfortunately, Veronika's issues do tend to lead to physical altercations. For your last few weeks here, I advise you maintain a comfortable distance from her. We would not want any more harm to come to you before your big day, now would we?"

Was this woman for real? She made my impending execution sound as if the days were leading up to some big celebration, like a wedding or something. I narrowed my eyes and rubbed my forehead, avoiding her question and hoping she would get bored of me and leave. Just my luck she thought today was a good day for a chat.

"I had been hoping that your time here would lead to you finally admitting what you did, Alana. Your poor father was one of the best men I ever had the pleasure of working with and your lies only sully his reputation. Come now, do you not think that confessing and lifting that terrible weight off your shoulders would make facing death easier? I am a woman of science and can admit freely that I struggle with this little story of yours. It's difficult for me to believe you do not remember your actions. How could someone lose a year of her life?"

I shifted uncomfortably as Theresa continued talking down to me.

"Alana, I don't want to hear excuses, but I must abide by the rules of the Grand Masters and keep you safe until your birthday. Confession is good for the soul, Miss McCarthy."

Wishing I could tune out the sound of Theresa's incessant droning on, I remained silent.

"Your father spoke out many times against the death penalty for minors trying unsuccessfully to convince the council of Grand Masters of Justice that young offenders could be reformed, given the right opportunities and time. He introduced most of the programs now run in this department. Did you know that? Cormac told anyone who would listen that there needed to be some leeway with certain offenders in order to prove that society cared about our future. Your father was an idealist, but the good he may have done died the night you murdered him, Alana, and because of you, his beliefs will never come to pass."

I sat up in the bed, a lump forming in my throat upon hearing my dad's name spoken so casually, and I pulled the sheet with me so my body was covered. It was difficult enough being subjected to a verbal tongue lashing by this woman I didn't trust. My only defence was holding onto what little dignity I had by keeping my battered body out of sight.

"He always spoke of how proud he was of your achievements, Alana. Always said what a fine officer you would make. Willingness to do what is right is a tremendous attribute to one's character. I find it repulsive that your father's opinion of you, along with his work, now remains stained by your lies. You won't have many more chances to come clean. Think about that until you are returned to your section this afternoon."

"As I have told every single person who has interrogated me since that night, I really can't remember. My last recollection was of heading off to the training centre. The next thing I knew, I was being dragged out my own front door covered in blood. Goddammit, I want to remember. Either way I want to remember."

Theresa drummed her fingers against her thigh. "And your sessions with Dr Costello. How are they proceeding?" Something in her tone bothered me, but I couldn't quite put my finger on it. Regardless, warning bells rang in my already pained head.

"Dr Costello holds onto his faith that he can trigger my memories. He believes that I may have blocked out the year in order to protect myself from what happened. He seems to know what he is talking about, so I have to trust him, don't I? It's not as though I have many other options left, right?"

Something crossed the warden's face but instantly disappeared. Theresa studied me, running her steely gaze from head to toe before she rose, her heels click-clacking against the tiles as she did. Smoothing out her jacket, she looked at me with a pursed smile slipping onto her lips.

"Dr Costello speaks highly of your progress, as well, Alana. He is by all accounts a rare commodity in this day and age… a man who absorbs knowledge and wants to use it to better the world. Be thankful that he wants to spend his resources on you, even when it seems to me to be a waste of his talents. If I had my way, you would spend the rest of your sentence in solitary, but the Grand Masters have ruled in your favour this time. Enjoy the reprieve."

I didn't get a chance to respond because the warden swept from the room like a tornado, pausing and looking over her shoulder. Her smile transformed into a sneer and her obvious hatred for me written all over her face. She snapped her fingers and one of the guards followed her, leaving one to watch my door.

A sigh escaped my lips, and I rested my head against the cool, metal frame headboard. This was all I needed. Sure, I might as well paint a target sign on my back. More than ever it seemed as if the vultures had begun to circle my dying body, ready to pick it apart at the first sign of weakness. Someone really needed to give that bitch a swift kick somewhere it was bound to hurt.

While trying to relax, I shut my eyes and listened to the sounds around me. Shoes squeaked as nurses passed by my room. Hushed conversation between colleagues, far too soft for me to hear or fully understand. A nurse briefly entered my room and checked my vitals, failing to utter a single word before she promptly exited again. She left the scent of her overly floral perfume behind. I tried unsuccessfully to empty my mind of all these conflicting thoughts, willing the warden's words away. Was she right? Had my memory lapse happened because I was guilty? If I were guilty, then what kind of horrible stimulus would make me kill my entire family and leave me marked for death?

Continuing to mull over things in my head brought back the headache that had barely begun to subside. Tears welled up and I let them fall, wishing the salty streams rolling down my cheeks could magically return to me all that I had lost and allow me to die with some semblance of peace.

Heavy footsteps thundered down the hall, halting outside my room. Murmured voices floated across the almost silent infirmary, and I kept my eyes closed. I rubbed my tear-stained face with the sheet, wanting to avoid any show of weakness, unsure of who would come in next and try to have another go at me.

Finally, the voices uttered a goodbye and the heavy footsteps entered my room. I felt the presence watching me before the scrape of metal legs on the floor indicated the chair was being dragged closer to my bed. Trying to regulate my breathing, I waited until my visitor seemed to settle down before opening my eyes.

Connors sat slumped in the chair, his usually mischievous face sombre. His eyes travelled over my face, observing me as I winced trying to sit up in the bed. Concern darkened his eyes, and his ever smiling lips clenched together awkwardly as I struggled to get comfortable.

"It looks worse than it is. I swear." I tried, but the situation must be dire if I couldn't drag a grin from Connors. After a few minutes of uncomfortable silence, I began again.

"Hey, Connors, this isn't your fault. You know that, right? I got involved in something I shouldn't and had my ass handed to me. No big deal."

"No big deal? You gotta be kidding… McCarthy, you could have died. You understand that, right? I've been pacing the corridor for two damn days waiting for you to wake up, and you tell me it's no big deal."

"Two days? Wow, that's the most sleep I've had in months."

Shaking his head caused his ginger hair to slip into his eyes before he swiped it out of his face again. "How can you joke about this, McCarthy? It was my job to keep an eye on you. Some protection I've been when you end up unconscious after getting your skull cracked."

Why was he so upset? He just happened to be the guard on duty. Maybe I was wrong and Connors took his job way more seriously than I thought.

"Connors, it really is okay. I'm fine. Well, not fine, but I will be. Don't beat yourself up about it, you hear me? Veronika has had it in for me since I got here and eventually would have used any excuse to try and take me out. I think she wants to be the one to kill me… doesn't want to wait for my birthday and see the pleasure of my last breath belong to someone else." I managed a weak smile, but Connors' face remained impassive.

"So are you here to take me back or what? I hate to admit it, but I'm starving."

The chair screeched as he stood, and Connors rose to his feet, reached into the bedside cabinet and tossed my clothes on the bed.

Yeah, 'cause I was in a hospital gown and getting up would show Connors parts of me I did not wish for him to see. Ever the gentleman, he turned his back as I dressed, slowly pulling my jumper over my bandaged midsection, the weight on my left leg burned as I forced myself to stand.

As if hearing my unspoken question, Connors said, "You have bruised ribs which will heal in time, a nice shiner on your right eye, bruising along your jaw and cheekbone. You're lucky to have only a slight concussion. Amazingly, you avoided any broken bones. Apart from that, your injuries will heal in a couple of weeks."

"Just in time for my execution."

"Yeah, I guess."

When I struggled through the pain of putting my shoes on, I said, "I'm decent, Connors. Let's go."

He didn't answer, just mumbled something before turning around and letting me pass as he followed me out. The activity stopped in the infirmary as I hobbled through the corridors, keeping my head down in order to avoid any looks of pity anyone might decide to throw my way. I was a big girl; I messed up and would deal with the consequences but didn't need or want their pity. Maybe I was proud and stubborn, but, hell, I didn't have much left to hold onto.

We exited the infirmary and walked in silence down the long corridor. The stillness was almost deafening, and I longed for Connors to say something inappropriate or witty to take my mind off things. The eerie awkwardness and strange unease between us irked me, causing my mood to darken and the hopelessness of the situation to bore down harder on me.

"Veronika returned to the wing this morning after two nights in solitary. She's bragging about what she did to you."

"And so she should. I would have beaten her as badly as she did me."

Connors shook his head again. "You really are a little ball of mischief, aren't you?"

I shrugged, cringing as the movement pulled on my sore midsection. As we rounded a corner and arrived at the door leading into the main mess hall, Connors put a hand on my elbow, and I looked up at him. Face grim and drawn as if he were thinking too hard, Connors leaned in close and spoke softly.

"They have eyes on you now, Alana. Nothing will stop them from making sure you are held accountable for what you supposedly did. Watch your step. Trust no one."

As I opened my mouth to reply, Connors keyed in a code. The door rattled open, freezing the words on my tongue. I stepped into the mess hall and immediately everything ceased. Nobody spoke or ate or made even the slightest noise. I was starving, and we had entered the mess hall at the far end, meaning I would have to shuffle all the way up to the serving area, passing dozens of rows of inmates who knew what had happened between me and Veronika. Nothing added more to your celebrity status than getting beaten up by the resident psycho.

I nodded to Connors and held my head up as I struggled across the floor, feeling the weight of everyone's eyes on me. From the smells wafting at the front of the room, minced something was on the menu. Finally managing to reach my destination, I kept my eyes forward and muttered a soft *thank you* under my breath as I collected my meal. Sitting on the nearest available free seat, my legs threatened to cause me more embarrassment, and I almost nosedived into my mince concocted meal.

Once I was fully seated, people returned to their own meals. I dug hungrily into mine guessing that two days of being unconscious and not eating would take away any reservations one might have about institutional food. After I had inhaled the meal, not tasting anything but needing the sustenance, I looked around and my eyes lead me to Veronika. Of course, she was staring daggers at me.

Some might say I had acted stupidly. Others might call it arrogance, but something lurking deep inside me made me flash a satisfied grin at her as if I were goading her because she hadn't quite finished me off. Her face lit up a glorious shade of red as fury danced in her eyes, but I simply inclined my head and shrugged. I was already dancing with death, what harm could it do to antagonize her? If she didn't kill me, I was dead soon anyway.

She sat taller and straightened, rising to her feet, but one of the Russian boys put a hand on her arm and yanked her down. They each repeated the action like some kind of strange dance, the sound of angry Russians gaining an audience. Veronika used her favourite intimidation technique, picking up her knife this time and running it along her neck. I waved a hand dismissively in her direction and pulled my eyes from her gaze.

My heart raced faster than it did while poking fun at my Russian psychopath. For a moment, the world seemed to disappear and I released a breath I hadn't realized I was holding. Standing at the far end of the room with Connors stood Dr Costello, Daniel. His steely eyes firmly focused on me as Connors leaned in and spoke to him. Daniel nodded in agreement, but his eyes never left mine, and I shivered under the scrutiny of his gaze, not wanting pity or sympathy, especially from him.

Theresa's words came back to me, and I wondered why he wasted so much time trying to help me remember what I had lost. Connors nudged him slightly, and he broke from our stare, a hint of red tingeing his cheeks. It gave him a certain boyish charm, and I scolded myself for thinking of him as anything other than my shrink. *Don't be stupid, Alana. You are merely a means to an end, a way for him to advance his career by retrieving the memories of the girl who protests her innocence way too often.*

Something must have registered on my face because Daniel looked at me once, blue eyes narrowing and his eyebrows almost meeting as he frowned. And then, with a quick turn, he patted Connors on the shoulder and made a quick escape out the door.

A sick feeling tensed in the pit of my stomach, and all my glory at taunting Veronika vanished, leaving me anxious and worried that I had somehow disappointed Daniel by my actions. Pushing my empty bowl away, I stood and made a quick escape, wincing with every step I took up the stairs.

My exit seemed to alleviate most of the tension in the mess hall, and the inmates returned to their chats and laughter. Life would go on, even if my own didn't for some godforsaken reason. Daniel's facial expression tonight had brought me to a dark place... where I stayed. I would never grow old, fall in love, have kids or have a quiet moment to drink life in. I would be dead, and the world would continue on without me until the people who once knew me regarded me in the distant corner of their minds. Probably sooner than later, I would fade from existence altogether.

A sob threatened to slip free, but too many eyes remained on me to allow myself to break down in front of them. Once in the safety and familiar surroundings of my cell, I crawled into bed and pulled the sheet over my head. When the cell door clicked into place, I allowed myself to cry until I struggled to breathe from the pain in my chest. Salty tears lulled me to sleep.

DANIEL

"He had the eyes of a fighter, never did nobody harm."

(JACK SAVORRETTI: ONCE UPON A STREET)

THE LAST TWO DAYS HAD BEEN EXCRUCIATING. IT WAS WAY worse than having to wait months and trying to get relocated to this section of the prison. At the time, the apprehension I had felt waiting to meet Alana's family for the first time, or waiting for the official letter to say that I had been accepted to the program was pure agony. Achieving this could leave the stigma surrounding my family's name behind me and carve out a life for myself that did not revolve around my rebel parents.

I told Alana all about my family that day over coffee, my need to get the dirt out in the open before she wasted any more time on me. You see, my great grandfather was one of the rebels who stormed the government many years ago. My grandfather was a very vocal man who had spoken out at rallies against the United Parliaments and what it meant for the country. In true family tradition, my father continued on in that legacy until my mother died in a rally gone wrong. The United Army fired on civilians and my mother had been crushed in the fray. I was twelve.

Later that night, my father fled the country, leaving me behind with my aunt. I never quite understood my father's need to rebel, but I suppose doing what I was doing in the current situation made me a chip off the old block. Eventually, my father moved to a ranch on the

Free Islands of Australia where he remarried and had more kids. He never once suggested I come join him. *I am unsure if I'm sad or happy about that.*

But Alana hadn't cared. She assured me that I would not be judged on the actions of my father, and I told her the same. During the rest of the date, she had asked me about my studies and what I hoped to achieve in life. Once we discussed our families, it was done, never to be asked about again unless we brought it up ourselves. We were both lost souls trying to shine under the umbrella of our individual family histories, but to us, we were just Daniel and Alana, students of the centre. I fell for her that very day.

When Chris Connors had shown up at my door two days ago, the boy had guilt written all over his face, and his voice cracked more than once as he explained what had happened to Alana. I longed to go to her. What psychologist would visit their unconscious patient? I had to wait on tenterhooks for Connors to update me on her condition, knowing full well that I would not be satisfied until I saw Alana myself.

Connors explained the extent of her injuries to me, blaming himself for not checking that the shower room was clear before he sent her in. I tried to reassure him that Veronika's actions were not his fault. Neither Alana nor I would hold any blame against him. My light-hearted friend took too much on his shoulders, and I believed it really was my fault in the end. He had watched out for her from day one and every day after that until I could get positioned to be there myself. I knew he still cared about her.

On his way to collect her, Connors let me know that Alana was awake, and I assured him again that what had happened to Alana was not his fault. He immediately dragged me in for one of those awkward man hugs, saying that he was honoured that I had placed the love of my life in his care. Connors took that responsibility to heart and swore he would not let her come to any harm again. They had never met, Alana and Connors, during our six months together, but I had told him all about her. At the time, my friend replied in only the way he could... that the girl was far out of my league. I knew he was right, but it didn't matter.

Calmly, I had walked into the dining hall in time to see Alana limp over to an empty table and sit. A slow smile quirked my upper lip as my girl dived into her food like a starving animal. Her eyes scanned the room as she took in everything around her. Hidden in the shadows of the doorway next to Connors and out of view, I watched as her eyes latched on to Veronika's. Tension built in the room as the two exchanged non-verbal threats to a captive audience.

One careful step forward and I eased up to stand by Connors. He leaned in and whispered that the guards were placing bets on when the next fight would be. I shook my head in disgust, but when I spotted Alana's eyes firmly focused on me, I nodded at Connors as if I understood his comment. Whatever he had said to me went unheard as I held Alana's gaze. She must have read something in my expression because she pushed her food away and got up to leave, her arm wrapped around those bruised ribs. With one final look in my direction, she ducked into her cell. That's when I remembered to breathe again.

Left to apprehensively wait for Alana to arrive at her next session, I found myself unable to relax. What had she read in my expression that stopped her from goading Veronika? Had I given something away? Was she suspicious? If I told her who I really was, would she think I was the crazy one? My stomach did somersaults while I kept checking the time. I made a conscious decision to broach this session from a different perspective.

Stepping away from my desk, I walked to the side and pressed the button to heat the water on the percolator. Opening up the cupboard, I removed two mugs, putting a sachet of coffee in one and a tea bag in the other. Coffee is okay, but I was jittery enough already. As the machine beeped to let me know the water was ready, I took turns putting the mugs beneath the stream of hot water, filling them and adding condiments to our liking. I set them on the coffee table between the chairs in front of the desk.

Soft, hesitant footsteps echoed down the hall, and my heart raced slightly. No banter or chat accompanied the forward progress, only awkward, irregular thumps in the hall. Soon after the keypad was accessed, the door slid open, and I settled into one of the chairs and waited.

Alana limped into the room, her dark hair falling over her forehead, blocking her eyes from me. She slowly approached her favourite chair across from mine and started to sit with her legs tucked under her, but her knee was far too sore for that. I waited while she settled in and gave Connors a nod. He almost laughed when he spied the mugs and winked, a familiar grin returning to his face.

Before I realized he'd left, the door whirred closed, and we were alone. Alana eyed the mug suspiciously and then looked at me. I smiled, hoping to ease some of the obvious tension that had built up in her shoulders, but her gaze only narrowed.

Pointing to the mug, she asked in her softest voice, "What's that?"

"Coffee," I said. When she didn't respond, I continued, "Coffee... three spoons of sugar and just a smidge of milk so as not to dampen the sweetness of the sugar.

Or did I get it wrong?"

Alana did not answer but simply leaned over and wrapped her fingers around the mug and lifted it to her lips. A dazzling smile lit up her face and eyes as she swallowed the liquid and exhaled.

"How do you know how I like my coffee?" Her voice was accusing but without a hint of malice darkening her tone.

Mimicking her actions, I sipped my tea and leaned back in my chair before answering, "I did my research. I thought after the last few days… you would like something… I dunno… nice."

"Thank you."

Her eyes returned to glance at her mug, and we sat in a comfortable silence for about twenty minutes as she savoured her coffee. I had finished mine well before her but waited, giving her time to feel safe before we got down to things.

When she laid her mug down on the table and sat back in her chair, her fingers started twirling the ends of her hair in a nervous attempt to avoid eye contact. "Do you want to talk about what happened with Veronika? Or would you like to tell me what you hoped to achieve by antagonizing her?"

"I wasn't trying to *antagonize* her. My purpose was the opposite. I needed to stop her continued efforts of intimidation, to prove that what she did meant nothing. People needed to see someone stand up to her because she will continue picking on the weaklings if they show fear."

"And is it important to you not to show fear?"

"Yes, because bullies can't be allowed to win." Alana folded her arms across her chest and winced as her elbow dug into her rib.

I drummed my fingers against my leg and waited, contemplating my next question. "Why was it important to protect Afsana? Why did you not call on Connors and let him remove Veronika from the showers? Have you thought about why it had to be you to save Afsana when it didn't need to be?"

Alana mumbled under her breath so I couldn't hear, so I asked her to clarify. She exploded, her voice ringing in my ears as she snarled.

"If I let that psycho beat up Afsana, the mouse, then it confirms that I am the monster they tell me I am. If I stood by and let Veronika torture that poor girl, it makes me think that I might have actually killed my sister in cold blood. Maybe, in my mind, getting my ass kicked means that I'm not evil."

"So by helping Afsana you feel you might be able to redeem yourself... even if you killed your family?"

Alana's shoulders shrugged, and she slumped down in her seat. She appeared pitiful, defeated, hopeless, and my heart banged like a drum against my chest. I wanted to wrap her up in cotton wool and protect her, but with the grains of sand dropping in the hourglass, we didn't have time for subtle. When she remained quiet, I pressed on. Anger was good, but I needed her to feel it, really feel it.

"Did you practice the technique I asked you to during our last session? Did it bring anything to the light, any-thing at all?"

"I did as you asked and cleared my mind and all that, but it turned out to be useless. I dreamed of a memory I already had, me and my sister in our garden, the night before I headed off to the centre. It was a time before I lost my memories. She asked me not to forget her. That's all."

Instinctively, I reached over and took her hand in mine, trying to ignore my body's reaction to her touch. "But it has worked, can you not see that? Your sister and your memories of her are what will set your mind free, Alana. I know it's hard. Time is not on our side, but try with me now, please. I promise you are safe here."

Alana pulled her hand from mine, and I missed the warmth immediately. She swept her hair away from her face, and I got a view of those brown eyes again. As she inhaled and then lifted her head, those deep, thoughtful chocolate eyes stared at me as she spoke.

"Okay, let's give it a go… I have nothing left to lose." God, if she only knew.

"Right. So what I need you to do is sit as comfortable as you can and close your eyes." She wiggled around in her seat before closing her eyes, waiting. "Now, Alana, I want you to count backwards from ten until you reach one. When you get there, I want you to picture your house as you remember it. Are you okay with that?"

No answer. Alana simply started counting down from ten and stopped at one, her eyes clenched closed. "I see it," she said in a bland voice, trying to avoid the emotion that occurred while dredging up her past.

"Can you describe the room you're in for me, please?"

"It's the front room. There is this hideous olive carpet on the floor, and the walls are painted sunshine yellow. Along the fireplace are family pictures, even more hang on the walls. My dad's armchair sits beside the fireplace with a coffee table in front of it, and a couch runs along the wall barely inside the door."

I leaned forward, clasping my hands in my lap. "That's very good, Alana. You're doing great. Now can you put your parents in the room for me, please, and tell me what you see."

She swallowed before speaking, but this could be it— the breakthrough we were waiting for.

"My dad sits in his chair, piles of hard copy files all over the coffee table. He has his *work frown* on, scowling at the paperwork. Mom is on the couch, her legs crossed like a proper lady, her feet hooked, one behind the other. She has one of Sophia's school dresses in her lap and her sewing kit next to her."

Alana's voice trembled, but we still had a way to go. "Now, Alana, it may be hard, but I need to see Sophia in the room. Can you tell me where she is?"

"Soph... Sophia is sitting on the floor reading one of Mom's old books, ones she thought we would like to read from a proper paperback instead of on our computers. I think it's her favourite, *Alice in Wonderland*. Her hair is pulled back into a French plait, and her mouth moves as she reads the words in the book."

Now for the hardest part. "Brilliant, Alana. You are doing so well. Next, I just need you to think back and try and picture that room as it would have been that night. Don't visualize it as others have told you it was. Try very hard to think about it as you imagine or believe it to be. I know it's difficult, but all I ask is that you try. Can you do that?"

She must have tried because her eyes darted from side to side behind her lids. I also watched as her breathing became laboured, and she bit her bottom lip so hard it bled. "Alana, please describe what you see."

"Blood, so much blood, it's everywhere... I never knew a person could bleed so much... Oh god, I can't... Sophia... oh god, I'm going be sick."

Her eyes sprang open and she bolted, faster than her sore limbs would have normally allowed... into the bathroom where she wretched into the toilet. I thought about leaving her to her privacy, but a voice inside my head said *screw that*, and I softly rubbed her back as she vomited. When she had emptied her stomach, she wiped the back of her hand across her mouth, and I returned to my seat. She collected herself, wiping away a few tears and sat back down.

"Can you tell me what you saw?"

"I don't know if I can without being sick again." Honest words.

"Whatever you can say will help."

"I was standing in the doorway looking in at my parents' dead bodies. My dad had a bullet hole between his eyes, and something oozed from it. Mom's blouse was soaked through with blood, spilling out onto that horrible olive carpet. I braved a step into the room, and that's when I saw her... Sophia. Her empty eyes just stared up at me. Her hair was matted with blood and... did I do that? Daniel, please tell me I didn't do that."

It was my turn to ignore her question because I didn't have an answer for her. My silence must have confirmed whatever ran through her head as she rose to her feet and spoke in a hushed tone. "Can I go back to my cell, please? I don't feel very well."

Looking at my watch, I said, "We still have time left, Alana. Do you not want to talk about it more thoroughly?"

She inched closer to the door. "I want to go now, *please.*"

I sighed internally but went to my desk and lifted the telephone to ask Connors to escort Alana back to her cell because she was unwell. Replacing the receiver, I waited about five minutes, watching as relief sagged her shoulders at the sound of Connors' boots down the corridor.

When the door slid open, Alana stepped out with some trepidation, and I bristled at the sound of my name on her lips. "Daniel?"

"Yes, Alana?"

"If that was a memory, and I did remember it, then where was my dad's gun?"

"I'm sorry. I don't get your meaning."

"If I did all that. Where was my dad's gun? I didn't see it in my hand or anywhere in the room when I pictured it. If I killed them, would I not remember the gun?"

She left me to mull that detail over as the door closed. It had always been a sore point for the investigation. How could a left-handed girl use her father's right-handed gun? And why... if she had remembered that night correctly, did she omit a gun from the memory?

Hope rushed through me. Finally, we were getting somewhere. I allowed myself the time to rejoice before my next patient arrived. Sitting behind the desk, I opened up my notebook and jotted down a few questions from today's session. Why had Alana escaped from being shot? The logical reason being that she had committed the crime and was guilty. The gun also played in my thoughts as did Alana's reaction to the blood. She had been physically sick at the recollection of it... how could she have had the stomach to gun them down in cold blood? Even if she had shot one family member, would her weakness for the sight of blood have allowed her to continue and kill the others?

The door slid open and my next patient strode into the room, escorted by Connors.

"How was she?"

"Quiet, Danny-boy. She seemed as though she were on auto-pilot. Went straight to her cell without a single word."

"We might be making progress," I said.

"Hopefully, Danny-boy. Hopefully. We have all worked far too hard for there to be any fuckups now," Connors retorted before he left the room.

I turned my attention to the boy sitting in front of me and couldn't help but laugh as he put his feet up on my desk and waited.

"If I told you to get your feet down, I suppose you

would just ignore me, right?"

"Sure… but you have to be nice to me because I'm helping you."

"And you get nothing from our arrangement?"

Grinning even wider, he snorted. "Of course, I am. It's why our friendship works, Daniel. We both get something out of this."

Yes, we did. I was quickly amassing a network of people to help me with my plan, and this boy was only a minor piece on the chess board. I rested my chin in my hands and simply said, "I think it's time for phase two. You know what you have to do?"

The boy nodded. "Yup. Once you don't forget our deal, everything will run smoothly."

Soon after that, he left me alone in my office again. Phase two would now be set in motion, hopefully leading to an acceptable outcome. My hands were clammy, and I stared anxiously at the telephone. Time to pick it up and proceed.

I focused on Alana and how brave she'd been as she fought to remember things that were surely more horrific than not suppressing the memories. Drawing on her strength, I picked up the receiver and dialled a number that replayed over and over in my head for the longest time.

The call connected, and I waited as the dial tone sounded in my ear. It rang five or six times before a familiar gruff voice answered. For a second, I couldn't speak, but when the voice repeated his greeting, I finally answered.

"Hi, Dad. It's me, Daniel. I need your help."

ALANA

"So I'll stare into the darkness just to see how deep
it goes."
(YOUNG GUNS: DOA)

LAST NIGHT I DREAMT OF NOTHING BUT BLOOD. IT WASN'T the same as what I had pictured during my session with Daniel, but it seemed everywhere I turned the world was haemorrhaging blood. I had been walking down to breakfast with the hallways eerily quiet, and there were no guards around. Stepping out into the hallways, I stopped abruptly. My hands were firmly on the railings as I looked down into the mess hall, full to the brim with prisoners. All at once, hundreds of inmates turned and focused up at me. Blood seeped from their eyes, noses, ears, and mouths. Every colour of jumper was drenched in crimson, and while the blood dripped into their porridge from their orifices, I felt a strong urge to vomit. They continued shovelling the blood-covered cereal into their bleeding mouths. My nose itched, and when I wiped it with my hand, my fingers were soaked with blood.

The beige walls bled, red dripped down in long streams until it pooled on the floor causing puddles of blood that I had to step over on my way. The puddles spread across most areas of the floor. If I kept walking, I soon would have to wade through an ocean of blood.

Then, without knowing how it happened, I was back in the room and my hands were covered in blood. I could not escape it as it trickled down from my nose. I cried uncontrollably and tears of blood spilled from my

64

eyes, blurring my vision. When I heard a voice call my
name, Daniel ran towards me. His eyes were full of fear,
and a loud bang echoed through the wing. Daniel keeled
over, his knees hitting the hard ground as a gaping hole
appeared in his chest, blood gushing down his shirt. He
tried to say something... his mouth was moving... but
I could hear no sound. Staring back at my hands, I saw
my dad's gun. It was pointed directly at Daniel. I raised
the weapon and placed the barrel calmly at the side of
my head. In slow motion, I pulled the trigger, screamed,
and woke up. The piercing scream continued even after
I was fully awake, only muffled when I clasped a hand
over my mouth.

My nose tickled, and sure enough, as I pulled my
hand away from my mouth, little drops of blood stained
my pale fingers. Carefully, I swung my legs out of bed,
trying not to aggravate the broken and bruised ribs, and
I hobbled into the bathroom. Filling the sink with cold
water, I proceeded to splash it on my face in the hopes of
waking from the nightmare. When I saw my reflection
in the mirror, it was a scary reminder that the last few
months had been less than kind to me.

My skin was pale, surely due to the lack of sunlight
available to me since I had not seen the outside in a long
time. Eyes that I once believed were pretty were sunken
into my skull; large bags drooped beneath my eyes, making me appear even more pathetic. How could I have
ever thought that Daniel or even Connors found me attractive? *Yeah, sure. Skeletal features are all the rage among the
prison community these days.* I shook my head at the reflection in the glass before throwing another handful of ice
cold water on my face and pulling my hair back into a
ponytail.

Once I returned to sit on the bed, I tried to close my
eyes. I had a strong need to see anything but the blood-

soaked walls. After half an hour, I realized that my mind was still playing havoc with me. Closing my eyes only brought repeated images of me shooting Daniel. Talk about your Stockholm syndrome issues. First, I began by crushing on my shrink. Now, I had dreamt of shooting him. *What's up with that?*

Because I had woken up long before the time for breakfast, I had hours to dwell on things. I tried hard not to think about my family but kept going back to that memory of me and Sophia playing in the garden. Why would my mind have blanked out just two short weeks later? I really was ready to deal with it now. I had to, didn't I? Deep down inside my gut I didn't want to die, but dying without knowing the truth was unthinkable.

While studying the shadows as they turned to light on the floor, the night eased into day, and I waited for sounds of waking inmates ringing out through the corridors. Most of those lucky souls would eventually be free and educated, rehabilitated into society so they could use the skills and knowledge they learned to better the human race. Some knew when they would be getting out and ticked off the days until they could breathe fresh air again. Each day I heard happy conversations from those inmates as they shuffled past me. It shouldn't have grated on me... but it did.

Cautiously, I waited until my cell door opened, and upon exiting I half expected to see the river of blood surround me. One deep breath later, I headed down for breakfast. It was Saturday. No session with Daniel today. Disappointment welled up, but I quashed it down as far as I could. Even so, my shoulders slumped, and an involuntary darkness swept through me.

Because of the nightmare, I wasn't sure I could stomach the porridge, so after skipping the line, I grabbed a bruised apple and plonked down in a corner of the room.

As soon as I had settled, I noticed some of the guards had manoeuvred themselves closer to me, avoiding my glances but close enough to intervene if necessary.

That's when I gazed up and spied the warden, deep in conversation with Connors. Theresa blatantly pointed her finger in my direction, and Connors frowned but nodded in compliance. She was apparently telling Connors off, and he did not look happy about it. He nodded but turned, heading away from her. Evidently, he must have sensed my stare because his head spun in my direction, and his gaze met mine. When it did, Connors winked and stuck out his tongue, sending me into fits of giggles.

Theresa's head snapped in my direction, and I almost choked on my laughter while trying to mask my amusement. I bit into the apple, and the bitterness of it made me swallow hard. How difficult would it be for such a high tech facility to at least have something edible on the menu? My stomach growled while I continued to munch away on the sour tasting fruit. During the rest of breakfast, I kept my head down, waiting to return to my cell. Out of nowhere, a shadow appeared in front of me.

He was a boy about my age who sat down on the bench in front of me and chuckled as I raised an eyebrow. I continued to nibble on the apple, and the boy waited for me to finish. He watched in silence as I tossed my leftovers into the bin and began to rise.

"So you're just gonna be rude and leave without so much as a 'Hi. How you doing?'"

"When people are *friendly* to me, I normally end up in the infirmary, so you'll have to excuse my lack of manners."

He leaned closer to the table, resting his elbows on it and then his chin on his hands. "Veronika's a nasty bitch. Thanks for helping Afsana out like you did. Poor girl never says boo to anyone, and she gets pushed around a lot. You would think being in here for *acts of terrorism* would scare most people away from her... but not Veronika." He used air quotes when saying *acts of terrorism*, pointing out to me that the little mouse of a girl could not be a terrorist.

This guy spoke of her in terms similar to the ones I used for Sophia as if he were a big brother looking after her. That's when I took notice of him. He stood a few inches taller than me, but that wasn't hard for most people. Hair trimmed down to his skull, he had fine bristles of blond barely shimmering in the winter sun. Built stocky with strong shoulders and a cheeky grin. One of his most distinguishing features was a very intriguing scar that trailed from over his forehead and disappeared behind his ear, but I couldn't get a clear view of the rest of it. He wore black. At least we had that in common.

People had avoided me since I got here, and I grew suspicious of the boy immediately, surprised when he reached out his hand and said, "Name's Jayson, friends call me Jay. Pleased to meet you." Nothing was given away in his accent. He spoke in a level tone, and I decided to play along.

I wrapped my fingers around his and shook, his grip firm and strong. Allowing a smile to dance on my lips, I answered, "Alana McCarthy."

He let go of my hand and returned to his position of resting his head on hands as he waited for me to speak again. I didn't. Instead, I leaned back in my seat and folded my arms across my chest. He chuckled again and held up his hands in mock surrender.

"Don't worry, Alana. I came here as a friend, an ally really. You helped one of my people out, so I am extending the hand of friendship. Come join us anytime. Your hostility doesn't seem like the best of company."

I narrowed my eyes at him. "Your people?"

Jayson sighed. "Yes, Afsana and a few others. We look out for each other. The lifers think it's fun to pick on the part timers for whatever reason. So I try and gather as many of them together during group times to avoid what would have happened to Afsana if you hadn't stepped in. Thanks again for that."

"Jealousy," I muttered.

"Sorry. What did you say?"

"Jealousy. That's why Veronika does it. She knows that they will eventually get out of here while we waste away gathering dust until D-day."

Jayson rubbed his chin, his grin widening. "I knew there was a reason I liked you, Alana. You are not afraid to speak the truth."

"When I can remember it, I do." The words had slipped from my lips before I had a chance to stop them, and I should have been horrified, but Jayson simply laughed as I clasped a hand over my mouth. Soon another rumble of laughter came from my right. Out of the corner of my peripheral vision, I noticed that Connors had replaced one of the guards. His shoulders shook at my words.

"Damn, Alana. If we had met under different circumstances, I'm sure we would have had a lot of laughs. Feel free to join us anytime. You are entitled to some fun before you die... you don't have to be alone."

I couldn't say anything as a lump formed in my throat. Why the hell was this guy being so nice to me? Sure, I had intervened on behalf of Afsana with Veronika, but that had been more for me than the girl. And then he said something that just about gave me a heart attack.

"We've met before, Alana."

"Whaaat? Yeah. I remember you being here when I

got brought in."

Jayson leaned in closer until his face was inches from mine. As he spoke, my heart pounded against my chest, and I fought hard not to let the threatening tears spill over.

"We met before that, Alana. You just don't remember. I'd say it was about ten months ago. You were on a field assignment for the centre. I don't want to tell you if it is going to upset you, but it might help for someone to tell you about part of your missing year."

I nodded, afraid to speak. Jayson sat back and began to tell his story.

"My sister always seemed to be sick, even when she was a tiny baby. Our mom always had to sell our stuff to get medicine for her. Dad had left us long before that, and with the reduction in money being given out to single parents, sometimes we barely ate. Mom went out at night and came home with money, but it never seemed enough. Ellie just got sicker and sicker. That was when my mom started drinking. You can guess where things were heading.

One night, Mom went out to buy medicine for Ellie, but she just never came back. So here I was, this fourteen-year-old kid raising his ten-year-old sister. I got food and money doing odd jobs around the markets, but then Ellie got an infection, and her medicine was just too fucking expensive for me to get. I snapped…

I asked the pharmacy for the medicine up front and told them I'd work off the debt. The stupid idiot made a comment about me not being able to pay like my mom could have, so I dived over the counter, grabbed the medicine and headed for the door. I knew I would get arrested and Ellie would be taken into care, but at least she would be alive."

Jayson paused and cleared his throat. I admired his

willingness to go to extraordinary lengths for his family. Anxious to get to the part where we'd crossed paths, I struggled to politely wait for him to continue his story. To be honest, something about his story was strangely familiar, almost as if a fog had cleared, and I saw through it.

"I fought with the cashier and pushed him away. He fell, knocking down a shelf, spilling meds all over the floor. I scrambled out of there while he tried to stop the few customers who got down on their hands and knees to pick up their own medication. The wail of a siren came closer and my eyes averted for a second as an officer gave chase. When I ran from him—"

"—You ran into an old man, and he hit his head and died."

The words flowed from my mouth as something clicked into place. I remembered details of Jayson's case. A rush of excitement overtook me, and I ignored the guards' gasps when they heard my recollection. I had remembered something… or let it slip.

Jayson smiled. "That's right. I accidently bumped into the man as I tried to escape, and he cracked his head on the pavement and boom! Instant manslaughter charge. You came with the field kit when I was being brought over from London. I remember thinking how nice you were for giving me water when the officers weren't looking. You smiled at me and whispered something in my ear. Do you remember what you said?"

The memory crashed into me as ferocious as a tidal wave into a ship, causing its inhabitants to hold on for dear life as the monstrous waves threatened to drag them into the undercurrent.

With a shaky voice and dry mouth, I said, "I told you that I would have done the same thing if my sister had been ill."

Jayson nodded. "Small comforts that I held onto in

here. I have another year before my eighteenth birthday but knowing my sister is well and being cared for means a lot. I heard you ask one of the retrieval officers what had happened to my sister. You repeated very loudly that she had been fostered to a nice family who ran a cafe and had no kids of their own. One of the few small acts of kindness which has kept me sane in here. So, Alana, I owe you one... Don't be afraid to cash it in."

I had no words. My brain refused to cooperate with my lips as a piece of the puzzle from the last year slotted into place. Jayson rose, and I stood with him. The boy came around the table and engulfed me in a hug. I awkwardly hugged him back, ignoring the slight ripple of pain in my stomach as I revelled in the most physical contact I'd had in months, and I patted him on the back.

His warm breath tickled my ear when he whispered, stepping out of the hug and sauntering back to his little circle of friends. I froze in the moment before shaking out the cobwebs and quickly vanished from the room. Amazing. I had remembered all on my own! Well, with some prompting. For a long time, hope had been a distant thing, too far away for me to cling to, but I hung to my lifejacket now as sharks circled, waiting. I will remember... I will.

By now word would have filtered around the wing and spread to Theresa Lane, who would say that I knew everything all along, and my lies were starting to unravel. Would Daniel know? Of course, he would—Connors was bound to tell him. I had a sneaky suspicion they were friends outside of work, but Connors never spoke of Daniel other than in passing, and Daniel did the same.

The initial high at finally remembering something, evaporated, leading me to question myself again. Sure, I had something to work with and obviously had passed my first exam to be taken out in the field, but how could

I trigger more memories? Jayson had practically pulled that one from me... what if I couldn't continue doing the same?

Upon entering my cell, I let myself slide down the wall until my ass hit the cold floor, and I stretched my legs out in front of me. Oh, to get through Sunday. Then I could talk to Daniel and see what he thought about all of this new information. It was okay to be optimistic, right?

My thoughts reverted to Jayson. I really did feel sorry for him. In my opinion, the boy had done nothing wrong, but as a member of the UPDC it was not in my job description to question the Grand Master's rules and punishments. They had been set into law long before I was born. I closed my eyes and replayed the memory in my head.

I remembered accompanying a retrieval officer, Sommers, into a detainment centre in central London. I had never left the Island before and excitement sang in my bones. Dressed in my navy uniform, I felt powerful and respected as we were greeted by nods and hellos as we sauntered into the building like we were in charge.

Sommers had told me to hang back and observe while he went to the desk and signed the paperwork. I followed orders. Only one cell was occupied, and it was an old one, all metal bars, and key locks. For me, it was like the words I had read on paper to describe the cells coming to life. A young boy sat in the cell, his head in his hands. I felt sorry for him being stuck in there.

My partner finished up with the officer at the desk, and they both approached the cell. The desk officer, who smelled of cheap beer and cigarettes, put a rusted key in the lock and with a groan, the door opened and the boy darted to his feet.

"Jayson Ferguson. You have been charged with manslaughter and have been sentenced to execution on the day of your eighteenth birthday. Step forward, arms out, please." Shock sent a shiver through me as the boy stepped out and held out his hands. Sommers motioned for me to do the honours, and with a heavy heart, I snapped the metal cuffs in place. At the time, it was our only way to restrain him until his behaviour chip was installed.

Sommers pushed Jayson forward, and he walked between us. The ride to the plane was silent except the whir of the car's engine which dominated until we boarded the plane and tied Jayson in with his seatbelt. He finally relaxed into his seat.

When Sommers went up to speak to the pilot while waiting for one more prisoner to board, I slipped Jayson the water and whispered in his ear. Today, I had perfect recollection of the event—from the smell of the gas-guzzler of a car to the stench of the heat riddled plane.

I had shown some kindness to a prisoner, even empathized with him. Karma had returned something small, but important, to me. Jayson's last words rang in my head. "You don't have to do this alone."

And from now on, I wouldn't.

DANIEL

"I've been thinking of everything I used to want to be.
I've been thinking of everything, of me, of you and me."
(30 SECONDS TO MARS: THE STORY)

SPEAKING TO MY DAD AFTER SUCH A LONG TIME DID NOTHING to brighten my mood. In fact, it ended up being a rushed fifteen-minute conversation that left a bad taste in my mouth. We refrained from exchanging pleasantries, leaping straight to the point of my call. I did not ask about his new family, and he never asked how my aunt was. I explained a few things to him, and when I had finished, the cruel bastard laughed. As a boy, I had objected to his activities, so he saw no need to provide me with any help now.

It had taken a lot out of me to phone my father, and he had proved me right after all these years by hanging up on me. Apparently, escaping to the Free Islands had done nothing for his fatherly skills. My mother would be turning in her grave if she knew we were so estranged and that I didn't even know the names of my siblings. My aunt never spoke of her brother much, and I always thought she did it so I wouldn't feel uncomfortable.

Staring at the phone, I half expected him to call back. It never happened. I suppose it did make me angry, but in hindsight, what did I expect from a man I shared nothing but DNA with? Time to come up with a plan B.

A slight rap on my door startled me back to the present, and I looked up in time to see a piece of paper slide under the door. When I approached the door, I crouched down and picked it up, turning it over in my fingertips. Recognizing the scrawl of handwriting of my name, I unfolded the note and read it:

Danny-boy,

Your girl remembered something. Jayson did as you instructed, and Alana ended up remembering in front of a few of us. The incident that Jayson told you about... where he had first met Alana... that's what she remembered. It's a good sign, right? But be wary. The warden has told us to keep a close eye on your girl.

The note wasn't signed, but I recognized Chris Connors' handwriting. He was also the only person who called Alana *your girl*. Was it too early to get excited? It was just a small memory that had returned—nothing major. But until the day I saw the light go out of her brown eyes for the last time—I would grasp hold of that tiny spark of hope. Then I would pray for it to ignite the flame that would uncover the truth Alana so desperately needed.

Glancing at my watch, I realized I was going to be late for our weekly staff meeting if I didn't get a move on. Monday mornings always brought trepidation that I would be discovered, that someone would turn up in the UPDC from the centre who'd seen me and Alana together. That would be it—no epic end to our story—a failure so immense I would never recover.

I left my office, a folder in my hand, and headed down the hall away from the prisoners' section. Swiping my ID over a panel, the door slid open, and the metal elevator doors appeared. Standing still for a few minutes, a camera rotated above my head, the doors opened, and I stepped inside. I pretended to flip through paperwork as the elevator crept upwards. The cameras hummed and the elevator whirred, but I tried to ignore them. The sound was as annoying as a fly that occupied your bedroom at night and just would not leave.

Finally, the doors opened, and I exited and made my way along the corridor. From up there, you could see down into the mess hall from all angles. Windows and floors were made of special types of glass where from above you could see everything below while the general population below saw only a beam that ran from one side of the ceiling to the other. Even though every inch of me longed to sneak a peek and search out a familiar mess of curly hair, I restrained myself. The camera rotations were a stark reminder that I was being watched.

I scanned through the next door and entered, exchanging brief pleasantries with a few of my colleagues who were already seated. I took my usual spot at the far end of the table, creating as much distance as possible between me and the warden's head of the table location. Listening in on the conversation that had begun prior to my arrival, I nodded at the appropriate parts although I had no interest in what they said.

The guards' conversation stilled as Theresa Lane entered the room and strolled over to her seat. I hardly knew anything about the woman, but she made me feel very uneasy. Plus, should I be found out, it would be her signature that signed my own death sentence. In my case, there would be no waiting; I was almost twenty-three.

Mine would be a quick death.

Theresa called the meeting to order, and I listened as officers droned on about security protocol and how well the new education programs were going. One of the security guards, I think his name was Sullivan, spoke of one or two instances where some of the boys had tried to sneak off with girls during common time. They had been sent to solitary. The warden brushed the incident off as a minor offence and said that in future, save solitary for those who needed it, to just implement the behaviour chip.

"A dose of reality will surely stop them from thinking this is a holiday camp and not a prison. If the chip does not deter such behaviour, I give consent to use force to set an example."

Sullivan was a burly mountain of a man. It might require a bulldozer to shift him. He looked overly cheery at the warden's comment, and his lips curled up into a sadistic smile that assured me he would take pleasure in inflicting pain.

A few more items on the agenda were discussed, and I tried to take it all in but had more important issues on my mind. Although my interest was piqued when I heard Veronika's name thrown out, I chewed on my pen and remained silent. Head of security, Matthews, suggested they do something about Veronika's behaviour.

"I mean the girl actively seeks out trouble. Her perception of power over the Russian inmates and her enjoyment at hurting the weaker inmates is progressing at an alarming rate. Would she be an ideal candidate for Treatment?"

Theresa stared down at Matthews and pursed her lips. "Treatment has not been proven to help those who lack the capacity for emotion. Veronika does not see her actions as wrong. That is what brought her here in the first place. She murdered her roommates out of rage and plastered their blood on the walls. Why should I waste the advances in science on someone who will be dead in two years?"

Her words were crass, but I was intrigued by whatever Treatment they had in mind. Psychologists were excluded from meetings where physical or chemical remedies were discussed. Yes, thanks to Connors, I knew that a scientific lab existed beneath the prison where studies were being conducted to advance methods used in all prisons. The behaviour chip had been created there.

Matthews cleared his throat and wiggled his caterpillar-like eyebrows before he spoke again, "Warden McCarthy suggested that Treatment might be of use to help eradicate the death penalty altogether. Surely, we can be allowed to view his research and see if it is beneficial."

Theresa sat back in her chair and folded her arms across her chest. Her eyes narrowed, causing her brow to crease. I noticed a slight tick in her jaw. She was not happy when the subject of Alana's dad was brought up. But I had to hand it to her, even as I studied her reaction, she took the time to calm herself before replying to Matthews. "Cormac is dead. His idiotic ideas that everyone could be redeemed were idiotic and ludicrous. Treatment, once it has been scientifically proven, will only be available for those who are to be successfully integrated back into society. For those on death row, their fates are sealed, regardless of the empty dreams of a dead man."

The room because eerily quiet as guards and officials were taken aback by the cruelty and tone of her words. Whether they agreed or disagreed, no one spoke. As the meeting ended, I gathered my papers together to make a quick exit. Sensing something at my back, I looked up.

"Speaking of the McCarthy family, Dr Costello... I hear your pet project has finally begun to crack. Is it true that lies are being uncovered?"

I clutched the files to my chest trying to ignore my shaking hands. "What lies have been uncovered? We have no evidence to prove the girl is less than sincere about her memories. There is significant reason to believe that the trauma leading to that night forced Miss McCarthy into burying the incident deep within her mind in order to protect herself."

"But there is also no evidence to say your findings are fact either, Dr Costello. By all reports, the girl was top of her class with a high IQ. It is not beyond reasonable thinking that Miss McCarthy is so smart that she devised this memory loss ploy as an elaborate plot to avoid her inevitable death?"

The others around us stayed glued to their seats, witnessing the verbal ping-pong. I pushed my glasses back up on my nose and replied, "I reserve judgment on Miss McCarthy until such time as her memory returns, which I do believe will happen. Until then, I must remain impartial so I may treat her to the best of my ability. Having spent a significant amount of time with Miss McCarthy, I can say that, in my professional opinion, she is not faking her memory loss and has always been open and honest about her willingness to try."

All eyes were on me.

"I have begun to use techniques to try and lull her subconscious into remembering. By all accounts, her recollection of the time spent on field assignment is the first step to unlocking the truth about how her parents died. Until that happens, I am willing to presume her innocent until proven guilty."

The warden leaned forward, a sneer almost as sadistic as Sullivan's uglying her face. "But, Dr Costello, she has already been proven guilty by means of physical evidence. Her death has been set. Memories or not, the girl will die."

I held her gaze as bile crept up my throat. "Then so be it… but I would rather her die knowing the truth than us never finding out what happened to Warden McCarthy. Don't you agree?"

She never answered me, so we all assumed the meeting was over and people started filing out of the room as I stepped into the flow. I froze when my name was called.

"Dr Costello. A word, if you please."

I stepped back and waited until the room had emptied, leaving only me and the warden. Telling myself to keep calm, I struggled as sweat beaded on my forehead and the room felt suddenly far too hot. Theresa poured herself a glass of water and took a sip, keeping me waiting while she assessed my mood.

"It's easy to forget how young you are, Dr Costello. If it were not for someone going over my head, I would not have allowed you to carry on with your silliness regarding Miss McCarthy. How old were you when you got your first degree?"

"I had just turned sixteen. But while I accept that you never wanted me here, warden, I am here and my work is not silliness. The mind is a powerful thing, far greater than any scientific advancement that may or may not happen. The brain protects itself in ways we can only imagine… whether it's keeping someone in a coma so their body can recuperate or suppressing memories that may be difficult for the subject to deal with. I would gladly show you numerous studies related to my research, but I doubt you have time to pour over that many pages."

She tapped her fingernails on the glass, and I waited. Suddenly she laughed, causing me to jump slightly in surprise. "Forgive me, Dr Costello. I am a woman of science, and it is difficult to trust something that cannot be proven and seen with my own eyes. You are also aware that this case is close to my heart. Warden McCarthy and his death caused me much pain. Such a waste of a family."

I nodded in agreement, but something in her voice was not quite right. "No offence taken, Warden. I may be young, but I am determined to unravel this mystery in time. Miss McCarthy has begun to recall things from her past. It is my hope that she will do so in time so we can all rest easy knowing that the true culprit will be punished for their crimes."

She regarded me for a moment and spun in her chair to glance around the mess hall as she said, "Yes, they will." I took that as my dismissal, and I was free to go. Turning on my heels, I high-tailed it out of there before she could say more. Relief flooded through me when I retraced my steps and returned to the safety and comfort of my office. Once inside behind closed doors, I allowed the folder to drop to the ground and me with it. My hands shook, and before I could stop myself I heaved into the wastepaper bin, emptying the contents of my stomach in one go.

I really thought she had caught me, figured it out. Damn it, I was a nerd, not an international spy! Time was my worst enemy, and I had barely weeks to wrap everything up in a nice bow. My nerves faltered.

Upon regaining my composure, I collapsed onto one of the chairs and closed my eyes, eager to cling to an early memory of me and Alana. I needed something to help get through this.

I had changed my clothes about seven times, but every time nothing seemed quite right. Alana had told me to wear whatever I was comfortable in, but I rarely went to pubs and did not want to stick out like a sore thumb. She knew I would go. How could I refuse, with such a beautiful girl by my side?

Despite having had coffee a few times, this was our first official date and "nervous as hell" did not accurately describe the feelings in my gut. In the end, I settled for faded blue jeans, a pale blue t-shirt, and a black short-sleeved shirt over it. We were only going to the pub on campus, but I did not want to embarrass myself by proving why Alana and I weren't logical together.

Knocking on the door of her room, I waited, and my jaw almost hit the floor when Alana stepped out of the room. She was a knockout in a short purple shirt dress, the sleeves rolled up to her elbows and black heels that almost brought her up to my height. Alana smiled at my reaction and linked our arms, laughing as she said she needed to lean on me for support so she did not fall over in the heels.

I liked having her so close to me, and with her dressed like that, it was hard for my brain to remember that she was barely seventeen. My self-esteem soared when Alana ignored all the admiring glances and remained focused on me.

We entered the pub and went straight to the bar where I ordered a pint for me and a Coke for Alana. After finding a private table, we chatted about our day and slipped into a familiar pattern. My knees grazed hers beneath the table. The beer made me feel brave, and I reached for Alana's hand across the table.

As she held my hand in hers, the glint in her eyes made me deliriously happy. We discussed her impending field trip, and she blushed when I said I would miss her over the next few days.

"You'll be working too hard on your presentation to miss me."
She mused.

"Or... missing you so much that I can't concentrate."

She smiled and leaned in close enough that I could have kissed her had I had the nerve. Her eyes twinkled. "Smooth, Costello... very smooth."

It was my turn to laugh then because smooth and Costello didn't belong in the same sentence. A group entered the bar and Alana tensed as one of the girls and her little flock spotted us and made the way to our table.

"Alana, darling, you never mentioned you were heading out to-night."

"I didn't mention it because it was private." Her tone was clipped and sharp, and I wondered if she were embarrassed by my presence. When I tried to ease my hand out of hers, she held on with such a grip that I was bound to have indents of her nails in my palm.

"I had a date with my boyfriend, Dara. It's hard enough to get time together when our schedules are so busy."

Boyfriend? I liked the sound of that.

This Dara person looked me up and down and flicked her blonde hair off her shoulders. *"Oh, you kept that one quiet, missy. Boyfriend of Alana, I know you from somewhere, don't I?"*

"The name's Daniel Costello. I'm sure you would have seen me around campus."

"That's not it… I remember now… you did a couple of lectures for Professor O'Neill, right? On offender profiling?"

"Yeah, that's me."

"Oh, Alana you picked a good one there… a lot of the girls were swooning over your Daniel during his lectures."

Swooning?

Alana cocked her head to the side and flashed Dara her most radiant smile. *"I know, right? And I get to have him all to myself. I am such a lucky girl. S'cuse us, Dara, but I love this song and want to dance with my boyfriend."*

Pulling me from my seat, Alana led me onto the dance floor as the music suddenly changed to a slower tempo. I used the heel and height advantage and slipped my arms around her waist and pulled her close. She rested her head on my chest, and I closed my eyes not wanting this feeling to ever leave. As other couples danced around us, Alana looked up at me and smiled sheepishly.

"Boyfriend?" I asked and laughed again as she shrugged.

She replied simply, *"Our relationship was heading that way, and I'm not known for my patience. So it's official now, and that's that."*

"And I have no say in it?"

"Nope, get used to it. When we are old and grey and our grand-kids are running around the place, you still will have no say." She grinned in the dim light but had never looked so beautiful. Most guys would have run at the mention of kids and grandkids, but I had known from day one that she was the one for me.

Taking her by surprise, I lowered my face to hers and kissed her. Now some men would be reluctant to admit it, but I didn't care. The moment my lips met hers, and she kissed me back, our tongues tasted each other and we both savoured the experience. It felt like heaven.

When we finally broke apart, both of us caught our breath, and she looked up at me with one eyebrow raised. I smiled and simply said, "It seemed like something a boyfriend would do."

Without hesitation, she pulled me in for another kiss and as she laughed, the world faded away. It was just me and my girl and the kiss that made me feel as if I were the luckiest man alive.

The phone shrilled on my desk and dragged me from my happy thoughts. I rose from the chair and answered it on the fourth ring.

"Daniel Costello."

Nothing. But I could hear some breathing on the other end, so I waited and heard the words that flooded me with hope.

"Daniel... it's Dad. I've thought things over... How can I help?"

ALANA

"Build a bridge of memories, stretch it out overseas,
To the end of the world if there's a way."
(LIMP BIZKIT: BUILD A BRIDGE)

I BLINKED MY EYES OPEN, WAITING FOR THEM TO ADJUST TO THE darkened room, awakened by the raised voices that resonated from the kitchen below my bedroom. My parents had never fought while I was growing up, but it seemed that recently as I prepared to leave for my training, the arguments had become a regular occurrence. The topic of disagreement was always about the same thing: my father's job.

Even though the voices were raised, I couldn't quite make out the actual words being said. My mother never raised her voice, never shouted at us when she was mad, making her silence deadlier and louder than any screaming match. She never lost her cool or raised a hand to us, so what had changed in the last couple of months to leave my parents at each other's throats?

The wind howled outside, whistling through the house, and I heard the attic door banging from the hole in the roof that Dad had promised to fix ages ago. I listened as the rain bounced off my window, and it seemed that the storm outside was gathering as much force as the one downstairs.

Worried that the noise of their fight would wake and frighten Sophia, I slipped from my bed, careful to avoid the creaks on the floor just inside the door of my room. Twisting the handle, I pulled the door open and crept down the landing to Sophia's room. Gently, I pushed her bedroom door open and spotted the top of her blonde head under the covers. I watched her sleep for just a brief moment. Her light snores indicated the deep sleep she was in, and I closed the door fully so she would not wake up frightened by the argument in the other room.

Knowing I would be unable to sleep… and just because I was nosey, I quietly made my way back across the landing and passed my room. Instead of returning to my own bed, I sat down on the top step to listen. I shivered, although I didn't know whether it was because I could hear the frustration in my mom's voice or because of the chill that rattled through the old house. Goosebumps littered my skin, and I hugged my knees to my chest.

"Damn it, Sorcha, how many times must I tell you that my work is important."

"And as I keep asking you, Cormac, is your work more important than your family?"

"You know it isn't, but I have a duty of care for those under my watch."

"Those people you care about are criminals, some of them have raped or killed. How can you put those animals ahead of your family again? And what would you do if those in your care decided to seek retribution for being locked up? They could come for us."

"For God's sake, woman! That's not even an issue, and you know it. For some reason, your distrust of Theresa and your anxiety over Alana has made you crazy."

My ears pricked up at the sound of my name, and I leaned my head against the wooden railing in the hopes of hearing more.

"Of course, I'm worried about Alana, Cormac, which does not make me a bad mother. She is your daughter and wants to prove she can be like you. At least with Sophia I know she won't sign up and leave when she turns sixteen. My Sophia is far too soft to be an officer. But Alana takes after you and wants to right the wrongs of the world."

A loud bang broke the silence. For a split second, I was afraid that something bad had happened when the sound of my mom's voice pacified me.

"And that's going to solve everything, isn't it? Does it make you feel better, smashing cups like a barbarian? I swear, Cormac, I am

87

tempted to pack up and take Sophia with me and seek passage to the Free Islands."

My dad growled. "Over my dead body, Sorcha. Do not let that thought cross your mind again. Why must you make more of this than it is?"

"If you were me and I spent most of my free time with another man, would you be so coy about it? No, judging from the scowl on your face, I think not. That woman is a blight. She is power hungry and only follows you because she wants more. Whatever it is, whether it's you or your job, I don't know. Honestly, I don't care. Just don't rush off and spend time with her for work when your daughter is leaving in a few days. God knows when she will be back."

My dad laughed, but a hint of bitterness was hidden in it. "So you're jealous? Ah, come on, Sorcha. I'm not a spring chicken anymore, my love, and I already snared the most beautiful girl ever to walk into my mother's bakery."

"Flattery will get you nowhere, Cormac. I won't budge on this. I swear that woman is nothing but trouble and will put an end to everything you've worked for. Are those criminals and your work with her really worth losing your family?"

My mouth went dry. The sound of my blood pounding blared in my ears. Would she really do it? Take Sophia and leave me here? Yes, I was leaving in a few days, but she was my mom and if she wanted me to go with her I would... wouldn't I?

"Don't make idle threats, Sorcha, it's beneath you. I am trying to reform a system brought in during a time when crime raged across the world and people were scared. Forgive me if I think that children, yes Sorcha, don't shake your head, they are children who deserve a chance at redemption, are worth saving. Some of them are as young as Sophia, some as old as Alana."

I held my breath as I waited for my dad to continue. Taken aback by his words, I couldn't imagine someone as young as Sophia locked up in prison.

"I have tried for years to have my opinions on the death penalty

for young offenders heard, and I am almost there, Sorcha. It will mean a reform in the judicial system as we know it. Would you really threaten to take my family away from me for wanting to ensure that our girls get to live in a better world?"

"One man cannot change the world when it took hundreds to ruin it. What makes you think that your Treatment can do what others have failed to do? Let us live out our lives far from all this controversy and reforms. Are we not enough for you? I'm through discussing this tonight. Go to bed and try not to forget that you have responsibilities other than being warden."

A kitchen chair creaked as my dad stood and pushed away from the table. Far too many things danced inside my head and it took me a second to match the sounds as the kitchen door closed behind him. Before it registered, my dad stood at the bottom of the stairs, eyes narrowed at me.

"How long have you been sitting there?"

"A while," I said quietly. He started climbing the stairs in my direction. My dad appeared like a typical soldier, broad shoulders, thick legs and a buzz cut that tended to be from age, not choice. He had a stern face that I knew could soften, but he was an imposing man all the same. Before he had become warden, he worked his way up the ranks first as a soldier, then as a guard in the newly built prison before accepting the role of warden in the underage unit.

"I'm sorry if we woke you, Alana."

His voice broke through my thoughts as he sat down beside me. I gave him a weak smile as I answered, "S'okay... Guess I should get used to waking up at ungodly hours."

"Are you nervous?"

His question stunned me. "A little... but it's what I want."

My dad sighed and his shoulders sagged as he ran his hand across the stubble on his chin. "Once it makes you happy, that is all that matters. Don't do this for me or anyone else."

I wasn't. All I ever wanted to do was to travel the world and do what was right, to be a little piece in a bigger picture. I never saw myself as the stay at home and have a brood of kids and bake cookies type of girl. Although I respected the hell out of women or men who chose to do that, it wasn't for me.

"I'm sure it will, Dad. I'm just nervous to start training."

"But you have an advantage that others will not." My sideways glance was greeted with a grin. "You trained with the best of the best. Me." He nudged my shoulder with his and I couldn't help but laugh.

"You learned to shoot a gun at ten, Alana, and I showed you plenty of ways to defend yourself without violence. You're fast. Use that to your advantage. I have no doubt that my little girl will do famously well in training."

His voice boomed with pride for me, and I feared I might disappoint him. I would never want that.

"Will you and Mom be okay? I mean, I can stay and defer for a year if things are…" I searched for a word to describe what was going on, but it eluded me.

My dad put his arm around me and dragged me close for a hug. "No, my girl, you go. Your mother and I will be fine. It's nothing for you to worry about. Promise me you won't."

"I promise," I said, but we both knew my words were false, and I would worry, regardless.

He pressed his lips to the top of my head and gave me a final squeeze before saying, "Go on now… go back to bed, so I can clear the air with your mother. But never forget that we love you, Alana, and are proud of you, no matter what happens."

Dad stood and headed off down the stairs. I watched until he disappeared into the kitchen again. My mom picked up the argument where they'd left off, but he shushed her, probably telling her that I was sitting on the stairs. When I heard the rustle of cups, I knew she was making tea, and I left my perch on the stairs to slip back into my room.

Lying on top of the covers, I breathed in the silence. At the end of the week, I would leave my childhood home and carve out a future for myself, but I would still worry about my family and wonder if my mom meant her threat to take Sophia away.

A flash of light through my curtains lit the room, and I listened as thunder followed in the distance. My parents continued speaking in murmured voices below me, and I squeezed my eyes shut, trying to block out the sound. The kitchen door swung shut and my dad's footfalls echoed on the stairs. He paused outside my door, and I heard him sigh.

"Goodnight, Alana."

I didn't answer... couldn't... for fear that my voice would tremble and only add to the pain of the situation. After a moment he moved on, and I heard him check on a still snoring Sophia before coming back down the hall and going into his own bedroom. The familiar creak on the threshold groaned as he stepped on it.

Exhaling a slow, steady breath, I turned on my side, pulling my legs to my chest and relaxed my eyes as a tear escaped from them. Soon I was quietly crying in unison with my mother, her own sobs floating through the house as the attic door banged and the storm continued to rage on.

Waking from the dream only made it seem more real, and I cried. All my grief flowed into my tears, and I wished that by emptying them, the hole in my chest would be filled. It was a long shot, and I did not hold out much hope. How had I forgotten that memory? So my parents had fought. Big deal. But when my mom spoke of Theresa, there was so much hate in her voice, and she did not sound like my mom. Was there some other reason for her feelings? I hoped not.

It was a sobering thought that my parents had argued over his work and Theresa... worse that Mom really might have taken Sophia away. Had there been threats on our lives? What could my dad have been working on that might cause my mom to think there was? They weren't here, so I had no one to ask... no one but Theresa. Sure. Could I even imagine walking up and asking her why my parents fought over her work? And what the

91

hell Treatment had they talked about?

I closed my eyes and pictured my dad's face and the mirror of my own eyes in his. I'd heard his words repeated over and over and over until I memorized the sound of his voice, the feel of him as he hugged me, and even the familiar smell of diesel that wrinkled my nose.

"But never forget that we love you, Alana, and are proud of you, no matter what happens."

"Oh, Dad, I'm so sorry," I whispered aloud as if his ghost would appear beside me and take me in his arms. I knew that I had been loved and safe but had not felt that way for a very long time. I tried to think of a time when safety was as simple as being in my dad's embrace. The image of him changed and it was Daniel's arms that were wrapped around me, his lips kissing my cheek as I leaned into him. The smell of cut grass and summer delighted my senses. We were sitting on a blanket in the grass. Daniel was at my back with me sitting between his legs, my head resting on his chest, his arms snared me from behind. It was natural and easy for us to ignore everyone else as they bustled around us, rushing to classes or home, enjoying a rare day where the sun shined down on us.

I sighed, content, as I watched Daniel out of the corner of my eyes. His own eyes were a vibrant blue against the sunlight and he appeared so relaxed, in jeans and a T-shirt. His smile sparkled with a certain brightness that I had not seen before, and I felt safe in his arms. I tilted my head to get a better look at him while he bent down to kiss me, and I eagerly awaited his lips on mine.

When my eyes opened, I shook my head thinking I really must be going crazy now. That couldn't be an actual memory. Could it? Surely it was only a dream… all in my head. Daniel was the only one trying to help me, so I must have morphed my feelings into something that wasn't real. Next, I would be crushing on Connors and making goo-goo eyes at him. He was so not my type. But Daniel on the other hand…

I let out a hysterical burst of laughter and it continued even harder, becoming uncontrollable. One or two of the inmates shouted for me to quiet down. For some unknown reason, I could not stop laughing and my sides hurt, tears running down my face. I sat up on the bed and placed my bare feet on the ground hoping the chill would bring me back to reality, but the laughter failed to cease, and it was difficult remembering to breathe at the same time.

The door to my cell opened, and the female guard popped her head in.

"Everything alright, McCarthy?"

I couldn't answer her because the laughter was still bubbling under the surface. All I could do was wipe tears away from my eyes. The guard watched and waited for an answer. I must have looked psychotic to her, all bed head and laughing my head off.

Finally, I was able to nod because I was still afraid to open my mouth for fear that another burst of laughter would explode. The guard studied me for a second to make sure I wasn't a danger to myself. When she turned and left the cell, I started into another hysterical bout of giggles.

Where was the laughter coming from, and why would it not just go away? Yup, I was now officially a crazy person. I needed help differentiating reality from dreams and memories from my overactive imagination. The real reason I hadn't answered the guard was because the answer she got would not be the one she sought. She just wanted to do her job and go home at the end of her shift and forget the criminals she was forced to guard.

Why did I keep my answer to myself and succumb to the insane giggling?

Because nothing would ever be all right ever again.

ALANA

"We've got nothing to lose except everything we are."
(WALKING ON CARS: DON'T MIND ME)

SOMEHOW I HAD FALLEN INTO A DREAMLESS SLEEP. I MUST admit, it saddened me, although I didn't know if it was because I hadn't remembered anything new or because I wasn't allowed to experience that warm, happy feeling when my pretend version of Daniel had put his arms around me. Oh, and there was the *almost kiss*.

I spent most of the morning in a daze, forgetting to eat breakfast, or basically playing with my food while I stared into space. It was a Monday, so my session with Daniel wasn't scheduled until later in the day. Monday mornings meant meetings for the staff. So I just sat there for what felt like forever, while some inmates shuffled off to their daily activities. The lifers hung around with nothing to do.

Jayson tried to catch my eye a few times, but I really did not feel in a sociable mood. He, Afsana, and another of the lifers were playing cards. The sound of their easy laughter twisted a knot in my chest. I still found it really difficult to understand how, as young as they were, some people could shirk off their impending demise like a bug on their shoulders, when all I could do was wallow in self-pity and delusional daydreams.

I made the decision to join them on the spur of the moment, but when I spied the Russian vulture swooping in, my mind was totally made up. Veronika and her boy-

94

friend proceeded to sneak up on the unsuspecting trio before I could get across the hall.

As their shadows loomed over the table, Jayson glanced up. After a fleeting look of surprise, he flashed Veronika a megawatt smile and gathered the cards, shuffling them together in his hands as he spoke. "Hey, guys… sit down and join us… makes it more fun with more players."

Veronika sneered at him, and I sensed that the girl was just out looking for trouble. I hovered, shy of the cluster, waiting to see if the bitch started something. Placing both hands on the table, the freakishly tall sixteen-year-old leaned in close to Jayson and sneered. "I vant to play vith the cards. Give them to us."

Jayson leaned back calmly and said, "Sorry, Veronika. The only way you can play with the cards is to join us. My cards, my rules. But by all means, sit and join us."

Veronika struck out and knocked the cards from Jayson's hands, and the deck went flying in the air, scattering all over the floor. I took a quick glance around the room. None of the guards even flinched. Why intervene when you can depend on a trusted behaviour chip should things get messy, right? I spotted Connors' freckled face amongst the guards and adverted my eyes as he begun to shake his head, probably advising me to steer clear of the situation. He knew I had always believed in doing the right thing and still did.

Jayson slid out from his seat as Afsana buried her head in her hands. Jayson stepped forward, and I put a hand on his shoulder. He peeked back, and I nodded. There was no way in hell that I would let the bully best me twice. If David could slay Goliath, then my tiny self could take down the Russian equivalent… even if my ribs still protested.

"Now, Veronika that wasn't very nice, was it? Pick

up the cards and be on your way, and the situation won't have to get physical," I said, no waver in my voice.

A pure look of absolute hatred spread across her face, and my smile widened. This was her weakness. For some reason it was personal for her. Her emotions would get in the way, regardless. But why did she hate me so much? Did this all lead back to my dad?

"Stupid girl. I will finish what I started, and your life will end."

"In case you haven't heard, my life's already going to end. Not much to hold over me, is it?" I had no idea where the bravado came from because my stomach was tied in knots.

Jayson stepped forward as Veronika's boyfriend inched closer to me, and their other friend gave up the ghost and fled the scene. Afsana muttered to herself as her entire body trembled, and Veronika's eyes latched onto me simultaneously while she reached out a taloned hand, ready to grab the petrified girl by the scruff of the neck. I didn't think. Gut instinct took over, and I just reacted to stop Veronika from harming the poor girl again. Balling my fist up tightly, I lunged forward as my fist connected with Veronika's stomach. She let out a strangled sound. *Ha... that's for my ribs, bitch...*

Her eyes widened in fury, and she growled before launching her massive body at me. She was so fixated on her rage that she failed to notice when I sidestepped, and she ran into an empty space with nowhere for her aggression to go. If this had been a cartoon, you would have seen steam coming out of her ears as she shrieked again and charged at me once more.

This time I listened to my dad's voice as he whispered in my head, *"Use your speed to your advantage."* While Veronika raised a hand to use her talons to try and relieve me of an eye, I spun to the side, crouched down, and Veronika's momentum led her straight into my trap. I flicked out my leg, tripping her as she crashed hard to the ground.

What happened next frightened even me, especially since I had dangled meat in front of the animal, and now she would eat me alive. The entire room had frozen while Veronika rose silently to her feet and turned, her face snarled into a vicious twist of rage and hate. She put her hands on the table where Afsana still huddled, and I realized what Veronika intended to do. I swiftly grabbed Afsana by the shoulders and jerked her back out of the path as Veronika imploded.

Shrieking like a wild animal she tossed the table aside, and it crashed into a nearby wall with such force that the wood splintered. The guards gathered finally, coming closer to see if they could diffuse the situation, but Veronika was too far gone for that. She grabbed hold of a stray piece of timber and swung it blindly, screaming. Not only did she smack Jayson on the hip but almost decapitated Connors as he tried to disarm her.

Afsana clung to me, the poor girl having wrapped her body around mine to avoid witnessing the carnage. I found it difficult to move as I watched Veronika stalk towards me, murder in her eyes.

"I will kill you! I will gut you and play with your insides while you still breathe! Your father promised to help me, and now you will pay for his lies… I hope he rots in the grave you put him in."

Time for me to lose it. I pushed Afsana aside with as little force as possible and when her arms were detangled enough for me to attack, I balled up my fist once more. Veronika readied her weapon to aim for my head, but I lunged for her midsection when strong arms wrapped around my waist and held me still.

I presumed it was Jayson who restrained me but was

too keyed up to notice. Veronika launched herself forward only to freeze and drop her makeshift weapon as her body convulsed. She hit the ground, twitching and screaming in pain for what seemed like the longest time before her body stilled, and her eyes rolled back in her head. Veronika was down for the count.

When I went to escape my captor's arms, I stayed a while longer when I heard a familiar voice whisper in my ear. "Alana, calm down, babe. Do not give Theresa an excuse to send you to Treatment. Think, babe, think." Babe? Had I heard him right or was my mind playing tricks on me again? Far too much adrenaline pumped in my veins, and I reluctantly spun out of his arms. Daniel stood before me with his hands held up in a sign of peace. I relaxed, slightly embarrassed at my loss of control. When I opened my mouth to speak, Daniel put his finger to his lips, and I waited.

"Miss McCarthy, please refrain from the use of violence. It would be such a shame to end up ill from the effects of your chip for a day or two when we have made such progress. Clean up this mess, and try to remain calm. I will see you at our session later to discuss this incident."

With a sneaky peek out the side of his glasses, those blues eyes peered up at the observation deck, and I could only imagine that the warden had been watching the whole time. I nodded, and Daniel turned, his lanky frame crossing the room and exiting the door leading to his office.

Turning my attention back to Veronika, I watched as one of the guards lifted her up. She sagged in his arms, her head lolling back as he carried her from the room. Connors rubbed the side of his head, and I did not miss the opportunity to tease him as I paraded past to help Jayson with the debris. "Might knock some sense into ya, Connors."

Connors chuckled lightheartedly and shooed me on. "It would take a harder punch than that to knock some sense into me, McCarthy, a hell of a lot more."

I smiled to myself and bent down, helping to gather the broken table pieces into little piles while some guards brought in a replacement and removed the rubbish to give the appearance that nothing had happened at all. Veronika's boyfriend scampered away once the clean-up was done, not as brave now that the numbers stacked up against him. Jayson sat down at the table after picking up his cards and indicated for me to join him.

Afsana stood at the edge of the table as if debating whether to join us or not. I tried to reassure her with a smile as she cautiously took her seat, and I said. "Hey, I'm sorry if I hurt you." She smiled back at me, and I got a clearer view of her face. Afsana looked younger than she was. Olive skin blended in with sea-green, innocent eyes. I knew this girl could never be a terrorist.

"Hey, Jayson, how's the hip?" I asked.

Jayson's lopsided grin made me laugh with his reply, "I've had worse knocks when I used to play rugby in school. Although Veronika hits nearly as hard as they did." He shuffled the cards and flicked them between his fingers. The tension had almost evaporated from the room. My session with Daniel was in an hour, and I tried to remember how to interact with people. I had not always been socially awkward.

But, of course, my mouth worked faster than my brain, and I studied Afsana while blurting out, "What are you in for?" Jayson cocked an eyebrow at me while Afsana tried to avoid eye contact. "I know what Jay is here for, and everybody knows my story, but I'd like to hear what happened to you."

Afsana glanced at Jayson, who shrugged. She brushed a strand of hair from her face. "I am terrorist."

"No, I don't believe that, Afsana. You don't have it in you… I can see it in your eyes."

She appeared startled for a moment before blinking and unfolding her story for me.

"I grew up in a wealthy family in Kabul. My father was a doctor and my mother ran the nursery in the hospital where my father worked. We had a good life. Money meant that my father could purchase the best education for his children. My brother leaned towards medicine like my father, but I had, how you say it, a knack for computers and fixing things.

We had been given a school project for sciences to replicate any item from past technologies, and I was excited. I had used my pocket money to go to the markets on my way home from class that day. All I bought was some wiring, an old battery, and a few other items so I could build an old radio, program it on a frequency and listen to music as they did long ago.

As I started to leave the market, there was an explosion. The ground shook. I was terrified. Dust billowed, clogging the air, and I had to pull my hijab over my nose so I would not inhale the dust. People screamed and wailed. Bodies littered the street. A siren sounded as the army filtered into the market, and the dogs were unleashed to sniff out further threats."

She paused for a moment and Jayson reached out and held her hand in support. I wanted to do the same, but we were practically strangers. She looked at Jayson with admiring eyes and squeezed his hand back before turning back to me to finish her story.

"I just wanted to leave. The scene sickened me with the maimed bodies that seemed to almost trip me up at every turn. Horrified, I paused to see a young child so badly burned I could not tell if it was a boy or a girl. The smell of burned flesh was putrid, made me sick. I clung to my messenger bag and was almost to the far side of the market when one of the dogs barked at me and reared up. The officer wielding the dog ordered me to stop, his gun pointed directly at my head."

A muscle ticked in Jayson's cheek as his face turned all protective while Afsana neared the conclusion of her story.

"He came to me and asked where I had come from and where was I going. I explained to him that I had come from school and had stopped to pick up some material for a project before I met my father at the hospital. He grabbed the bag from my hands and searched it, his eyes widening at the contents. He immediately pointed at me, calling me a terrorist. I was tackled to the ground and arrested for the bombing of Kabul."

Afsana paused as her voice cracked with emotion, and I fought the urge not to reach out and engulf her in a hug.

"I was never allowed to plead my case nor did they look into my story to confirm that I indeed had a project for science class. They said they found some bomb making techniques on my laptop, but it was false. My family disowned me publicly to avoid any further shame to the family name. And then I was sent here for the murder of twenty-seven people. I lie in bed at night, and all I can see is the empty stare of that child looking back at me."

The poor girl shivered, and I sighed. Three prisoners with a lot in common. Jay had only wanted to help his ill sister and got here by accident. Afsana had been blamed for something the girl would never even conceive doing. And me? Who the hell knew if I was guilty or not? Deep down it seemed wrong even thinking that I could have killed my family.

I reached out and took the girl's free hand as tears trailed down her gaunt cheeks. "Hey, I barely know you, and even I can tell there is no way you are capable of murder." She narrowed her gaze. I continued, "You can tell by a person's eyes. I see nothing that would lead me to think that you would mean anyone harm. Sometimes people see and believe what they want because it's easier that way. Stick with Jayson. He'll keep you safe." I didn't say the next part out loud because she would die as I would, and I would not be around to watch over her.

The quiet girl stared square in my eyes, and I had to admit that maybe she was tougher than I gave her credit. She focused on me for another minute or so before opening her mouth again. "I do not believe you are also capable of the things they say that you did, Alana."

I snorted out a laugh and asked, curious to hear her answer. "And what makes you say that?"

"You can tell by a person's eyes and I see nothing that would lead me to think that you would mean anyone harm." She repeated my exact words back to me with a silly little smile. It made me sad to think that she would have been a beautiful woman had fate carved a different path for her.

"Now that you guys are BFFs, can we play some cards, please? All this talk of dying is depressing as hell."

I laughed at Jayson's comment, and so did Afsana. She nodded for him to deal. After a few rounds of rummy, Jay got miffed when I kept beating him. I'd spent some of my youth playing cards with my dad and a few of his army cadets. Afsana proved to have an infallible poker face, her expression only softening when Jay batted his eyes in her direction. The girl was useless against his charms.

Despite earlier events, I enjoyed myself and lost track of time, a first since ending up in here. I continued to play a few more games with Jay and Afsana until a hand rested on my shoulder. When I looked up, Connors' smiling face beamed down at me.

"Sorry to break up the party, McCarthy, but you and the doc have a date."

A date, yeah right. I wish. I said my goodbyes and after promising to return to their table for dinner, followed Connors to face the music with Daniel. *Should I tell him about my dreams or would that just embarrass me completely?* I stayed lost in my musings as Connors led me out of the mess hall and into the corridor.

He held out an arm in front of me, and I stopped as two guards left one of the rooms carrying an unconscious Veronika with them. Her eyes were red and blotchy, evidence that she had been crying, but her gaze seemed unfocused. They dragged her by the arms down the hall, past Daniel's office, and I watched in amazement as a door slid open to reveal an elevator. They hoisted her into it and turned, facing us.

One of the guards had fingernail scratches trailing down his face and the other had blood trickling from his nose. They exchanged nods with Connors as the doors clanged shut, and I heard the elevator motor start. The noise sounded as if it was going down. I hadn't realized there was anything below this level.

Connors removed his arm from mine, and we continued on our way to Daniel's office. Connors opened the door, and I took a deep breath and entered, still unsure of whether to seek help to clear the clutter that was gathering inside my head.

DANIEL

"I can see through you, see to the real you"
(STAINED: OUTSIDE)

TODAY A NEW TWIST IN THE ATMOSPHERE SURFACED BETWEEN me and Alana: awkwardness. She kept averting her gaze, a faint blush creeping on pale skin when she peeked out through hooded lashes. Was she embarrassed that I had stepped in during her fight with Veronika? Or was this something else entirely? I had never seen this side of her, before or after her memory loss, and her coyness was completely alien to me.

"Would you like to talk about the incident with Veronika?" I asked softly, hoping my tone would reassure her that I was not angry or whatever the hell she thought I was.

She shook her head. Today she sat as far from me as possible, on the couch by my bookcase, hugging her knees to her chest. Her head rested on her knees, and apart from the few times she glanced out through the strands of hair, she avoided meeting my glances.

"Is there something new bothering you, Alana? You know you can speak freely here, don't you?"

She lifted her head as her face creased in a frown. "I don't have anything to say. We fought, she got shocked. Now I'm here. Do you have to overanalyse every single thing that happens to me?"

Her words were spoken in anger—but I didn't think it was directed at me—hopefully just at her situation.

104

From the way she dug her nails into the palm of her hands, Alana had become increasingly frustrated about her impending death sentence. With her birthday looming, we had precious little time left, so I pushed.

"I get the feeling you are angry at me for some reason, Alana. Would you like to share that so maybe we can go back to being friends?"

She snickered a cold, dead sound. "Friends? Is that what we are? You're my shrink. I'm your project, the broken little doll who needs her head fixed. Even if I get my memories back, I'm dead anyway. Nothing I want will matter either way."

"And what do you want?"

"I want you to stop asking me fucking questions!" Her voice rose, but I fought a smile. This was my Alana, fiery and fierce. I pushed my glasses up on the bridge of my nose, picked up a folder and began flipping through pages. It gave her a chance of letting the steam run out of her anger until she was ready to speak again. I looked out over the top of my glasses and watched as the frustration drained from her face. Her expression returned to looking sad. I pretended to focus on the folder as she stood and paced around my office as she had done so many times before. She stopped at the bookcase which held numerous paperback books I had collected over the years.

"Why do you bother with books when all the information can be stored on your computer?"

Setting the folder down, I pondered before answering, "Enjoyment has been taken out of so many things because of technology. That's not simply why I collect books, but I prefer to read from them. It's an important connection with history rather than leaving it behind as we evolve."

"Your house must be full of old junk... Your girlfriend must be demented from it." Another blush flushed her cheeks, and my heart skipped a beat.

"Most of my collection is in storage at the moment because I must reside here until my studies are complete. And not that it's relevant, but I do not have a girlfriend at the moment." *Actually, I do and she is standing in my office with no clue as to who I am.*

Alana opened her mouth to speak but clamped it shut again. She crouched down and ran her fingertip along the spines of my books including Shakespeare, Tolstoy, George RR Martin, Tolkien, Joyce, Yeats, Wilde, Beckett, and Keane. Her eyes examined every single title and absorbed the names and authors as she had done once before. My breath hitched, remembering her in my campus bedroom examining those same books as she did now, making fun of the fact that I had volumes of poetry.

Once again, she zoned in on my battered collection of poetry and pulled one out from the shelf. Sitting down on the floor, she opened the book and mock coughed at imaginary dust, bringing a ghost of a smile to my lips while I pretended not to notice. I listened as she swiped through each page, the rustle of paper against her fingers a more welcome sound than the previous stony silence.

I let her alone, lost in the sanctuary of words, but carefully watched her. Her nose scrunched up in a cute wrinkle and I could only think that she was trying to figure out the meaning of some forgotten poem. Without notice, she turned a page, her eyes moving slowly from side to side as she devoured each poem slowly and carefully. Alana chewed on her bottom lip and my heart skipped a beat again.

"Why do poems have to be so morbid... even the supposed love poems are all about loss and grief," she asked in a whisper. I was uncertain if she was talking to herself or to me.

"Maybe because the greatest loves of all always end in tragedy," I answered.

"Bullshit."

"Bullshit?"

"Yes. The greatest love *stories* may end in tragedy, but real love is never so epic that it can result in mutual death or suffering."

"So you basically think that all the great, epic stories that we all grew up reading and listening to are really just bullshit."

She nodded and returned the poetry book to its rightful place. "Take Romeo and Juliet. If you look at the core of it, Romeo was just a randy teenager who promised to marry Juliet so he could get into her pants or whatever. And Shakespeare just couldn't end it with her dying and him going on his merry way... so to make it a better story, he offed 'em both and boom... instant romantic tragedy to last the test of time."

"Aren't you far too young to be this cynical?" The words had left my mouth before I had a chance to mull over them.

"I won't ever get to experience it, so I'm within my rights to be cynical."

We stared at each other for what seemed like ages. I would have given just about anything to rush to her, take her in my arms and tell her that we have yet to finish our own epic love story. She fidgeted in her seated position, dragging her gaze from mine and returning to skim the shelves. Snatching *The Fellowship of the Ring*, she paged through it as if searching for something in particular. Once she found it, she smiled and turned to speak.

"All that is gold does not glitter;

"Not all those who wander are lost

"The old that is strong does not wither;

"Deep roots are not reached by frost." (Tolkien 1954)*

I knew she would eventually go there, and hope ignited a spark in my chest as I began a conversation that we had had once before.

"You've read Tolkien?" I asked.

"I've seen the movies."

"But nothing beats reading the book. It allows your imagination to be taken to a faraway world. Yes, the movies are great and true to the book, but there is something so magical about getting lost among the pages as you delve deeper into other worlds. If not for the books, that would not exist."

"I feel like I've had this argument before," Alana muttered to herself.

"Maybe someone tried to persuade you about the benefits of books over films?"

"No, that's not it... I dunno... sort of felt like Déjà vu or whatever."

Yes! This was what I needed, little reminders of the past year so it might jog something in her, and all at once she would remember our life together.

"Anyway, I only like it because, even though the ending is happy, you can still feel saddened that Frodo dies or whatever... seems more realistic that way."

"And does your story not seem real?" I asked, curious to know her true feeling on the subject. "Do you not feel like something is missing from your story that should be there?"

Alana pointed to her head and said, "Um, hello, memory loss here. Of course, I'm missing something."

"That's not what I meant—and you know it." I couldn't mask the frustration that had slipped its way into my tone. Alana's eyes widened at it. "I am trying to help you remember, but it seems that you are more interested in participating in fights than trying to unlock what's inside your head. Do you not want a chance to be proven innocent?"

She pushed herself off the floor and stood... hands on her hips. "And if I remember and am innocent, what then? I go back to the house where my family was murdered and live out my life as a recluse? I have no family, no career, no one to care about me."

"I care about you."

"Yeah, but you get paid to. I won't see you if I'm free, and I don't want to be alone. I'm better off dead."

The pen I held almost snapped in half as anger flooded me. I wished I could shake some sense into her and ask her if I risked my life for nothing. Was my love for her as easy to dismiss as her belief that epic love simply didn't exist? It did for me. She was it. Counting to ten in my head and closing my eyes, I breathed deeply to try and unleash something close to calm throughout my body. When I opened my eyes again, Alana had sprawled out on the couch, her small frame not even covering the whole seat. She had neatly tucked one foot over the other and her arms lay idly on her stomach. Her own eyes were closed and her breathing stilled and slow as if sleeping. I had an alarming vision of her in that exact position in a coffin and had to blink a few times to eliminate those thoughts from my mind.

"Daniel?" she asked without opening her eyes.

"Yes, Alana."

"Would you read something to me? I'm not being weird or anything, but it's been such a long time since someone read to me and I can't remem—" Her words caught in her throat, and I had the strange feeling she might cry. I rose and stepped away from the desk and stood in front of my bookcase, suddenly at a loss as what to read.

"Would you like anything in particular?"

She shook her head. "No. Surprise me. I like to listen to you. Your voice, it's as if it were made to tell stories. I just want to listen to you speak." A blush reddened her cheeks again, and I took another few minutes to select the perfect choice. Truly, it seemed like the only choice. I pulled the armchair over so we were only inches apart.

Clearing my throat, I became nervous as if I were that same awkward boy who attracted the attention of the bright, bubbly girl. I was a smitten teen again. Alana waited patiently for me to begin, and I glanced up at the clock to see that we had almost an hour and a half left for the session.

"It began with the forging of the Great Rings," I began and Alana smiled. "Three were given to the Elves, immortal, wisest and fairest of all beings. Seven to the Dwarf-lords, great miners and craftsmen of the mountain halls. And nine, nine rings were gifted to the race of Men, who above all else desire power. For within these rings was bound the strength and the will to govern each race. But they were all of them deceived, for another ring was made. Deep in the land of Mordor, in the Fires of Mount Doom, the Dark Lord Sauron forged a master ring in secret, and into this ring he poured his cruelty, his malice and his will to dominate all life. One ring to rule them all." (Tolkien 1954)*

I paused and looked over the top of the book at Alana, whose smile did not fade even though she had fallen asleep. Her faint snores were a welcome and familiar sound to me. Many a night she had fallen asleep by my side after a long day's training. I closed the book and returned it to the shelf. Pulling an old blanket over her, I noticed the time so she could sleep for at least an hour before I had to wake her.

Consciously being quiet, I sat at my desk and did some paperwork regarding her case. Soon I would be called to the warden's office for a discussion of her progress and would have to provide some proof that her memory was returning.

I outlined her memory of Jayson and how I had a sense that she was conflicted because she was uncertain if her memories were real or fabricated. It was all the truth, but I was certain the warden would have some choice comments about it. A lot needed to be put in place before the Hail Mary plan I kept close to my chest could happen. A few pieces of the puzzle were coming along nicely: Alana was beginning to trust me, my dad had agreed to help, and Connors and Jayson watched out for Alana when I couldn't.

I chewed the end of my pen and observed the sleeping girl while her eyes darted behind her eyelids and she tossed on the couch, fingers clutching the blanket for dear life.

She began to mutter in her sleep and I moved closer to her and knelt down beside the couch so I could hear what she said. "Blood, blood everywhere. I can hear the screams."

"Where is the blood, Alana... who is screaming?"

"All over the place... my dad... he's telling me to... oh god, there's so much blood."

"Think, Alana, think, babe... what is your dad telling you?"

"I can't... I don't want to... Daniel, there is so much blood... they're coming."

"Who is coming, Alana? Think hard, please."

And then her mouth opened to a blood-curdling scream, and she bolted upright. Her eyes darted around the room like a frightened animal looking for an escape, and I saw the start of a panic attack building up as tears flowed from her eyes.

"It's okay, Alana. It was just a dream." The words were barely out of my mouth when she wrapped her arms around my neck and pressed her damp face to my shoulder. I didn't say anything, just put my arms around her and whispered, "Shh, it's okay… it was only a dream."

We stayed like that for a while longer, and then she untangled her arms from my neck. Looking down at my tear-stained shirt, she spoke in a cracked voice. "I'm sorry. I just ugly cried all over you."

"You have nothing to be sorry about."

She straightened herself up, taking the handkerchief I had just pulled from my pocket, and blew her nose before stuffing it into her pants pocket. Her brown eyes were equal parts scared and confused.

"Would you like to talk about the dream?"

A string on her pants suddenly became very interesting and she focused her attention on the ground. "I don't really remember it, the dream, I mean. I was scared and alone and trapped. Did I say something?"

Now I had a dilemma. Should I tell her what she had spoken and frighten her more or tell her the truth in the hopes she could relay to me what her father was trying to tell her. I chose neither.

"Nothing that you need to stress about now. Have you had these nightmares before?"

"A few times," she replied in a low voice. "Sometimes I have other dreams."

"About what?"

Alana turned towards me for a second before shaking her head. "I'd rather not talk about it. Not today."

"Okay, Alana, but it might help to talk to me about it."

"Next time."

"Promise?"

"Promise."

She forced a precious little smile, and I had to resist the urge to lean in and kiss her. A thought had flashed

behind her eyes before I sat back, putting distance between us. The knock on the door startled us both and it
slid open as Connors strode in.

"Time to go, McCarthy."

She rose and joined Connors by the doorway. Without another word, I stood and watched them leave. Alana did not look back, and I was grateful because if she
had, my face would probably have given away a million
secrets. The door closed. I sighed in relief.

Sitting back down at my desk, I opened up the folder
and sought out a fresh blank page. On it I pondered Alana's dream as I wrote down my musings.

If Alana had killed her family then why would the
sight of their blood freak her out so much?

What could her dad have possibly been trying to tell
her?

And if she did not kill her family, then who did?

I had no answers to those questions, but I vowed to
find some. Determination to set Alana free gave me a
single-minded approach, and I would not rest until she
knew exactly what had happened and who I was.

Thinking along those lines reminded me of our earlier conversation about how she missed being outside in
the fresh air. Other inmates were allowed time out in a
small open air yard, but Alana and other death row inmates were considered dangerous and had not set foot
outside in a long time. During our time together, we had
spent many summer nights just walking around outside
and trying to put the world right. Now that I was sure
her mind was beginning to unlock its secrets, I would do
anything in my power to move this along.

Heart pounding in my chest, I lifted the phone's receiver and keyed in the extension number. The phone

rang, once, twice, three times before I heard a click and a rather nasally voice.

"Warden Lane's office."

"This is Doctor Daniel Costello. I would like to make an appointment to speak with Warden Lane, please."

A muffled click on the line aroused my suspicions that someone else was listening in or at least telling the secretary what to say.

"And may I ask about your business with Warden Lane that cannot wait until Monday's staff meeting? She is rather busy this week."

I inhaled and exhaled, calming myself so my voice did not tremble or give any indication of how nervous I actually was.

Instead, I spoke the words I needed to say. "I want to ask for permission to take a prisoner outside."

*Tolkien, J.R.R. 1954. *The Fellowship of the Ring.*

ALANA

"The fragile, the broken sit in circles and stay
unspoken. We are powerless."
(BRING ME THE HORIZON: HOSPITAL FOR SOULS)

FOR AN INSANE MOMENT BACK THERE, I THOUGHT DANIEL
had been about to kiss me, and for the first time in ages,
I felt alive. I saw something different in his eyes—a
longing—as if he had been waiting for me to lean in and
place my lips on his. That was just being crazy, right?

I could listen to his voice all day. Something in the
sound of his speech was soothing and melodic. I regretted falling asleep because I missed out hearing him read
Tolkien as if he had memorized the words and did not
need the book at all. He had watched me fall sleep, covering me with the blanket so I wouldn't get cold. There
was an intimacy in that too. Or maybe my mind was
over-thinking things again… it tended to do that.

While Connors led the way back to the mess hall, I
mulled it all over quietly to myself. Once inside, he gave
me a quizzical look and opened his mouth to say something but closed it again without speaking. He backed
away and returned to his post in the hall as if nothing
had been on his mind. I was inclined to return to my cell,
close my eyes and listen to Daniel reading to me again
in my head. Had I just wasted two hours being angry
and falling asleep? With so many questions to ask and
precious little time to do it, I struggled with the ability to
even do that right. Damn, I forgot to ask him about the
Treatment! Rounding the outside of the tables and head-

ed for the stairs, I held onto the banister. That's when I spotted a hand frantically waving in the air from the corner of my peripheral vision.

"Hey, Alana, come sit with us," Jayson shouted across the room, causing everyone to look in my direction. He sat with the rest of his group, and I shook my head, but he was already out of his chair and headed my way. As much as I would have loved to sit in my cell and daydream, I had enjoyed myself with that group the last time, despite Veronika's antics.

I approached the table and took the chair that Jayson had dragged over. All in all, seven people were seated at the table, including me, Jayson, and Afsana, who flashed me a brief smile. Two of the inmates wore blue from head to toe, one was dressed in a green jumper, and the one I was most worried about wore red. Red meant dangerous offender... not bad enough to warrant a seat on death row, but other prisoners were wary, regardless.

Jayson must have sensed the uneasy tension in the atmosphere, so he took it upon himself to get the conversation rolling. Plonking himself down on the empty seat next to me, he beamed at those gathered around the table and simply said, "You guys all know Alana... and as you can tell from the dazzling shade of black she is wearing, Alana is in the same boat as me. She has a slight issue with forgetting things, but we won't hold that against her now, will we? How about we do share time? You guys can introduce yourself so we can all be bestest friends."

I snorted out a laugh, just couldn't help myself, while the rest of the group remained shocked by Jayson's flippant attitude. The two dressed in blue locked eyes with each other, the girl nudging the boy with her elbow. Slightly chubby, the boy had pale skin and grey-blue eyes. His hair was pulled back into a black tangled mess of a ponytail, and he had a thin line of hair under his nose as

116

if he had tried to grow a moustache and failed. His caterpillar eyebrows wiggled as he thought, almost meeting in the middle when his gaze narrowed.

The girl seemed shy and kept glancing at her fingernails. Her strawberry-blonde hair was styled into a pixie cut with jagged edges at the end as if she had clipped the hair herself. She had a cluster of freckles on her cheeks, so I assumed that somewhere in her heritage was Irish blood. Didn't we all? She nudged the boy again and he sighed, his chest puffing out in annoyance as he fidgeted with the collar of his jumper. Jayson cast him a stern look.

"Uh… Hi… I'm Darren and this is Emily," he said. I made out a hint of an accent, although according to the United Parliament, due to the mass exodus from Ireland way back when, accents were dying out on the Island. Sometimes it might be picked up by a finely tuned ear. "As you can see, Emily and I are in for weapons charges. We have six months left on our sentence, and then we go home."

I tended to be on the curious side, but did not want to be rude and blurt out the obvious question. What sort of weapons charges? I knew it could have been anything from carrying a concealed knife to owning a gun without a licence or not paying the gun tax. My parents had taught me manners, so I waited for someone else to ask. Again, it was Jayson who spoke out.

"You're not telling the whole story… Emily, why don't you tell Alana what happened?"

"Why? It's not like she cares or anything. She's just looking for a distraction from her own death."

"Emily! Damn it, girl, why do you have to be such a bitch all the time?" Jayson growled. I put a hand on his shoulder to still him.

"It's okay, Jay, the girl doesn't have to tell me anything if she doesn't want to. It's her own business."

117

Jayson glared at Emily, who edged closer to Darren, her momentary burst of rebellion quashed down by Jayson's glare. Darren sighed again and said, "We raided a supply unit and got caught. Emily carried a knife. I had a gun. It was empty because I only wanted to scare them, but we got caught and sent here. We needed food for our families because where we lived was too far from any major town to make them send food or anything our way."

I nodded, understanding the frustration they must have felt. Although the Island did not have any city lines or boundaries, small towns were needed in order to provide it with a bountiful supply of workers and villages to call home. In some parts of the Island, sporadic villages had popped up, catering to those who would not be deemed suitable for work in the prison or any other desirable job. So many tiny villages with starving people still remained. I couldn't help but wonder if these two were better off in here.

Jayson nodded to the girl in green, and she smiled at me and proceeded to dart off into a conversation as if she were bursting to get her story out. "Hi! Alana. My name is Nikki. I'm here because I was selling my grandma's meds at school. The headmaster of my very prestigious boarding school found me out and sent me here. Just another boarding school for me. Once I get out, I'll be sent to another one and probably end up back here another time. No biggie."

I must have looked flummoxed because she giggled, a light-hearted, childish giggle and swept a hand through the air. "I know, right? You must think I'm mad, but if you can't get attention from your parents for doing good things, then bad is the way to go."

"So you basically got arrested and sent here for attention?"

"Yup. My parents are American dignitaries. Having

a daughter here just makes them look bad. Not ideal dinner party conversation, but it wouldn't surprise me if they pretended to only have one child. My sister is the golden girl who is engaged to a member of the United Parliament and is poised for great things. I'll be bounced around to various boarding schools until I'm twenty-one and then set loose on the world. Then I won't have to see them again."

Lost for words, I said nothing, but my eyes drifted to the boy dressed in red. He was a typical handsome jock, broad shoulders and defined arms from either sports or working out. His brown hair had some curl only on the left-hand side of his forehead. High cheekbones and a dimpled smile complemented his green eyes. Seeing him dressed head to toe in red made me extremely cautious.

The boy noticed my discomfort and smiled, my own frown deepening as he spoke. "Don't worry. I get that a lot."

Jayson nudged me, and my eyes averted from Red to him. "Do you really think I would associate with a sexual deviant? Well, other than myself, that is."

For some reason, I trusted Jayson and felt a little guilty for judging him when I hadn't heard his story. People were forever doing it to me. I held up my hands in apology and tried to soften my face. "Sorry."

Red shook his head and sparkled another dazzling smile in my direction. "It's okay. If I were in anybody else's shoes, I'd do the same." I didn't say anything and he continued on with his story. "Yeah, you guessed that I am in for apparent dangerous offences, but I'm innocent." I couldn't help it as I raised an eyebrow. Red laughed. "Yeah, I know. Everyone says it, but I mean it. I have another year on my sentence and have been here since I was sixteen. My boyfriend's parents caught us having sex. Rather than deal with the fact that their son likes guys, they accused me of rape. Jeremy didn't deny or reinforce their accusations, but in some places being gay was still a big taboo. Because of our ages, I ended up here. He was fifteen, almost sixteen, at the time, and in our backwater town it seemed easier for them to send me here than deal with it themselves.

When I turn eighteen and get out, I can't return to my hometown. It's part of the conditions of my release. My parents have been shunned and have since moved away, but Jer still lives there. I haven't seen or heard from him since. Not even a letter. We had been together for a year under their noses, but sometimes people can be selectively blind about things they don't want to see."

"I'm sorry... that sounds..." I searched for the correct word to use, but nothing came to mind. "Awful."

"Thanks... the name is Marshall, by the way."

"Typical American name there, Marshall."

"Yeah, the all-American boy. That's what I am." The words were dry, bitter even, but Marshall was smiling. It failed to reach his eyes. I knew that look. He was lost thinking about his past and the people who abandoned him and the ones he left behind. Been there, done that, except the people in my past are long dead or forgotten.

Now that the air was broken, we all chatted away with Jayson telling stories and jokes. Emily continued to stare daggers at me, for whatever reason. Why she had to look down her nose at me was anybody's guess, but I simply ignored her. Jayson and Marshall broke off into a conversation about football, and I zoned out a little, leaning back in my chair and listening to the noise of chatter around me. Looking upwards, I gazed out past the ceiling, watching as clouds gathered, greying as they did, blocking out any chance of sunlight. The sky darkened, and the patter of raindrops on the glass roof only added to the din in the room. It didn't take long for the rain to grow heavy, and soon it was pelting off the roof, sounding like sharp rapping on a door.

A commotion started up behind me, and I turned around in my seat to see what everyone was gaping at. Veronika had stepped into view and it was as though she'd undergone a complete transformation. Gone was the wild look in her eyes, replaced by a blank, empty stare. Her clothes were tidy. Even her hair was pulled back into a braid that held her usually unkempt hair off her face. I tensed up as she approached our direction and sat still, open-mouthed as she simply strolled past us without so much as a sneaky look. Had Veronika been replaced by a robot or a zombie?

Veronika continued her forward progress, slow and deliberate as the Russian inmates rose to greet their former leader. Her boyfriend pushed out past them and whispered something to her, but when she didn't respond, he shoved her away. To everyone's amazement, including my own, Veronika apologized in plain English with no hint of her Russian accent and then continued on her way. What the hell was going on?

The boy raced after her, put his hands on Veronika's shoulder, spun her around and began to shake her. He screamed at her to snap out of whatever daze she was in. I spied Connors stepping forward and the guards inching their way in the arguing couple's direction. The crowd shifted slightly, and I stood to get a proper look at what was happening.

While the boy continued to shake Veronika, blood trickled down from her nose. It was as if a light switch had suddenly gone out inside her, and her entire body shuddered, then she slumped to the ground. I rushed closer as Veronika convulsed on the floor. My view was blocked by the gathering crowd, so I slipped under the taller inmates and edged closer. The guards tried pushing everyone back. Veronika continued to tremble, blood now trickling from her ears, as well.

My own thoughts returned to the nightmare where everyone haemorrhaged blood, and I pinched myself hard to make sure I wasn't dreaming again. Another shift in the crowd allowed a perfect view as Veronika stopped moving. Connors bent down to check her pulse. I knew without a doubt she was dead.

I strained to hear and almost made out what the two guards in front of me were saying. "Treatment failed. Damn it, and it was going so well," one commented, shaking his head.

"Yeah. They'll need another candidate soon now," the other one replied.

"That bitch is going to be in some mood now." The guard looked up towards the control room.

"Let's hope our shift finishes before she hears about the Russian's death."

I stood up straight, ready to ask the guards what Treatment they meant when delicious blue eyes caught mine. Daniel was leaning against the doors leading to his office, observing the situation. He must have read something in my gaze because he lifted a hand up and held a finger to his lips, silently asking me to do the same.

An alarm sounded, dragging my gaze from Daniel's. When I glanced back, it was as if he had melted into the shadows and vanished. Another guard and Connors laid a sheet over Veronika's body as a few cries came from the Russian table. Connors stood, and in an authoritative voice he shouted. "All right, inmates, return to your cells immediately for lockdown." Nobody moved, so he tried again. "Now!"

The alarm shrilled again, and I backed away from the body and inserted myself into the crowd of inmates making their way up the stairs. I lost myself in a sea of unrest, inmates utterly shocked that a fellow inmate had died. Death was a daily occurrence, with some of our own deaths scheduled, but it rarely happened unexpectedly. Most prisoners either died on death row or were rehabilitated and sent back outside to be functioning members of society. The ripple effect of Veronika's death would stay with them for a long time, even though the girl had been disliked. Jayson was suddenly standing beside me, his hand in Afsana's. To say the girl looked relieved was an understatement.

"Is it inappropriate to say *ding dong the witch is dead?*"

"I don't think there are many here who will miss her... so no, not really."

"Something seriously weird is going on," Jayson muttered just low enough for me to hear. I nodded as we split off and went back to our cells. Before I reached mine, I peered down over the ledge and saw them carrying Veronika away. The alarm stilled.

Mention of Treatment again. Jayson was right, there was something very strange happening and I knew one person who could give me answers. Time for the good doctor to answer my questions for a change.

DANIEL

"Is it okay to be afraid of hope if you don't know
how to keep it?"
(CHARLIE SIMPSON: DOWN, DOWN, DOWN)

THE WORDS POMP AND PAGEANTRY WERE NOT LOST ON THE
warden. Her office had been decked out. One of the bland
beige walls was almost hidden behind framed diplomas
and degrees. A trophy case occupied most of another
wall. Medals for service to the United Parliament's
Department of Corrections, medals for being top of her
class in everything from strategy to aggression prevention
were laid out with care and precision. Anyone entering
her office couldn't help but be drawn to the excessive
shine.

My attention was centred on a small cluster of
photos that sat atop the trophy case. Some of the back-
grounds were familiar: the centre, the prison gates, and
even the pub Alana and I had gone to on our very first
date. I spotted the warden straight away in the photos,
but she appeared less serious than she was now. Theresa seemed happy, carefree, laughing, and even smiling,
whether she was dressed in casual clothes or her navy
prison uniform.

I stood, studying the photos while I waited and
quickly noticed a frame lurking in the back as if hidden
in plain sight. It seemed to draw me towards it, and I
instinctively reached for it and brought it forward to get
a clearer look. All the other frames were the same black
wood finish... but this one was fancy, with a black border

124

and another silver border inside it. This photo was special to her. Why?

After a long minute of study, I took in the warden's appearance. Dressed in dark denim jeans and a loose salmon shirt, her hair hung over her shoulders and she wore a faint hint of makeup. Theresa stared up into the face of a man, someone who was looking the other way as if watching something else. He had an arm slung over her shoulder, and a broad smile showed in his eyes. Theresa gazed adoringly at the man but as I studied him further, I couldn't hold back a gasp. Cormac McCarthy.

I had only ever seen other pictures of him with Alana, in the online bulletin when he died. The man in this photo was older and had far more facial hair than his younger self. As I focused on him, Alana's resemblance to him was obvious. They had the same shape face and nose, and the same colour eyes, a rich hazel. The photo wasn't a sharp original, obviously a poor reproduction with the image zoomed in. Had Theresa done that herself?

A clickity-clack of heels echoed in the hallway, getting louder as they drew nearer. I returned the frame to its place and sat in a chair in front of the desk, trying to appear normal. My skills as a liar would be put to the test. Something about the photo gave me the creeps.

The door opened behind me, and I stood, turning to greet the warden. Flashes of the carefree girl in the earlier pictures came to mind and were replaced by the harsh, cold woman standing before me. She looked less than pleased that I had requested a special meeting, and I knew if I had any charm at all, now was the time to use it.

"Dr Costello, please sit." She waved her hand in the direction of a chair, and I complied. Waiting until she had sat, she stared me dead in the eyes before beginning.

I spoke the words I had rehearsed over and over in my head all night. "Warden, thank you for agreeing to see me. I know my request is unorthodox, but I think we will start to see rapid improvements if you agree."

"You want me to let you take a highly dangerous inmate outside for your session with little or no security? Why on earth would I agree to that?"

"I believe Alana will remember more if she feels relaxed and realizes she can trust me. We have forged a bond, but if I get her one of the things she most wants before she dies, that faith will be cemented. I have suspicions that she has remembered more than she's admitting and want to give her the chance to find some peace before her execution."

My voice almost faltered at the words *die* and *execution*. It took every single ounce of strength to rein it in. I paused as wheels visibly turned in the warden's head while she contemplated my words. I crossed my fingers under the table, hoping, wishing that my plan would work.

"Do you really believe the girl has remembered but is withholding information?" The twitch in the warden's mouth indicated a hidden meaning behind her question.

"Not that she is deliberately trying to do that per se but that her unwillingness to trust anyone prevents her from divulging that information to me. Understandably, Miss McCarthy has lost an entire year of her life and had her family taken from her. In fact, I do not think she fears her execution at all. Her fear is wrapped up in not knowing the truth."

"And if I grant this little boon, then what?" Hope flushed through me.

"I believe that tactile experiences may bring back her memories entirely. If she has started to remember small things, then her mind is slowly releasing snippets of the past year. It would be our duty as members of the Parliament and advocates for the Grand Masters to try our best to help her unlock those memories." Dear God, my mouth was dry.

The warden drummed her fingers against the wood surface of her desk and ran her eyes over me. I held back a shiver at her stare and shifted uncomfortably in my seat. That seemed to please her.

"Okay, Dr Costello... you may take Miss McCarthy out for one hour today and take a guard of your choosing. I understand from the other guards that the girl seems to like Connors. He might be a possibility."

Eager to escape this uncomfortable situation, I stood before she changed her mind. "Thank you, Warden." In two quick strides, I was at the door and as it slid open, I prepared to step through and leave.

"Dr Costello." The voice stilled me, and I turned to face her. "I wish to be informed if Miss McCarthy does eventually remember. It would be of great misfortune for her to meet her death with her family's murderer still at large. You will update me."

An order not a request. I nodded, but she had already turned away and the door slid shut in my face. I didn't mind. Excitement and nerves overcame me at the same time. Treatment had been brought up a few times, and I would have to explain something to Alana to appease her because she would bite down like a dog with a bone until she got an answer. Memory loss or not, it was part of her character. She would not let it go.

I went straight to the mess hall to find Alana, but she was not there. Chris Connors inclined his head upwards, indicating Alana was in her cell. Then he raised his eyes in question, and I nodded with a smile. Only Connors could have beamed back at me like that. He leaned in and said something to one of the guards before moving away, heading for the door that would lead us out to the yard.

The door was open to her cell and she lay on the bed, eyes closed. She was not snoring, so I guessed she was just taking time out. I gladly interrupted her.

"Hey." At the sound of my voice, her eyes sprang open, and she sat up straight in bed. Her hair was tousled and I grinned at the sight. "Sorry, I didn't mean to startle you."

She combed her fingers through her hair. "It's okay. You didn't." My smile grew, and she laughed. "Well, not really anyway… Did I zone out and miss my session?"

I shook my head. "No, but our session will be cut short today. If you're free now, we could begin." A happy flutter jumped in my chest as the look of disappointment showed in her eyes. Before she could speak, I continued, "But I take it you'd be happy to sacrifice an hour of my time for the chance to go outside."

Alana blinked, processed what I had said and blurted, "You're shitting me, right?"

"No, not at all. Come on, get your shoes. Connors is waiting to take us."

She hesitated… and for a brief moment I thought she would refuse to go. Alana swivelled around and rushed to put on her shoes. She pulled a black piece of string from around her wrist and pulled her hair back off her face into a ponytail. I waited as she did, drinking her in before she faced me again and said, "Right, let's go."

Motioning for her to lead the way, I walked in sync with her. We descended the steps in silence, stopping at the end of the stairs. Since she did not know which way to go, I cautiously put my hand on the small of her back and steered her in the right direction. The doors leading outside were at the top of the mess hall corridor where staff enter and exit, away from prying eyes. Yes, there would be cameras outside, but no one would be able to hear our voices.

Alana had let out a sigh when my hand touched her back but did not shirk it off. We halted when we met up with Connors, who nudged Alana with his elbow and started whistling some really old George Michael song under his breath. She looked up at me, puzzled, and I shrugged but smiled.

The door slid open and we followed Connors through the corridor. He shuffled on ahead, still whistling his tune until we rounded a corner and then another before Alana spoke.

"How did you manage this? Death row inmates are never allowed outside... no need for vitamin D when you're gonna die, I suppose."

"I have my ways. Can't a man have some mystery about him?"

"There is nothing but mystery about you, Daniel." She pulled her eyes from mine.

After rounding another corner in the prison labyrinth, we stopped, waiting as Connors scanned his badge. The door opened and light billowed into the dark corridor. Connors went out first, and I followed him. Thankfully the weather was perfect, overcast but not very cold.

I watched the wonder on Alana's face as she stepped through the doorway, shielding her eyes from a ray of bright sunlight that peeked out from behind grey clouds. Taking her hands away, she blinked a few times adjusting to the new conditions. A tear fell, trickling down her face before dropping to the ground.

"Do you want to go back?" I asked, but she simply shook her head. I waited in silence. The yard wasn't exactly exciting. It was a square comprised of grass and a stone walkway surrounded by a high metal fence enclosing the area. If an inmate ever got over the fence, a full football field length stood between them and a massive ten-foot tall stone wall. A sniper perched in the security tower and guard dogs patrolled the perimeter. The grass had been freshly cut, and I held back a sneeze as the smell invaded my senses.

It had rained the night before our visit to the grounds, and the grass still had that wet look and fresh smell about it. No amount of moisture would have stopped my girl. She pulled off her shoes, tossing them aside, rolled up the legs of her cotton pants and walked barefoot in the grass, gingerly at first. Then a smile lit up her face, and she began running, kicking up loose bits of grass as she went.

Before I knew it, she started spinning around and around, her laughter floating on the soft breeze. Alana appeared carefree, alive and so beautiful. Connors nudged me, leaned in and whispered, "Danny-boy, I think your chick has finally gone crazy." He looked up, and I followed his gaze. Blurry faces were pressed against the security tower window. I let her enjoy her brief freedom.

Dizzy from her spinning, Alana flopped down on her back in the grass and lay there awhile. Connors gently pushed me forward, my brain forgetting that there was a reason we were here. I'd been content to watch the girl I loved, forgetting the purpose of the outing.

As I approached her, she regarded me with a smile. Her voice was low and crackled as she spoke. "Thank you."

"You're welcome. Shall we walk?" When she accepted the hand I'd offered, I reluctantly removed it once she was standing. She raced over to Connors, who held out her shoes, and she slipped them back on, dusting off the stray grass from her legs.

I began to stroll around the stone pathway, and she joined me halfway. We continued to walk the path quietly for a while, walking shoulder to shoulder, our bodies almost touching but not quite. We had completed one lap of the square before Alana broke the silence.

"Are you going to tell me what happened to Veronika?"

"She died," I said. She frowned her own special sarcastic version.

"That's not what I meant. You know it. What's the Treatment? I... I kinda remember my dad saying something to my mom about it."

My eyes focused forward, looking out at the stone wall that confined us. "There is so much I want to tell you, Alana, but I can't risk your life by telling you about it now. Treatment is a program that I know very little about, but it's the warden's pet project. Other information that I have was passed on to me by others, so I can't tell you any more details because I don't know... not yet.

All that matters to me is that you remember. You can trust me. You know that, right?"

Her hesitation was brief before she nodded, but that was all I needed. Glancing at my watch, I noted that we were running out of time. But when weren't we?

"I wish I could remember. Is it okay to admit that I'm afraid to? Maybe that's what is holding me back... fear."

Without realizing it, I gritted my teeth and resisted every urge that coursed through me. "Fear makes us feel our humanity," I said, "It is okay to be afraid of things, Alana, but fear should not conquer us. If you let yourself open up and admit to yourself that you are afraid, maybe your mind will accept it and allow you to remember."

She nodded but quickly refocused on the ground.

"You would tell me if you started to remember things, wouldn't you? Anything at all relevant or irrelevant... if something you have remembered has confused you in any way or you feel your dreams are misleading you, then you can tell me so we can figure them out together. Otherwise, I am of no help to you, and they will put a stop to our sessions."

Connors whistled and tapped his wrist indicating our time outside was up. The sky darkened and the rain began to fall, but I assumed neither of us cared about getting wet. Alana didn't answer, so I turned and walked towards Connors. I stopped abruptly when a hand landed on my elbow. Looking down at her, I kept moving.

"I'm sure I know you from somewhere. I really do... because you seem so familiar that I can't shake it off. I really want to remember."

My best response was no reply, and she didn't push. She needed to remember on her own, even if I was dying to just let the words spill out of my mouth. Telling her before she was ready to accept it might cause more damage than good, and I could not risk her safety for my own selfish means.

One last look around the yard before heading back inside, and I said, "I will try and get you some more time in the yard."

Alana stared at her feet. "I know you will, Daniel, and even if this was my last time, I don't mind... you came through on your promise and I won't ever forget it."

I exhaled and continued along, following the same path that brought us there. Far too soon we were back where we started. Connors left us alone, walking away without a word. The tension between us was awkward for a minute before I broke the silence and told Alana I would see her for our session tomorrow.

She acknowledged my words, and I watched her tiny legs carrying her up the stairs. Unable to turn away, I counted the steps until she disappeared into her cell. The mess hall was empty and quiet, so I took my time returning to my office. I had done all I could do to get her to trust me. This was make it or break it time. We had precious little time left for my plan to work.

Her words rang like music in my ears, a ballad of loss, love and, of course, tragedy. *"I'm sure I know you from somewhere. I really do... because you seem so familiar that I can't shake it off. I really want to remember."*

And as the shrill phone rang inside my office, all I could think was... *I wish you could remember me too.*

ALANA

"And it feels so real from the outside looking in."
(ONEREPUBLIC: TYRANT)

WHAT A RUSH! I HAD BEEN ALLOWED OUTSIDE. BREATHED IN real air and felt the rain-soaked grass tickle my toes. I was the first to admit that running around in the grass might make me appear even more insane than they already thought. And Daniel had done this for me. Day by day, I became more drawn to him and was now sure that I had seen him before… maybe even more than that. The way my body reacted to him had to be more than just false hope, right? Or maybe I was just deluding myself.

The fresh air must have worked wonders for me because I drifted off to sleep early that night and dreamt of nothing but Dr Daniel Costello.

While making my way across the campus, that familiar, happy feeling blossomed in my chest at the thought of seeing Daniel again. He had left a handwritten note, so Daniel-like, under my door asking me to meet him for lunch. He was a dork, my Danny, but he was my dork.

I had seen him before he spotted me, sitting with his back against the trunk of a tree, and I watched him push his glasses up his nose and couldn't help but smile. I had had many offers from other boys since arriving at the centre, but no one had grabbed my attention like Daniel. Smart and funny without trying, he was not typically handsome to attract certain female attention. The twits here were more interested in muscles than brains. But when Daniel

134

smiled, he was more handsome to me than any muscled idiot.

His brown hair was rumpled, constant bed head, so much so that I teased him about it regularly and his electric blue eyes were enough to take my breath away when he looked at me with such intensity. He made all the hardship about being away from home bearable.

A twig snapped under the weight of my step, and it caught his attention. When his head jerked up, a very sexy, deliberate smile crept across his face. Rising to his feet, I went to him, standing on my tippy toes to kiss him. It was a fleeting kiss, but a heated one, and I pulled away again.

"I thought you ninjas were meant to be stealthy… heard you coming a mile away." He chuckled, dodging out of my way as I tried unsuccessfully to swat him with my hand. Catching and grabbing hold of that hand, he pulled me down beside him, and I slipped comfortably under his arm, putting my head against his chest. He wrapped his arms around me fully. There was no other place I would rather be.

The shade of the tree cast shadows on the grass, the branches swaying from side to side, waving in the breeze. It was dry, had been for the last few days, uncharacteristic of the Island, but the forecast was for rain soon. Tomorrow, I would head home, my final trip there before graduating the first stage of my training. From there I would be out on assignment. It might be the last time I would see my parents and sister for a while, and maybe the last time I saw Daniel too until after completion of my first post. But in two days, he would come home with me, and I would get to show him off to my family.

"Are you nervous about meeting my dad?" I asked.

Daniel pulled me closer, and I heard the smile in his voice as he answered, "Me? Afraid of meeting your dad? Now, who in their right mind would be scared of meeting the warden of a secure facility? Certainly not the boy who dared date his daughter. No babe, I'm more scared to meet your mom."

"And why is that?" I laughed.

"Because it is a well-known fact that the more a father dislikes his daughter's boyfriend, the more the girl likes him… but moms are a different story. A mom who dislikes your boyfriend rings all kind of alarms in a girl's head."

"And you know all that from your profound knowledge and dating experience?"

"Sure, we can go with that."

"And what about the other way around?"

"My aunt is counting down the days till she meets you. In her own words, 'Any girl who makes you happy, Daniel, already has me won over.'"

"You're such a dork," I said, wrapping my free arm around his waist.

"Isn't that why you love me?"

I did love him, with every fibre of me. Sure, we had only been dating for six months, and he was older than me, but those things didn't matter. From my first week at the centre, and our first encounter, I had something to focus on other than worrying about following in my dad's footsteps. Someone who liked me for me. Nothing else mattered.

When I tilted my head up, Daniel lowered his lips to mine. And with that bare hint of contact, I was on fire. I ran my tongue over his bottom lip. He groaned. I pulled back and grinned as he shook his head.

"You'll be the death of me, woman."

I didn't let him say any more as my lips occupied his, reminding me that I had to wait another two days until he would be kissing me again. Twisting away from him, I lay down on the grass, my fingers on the collar of his charcoal T-shirt; I pulled him down with me. We kissed for a while, my fingers inching inside his shirt so I could feel his bare skin against my fingertips.

Another groan and a few whistles and catcalls made me laugh as Daniel braced himself on his elbows above me. His cheeks were flushed, and his gaze became hungry, but I put my hands on his chest and gave him a little shove. He chuckled again and rolled onto *his side and propped up on his elbow in the grass.*

"As I said... you'll be the death of me."

"At least you'll die happy," I joked.

He brushed his lips against my forehead and murmured, "Being with you, how could I not?"

My Daniel might not think he was a smooth talker, but deep down he was a charmer. The sun began to set, and the first hint of night crept upon us. We lay side by side, neither of us willing to make the first move. It may have been pathetic, but I already missed him.

So much left to do before I had to go. I still had to pack, shove a few things into a bag really, so I got up off the grass and said, "I'd better go."

"Need help packing?" he asked with a grin.

Shaking my head at the boyish, mischievous look on his face, I answered, "We wouldn't get much packing done. You know it."

He grinned, and I let him sweep me in for a tight hug. "I'm gonna miss you, too." When he released me, he nudged me forward. "Go on. I'll see you in two days. Try not to forget me while you're gone."

That was my key to laugh, and I stole another kiss before skipping out of his reach. I called over my shoulder, "I could never forget you, lover boy!"

Running back towards the dorms, I paused when I reached the door trying to spot Daniel in the distance. I watched as he disappeared into the shadows. In two days, the boy I love would meet my family and they would love him as much as me. If I were any happier, I would burst.

Blood pounded in my ears, waking me from a sound sleep. For a moment, I was unaware of my surroundings and tried to calm the rapid beating of my heart. God damn it! Why was my mind doing this to me? I let out a scream of frustration, not caring who heard me, unaware what time of day or night it was. Why would I be dreaming of Daniel at the training centre if he were not there?

My stomach was tied in knots, and I stayed in my cell for the entire morning, not bothering to go for breakfast for fear that I might vomit the nasty porridge. The pain in my stomach soon became unbearable, and I lay back on my bed, refusing to move.

Just after lunch, which I shied away from as well, Connors knocked on the cell wall. I kept still, but he stood over me, a look of concern on his face. Concern or pity? Now I really did feel like I was going to be sick.

"Time for your session with the doc, McCarthy," Connors said.

Shaking my head, I replied, "I'm not up to it today, Connors."

The concern deepened on his face. "Do you need to see the medic?"

"No... My stomach just feels weird. I don't want to be sick on his carpet."

"If you're sure you're okay."

No, really, I'm fine... I want to kiss my shrink, feel his hands on me like he did in my dreams. Then I want to see the lust in his eyes and feel safe as he hugs me. The sight of him would probably bring me to tears. Knowing that I imagined it all was almost as bad as not knowing if I killed my family.

I wanted my family to be alive and for me to awaken from this nightmare. It was important for me to be back in my room at home waiting for my boyfriend to come visit my parents for the first time. We would spend time with my sister and see her alive and well instead of this sick image I have of her lifeless and dead on the living room floor. I just wished for everything to make sense.

But I didn't say that. I nodded and closed my eyes so he would leave me alone. Sure enough, it worked. I heard his heavy footsteps on the landing, getting quieter the more distance he travelled.

Again, I was alone, lost in my thoughts, trying to figure out if the dream was real or not. But Daniel would have told me if we had met before? No, he wouldn't. Actually, his words from the day before rattled around in my head. *There is so much I want to tell you, Alana, but I can't risk your life by telling you about it now.* Why would he speak to me about risking my life? Could I be putting two and two together and coming up with five? And there I was again, imagining that there was an *us* when it might break my heart if he told me it was all in my head, and my dreams were not real.

I must have been lying there all through dinner because someone cleared their throat, and I reluctantly opened my eyes. Jayson stood in my doorway, holding something in his hand. My stomach lurched and growled at the same time causing Jay to smirk.

"I thought you might be hungry. You skipped all your meals today."

I sat up and looked at him. "Won't you get in trouble for coming in here?"

He jerked his head back. "I got permission from Connors before coming up. Seems he's a bit worried you might be ill. Does our freckled friend have the hots for the brooding inmate? What a movie that would make."

"Shut up, you idiot, and sit down," I grunted, taking what was in his offered hand. Unwrapping the paper, I picked at the few dried pieces of fruit, eating one or two so as not to appear rude. "Sorry, I just had an off day today. Needed time to myself."

Jayson sat on the bed and waited for me to eat some more fruit before he spoke. He rested his elbow on his knee, and then put his chin in his hand. "Everybody needs a time out every now and then... just don't avoid us. We might be able to help."

"Can you give me back the last year?" My tone was too sarcastic, but I regretted the words too late.

"Sorry, but I can be a roguishly handsome shoulder to lean on. Alas, I cannot work miracles." My lip twitched and he yelled, "Eureka! I got a smile... my mission is complete."

"Shut up, will you, you're such a dork." The words fell from my lips, and I suddenly felt as if a cold bucket of water had been thrown in my face.

"Hey, Alana, you okay? You've gone paler than normal."

"Yeah, I'm fine... just felt like déjà vu or something."

"That's good isn't it? Means you might be remembering stuff."

I was silent for a while, and Jayson tapped his foot against the floor. I turned to him and said, "Do you ever wish you could forget what happened to you?"

"No. I don't think so anyway. I did what I did to help my sister, and she is safe and happy now. Going to school and everything. That old man died, and I am sorry for that. It wasn't something I did on purpose, just wrong place, wrong time. But I would do it again in a heartbeat if I had a do-over. You understand why, right?"

I did. Jayson knew his sister benefitted from his crime and would lead a happy and fulfilled life thanks to him. If I remembered the past year, I would never be able to say the same.

"I'm beginning to get glimpses... but I can't tell if they are real or wishful thinking. I really want to remember more than anything. It all makes me feel like a broken teacup. You glue it back together, but there will always be a piece missing, leaking tea as you drink from it."

Jayson took my hand and gave it a squeeze. "Maybe you're better off... not remembering, I mean." I tilted my head sideways to look at him. "I mean, what if you do remember and it's far worse than you imagined? What if you remembered and you go about wishing you had never remembered? What if you just throw out the pieces and buy a new cup? Is any memory worth hurting yourself over?"

I gently yanked my hand free of his. "But if I don't remember, I'll die believing I killed my parents and my sister. That their blood was on my hands. I can't wash it off. Every day I have the feeling that I'm missing something. It's as if I should be doing something else. That remembering will solve everything."

He watched me cautiously.

"But then... do I want to remember and be proven innocent? What do I have to look forward to? A lifetime of loneliness with no family or anyone? What if I have forgotten something important?" My voice cracked and I hushed up.

Jayson stood as he said, "If it's important, you'll remember, I promise you. Is it possible you're trying too hard? By the way, you are not alone. There are a lot of people who want to see you happy with your memories back. I told you one other time that you're not alone. Talk to your shrink, Alana. He can help you more than you're willing to admit."

My gaze had met his before he turned to walk out the door. I lay back down on the bed staring at the emptiness of the ceiling, envying it. The ceiling, despite its blandness, was a clean slate. It could be painted over with a new colour and given a new life.

Returning my memories might not give me the clean slate that I wanted. My family would still be dead and I would still be in prison. I really believed that no matter if my memory returned or not, in two more months I would go wherever it is they take us to die. And that would be that. I would just remain a bit of gossip in the prison until something else happened, and I ceased to exist.

Suddenly I was angry… angry at my parents for dying and leaving me alone… angry at Sophia for being too small to defend herself… angry at Daniel for giving me false hope… angry at myself for letting pathetic fantasies take over my mind.

I jumped off the bed and screamed. The next thing I knew I had used what little strength left to overturn the bed, scattering all the bedding to the floor. I took one of the pillows and beat it across the wall. Then I kicked the bin with such force it smashed into the door with a sickening thud.

While continuing on my furious rampage, the door slid open and strong arms captured me from behind, holding my own in place. I struggled to break free and kicked out, but those arms would not let me go. I cried in frustration and tasted the saltiness of the tears on my lips.

"Shush, Alana, please… come on… calm down for me or else they are going to shock you. Hurts like a bitch. Come on, girl… shush. I got you."

Connors' voice sounded in my ear, and he kept shushing me until I stilled in his arms. My legs gave out, and we both went to the floor. Connors loosened his grip on me but still held me tight. My sobs became louder, and the pain in my chest was so bad that I thought I was dying.

Through my sobs, I heard Connors say that I was okay and to please just give him a minute. I heard someone argue with him, and he snarled and told them to piss off. The tears soaked my top, and I felt nothing but tiredness as I shoved against Connors, needing to breathe. He did not let go.

My god, I felt so lost. I closed my eyes and screamed out the last of my frustration and anger before tiredness won out. I gave in and let the darkness pull me under.

ALANA

"I thought I was close but under further inspection,
It seems I've been running in the wrong direction."
(PASSENGER: WRONG DIRECTION)

I HAD THE MOTHER OF ALL HEADACHES WHEN I WOKE UP
early the next morning, lying on my bed which had been
freshly made up. The floor was cleared of all evidence of
my little meltdown. My eyes stung, and I imagined that
my face was red and puffy from crying. Rolling over on
my side, I spotted Connors sitting on the floor, eyes closed,
head leaning against the wall. He must have stayed with
me all night to make sure I didn't lose it again.

Getting out of bed, I went to him and crouched
down in front. I put a hand on his shoulder and gently tapped him. His eyes darted open and he said, "I'm
awake. I'm awake." I allowed him time to take in his surrounding and have a seat on the edge of my bed.

Connors stretched out his long limbs and yawned. "I
never thought I would miss my lumpy bed at home, but
damn girl, how did you ever sleep on this floor?"

"It's comfier than the bed."

"That why you trashed the place last night?" he
asked, rising to his feet and leaning back against the wall.

"I'm sorry about that… hope I didn't hurt anyone."
I let my head droop because of the shame of losing it.
"My emotions got the best of me, keeping everything
inside until I exploded. I guess bottling things up really
doesn't help."

Folding his arms across his chest, Connors said, "I'm

143

surprised you didn't lose it long ago, McCarthy, because of the shit you have been through. I'd have put a gun in my mouth ages ago."

"Thanks for cleaning up."

He smiled. "Anytime. Are you okay now? I mean, can I leave you to get breakfast and freshen up before your session with Doc? You are going today, and I have to give a report on last night." I cast my eyes up to him and he looked away. "Sorry, but you made too much noise for it to go unnoticed."

"Sorry. I feel like I'm ten inches tall."

"Don't be. Talk it out with the doc. You scared me last night, Alana. I thought I'd have to sedate you or activate your behaviour chip, and I don't think I have it in me to put you down like that. I consider you a friend, girl, and despite the fact that we are where we are, I don't like seeing my friends hurting. I'm not willing to personally hurt them either. Now, go eat because I am so not spoon feeding you."

When Connors called me *Alana*, I knew I must have worried him. He pushed away from the wall and slipped out the door. I listened to his heavy boots clomp down the stairs. Once in the bathroom, I splashed water on my face and ran my fingers through my hair. I was certain I looked like a mess, but I didn't really care. Inside, I was hollow, empty... unsure how much fight was left.

That morning, it was easy to go through the motions. I headed down to breakfast, joined Jayson, and his gang of misfits, ate a spoon or two of revolting porridge and nodded at appropriate gaps in conversation. It probably didn't make a difference because I hadn't heard anything they said anyway. Fidgety and nervous, I wondered why no one asked about what happened because the gossip had surely gotten around. Even Emily kept her mouth shut, but I caught her looking at me on occasion. I chose not to react.

A door slammed shut, and I stared up at the control room, watching as Connors exited, his hands balled into fists. He stomped down the stairs, his face contorted into a nasty snarl. When he reached the bottom, he spotted me watching him.

His body relaxed, and he put a smile on his face and called me over to him. I said my goodbyes to Jayson's group and headed off to a chorus of see ya laters. Connors led me across the hall, and we left the noise and chaos behind us. He didn't say anything at first, earning his silence after last night. I restrained from asking him what upset him, but it also allowed time for me to think. Eventually, I knew I would have to explain about avoiding Daniel and my little exercise in redecorating to him.

Positioned to ask Connors to wait a second before he opened the door to Daniel's office, he beat me to it before I could speak. A nervous knot tied itself in my stomach and Connors, probably sensing my unease, leaned down and whispered in my ear. "It's okay, McCarthy. Just tell the doc what's going on in that complicated head of yours. You'll be grand."

He gave me a little push through the door, and I looked back at him, finding comfort in his easy smile but also noticing a kindness in his eyes. The door slid closed, and I was left alone with Daniel.

After the dream or memory or whatever it was, I didn't think I could stand being that close to him, so I perched on the couch. I pulled my knees up to my chest and concentrated on breathing, trying to remain calm while sneaking peeks at Daniel.

Just like in my dream, he shoved his glasses up his nose as he finished whatever it was he was writing. When those steely blue eyes turned to me, I forgot to breathe. He was wearing his serious face, and I couldn't tell if he was mad or concerned.

"How are you today, Alana?" he asked, turning over a page in his notebook.

I swept a hand across my face. "Yeah, I'm okay."

"Are you feeling better? I understand you missed our session because of illness?" I stayed quiet and he continued, "Or would you like to talk about what happened last night? Can you tell me what made you react the way you did?"

His voice was different, clipped and clinical, no emotion at all... with no hint of the friend he had been trying to be for the last few months. Did I do something to piss him off? Or was it that he somehow suspected that I was holding things back?

I shrugged my shoulders. "I'm not sure really. I— I just hadn't been feeling great yesterday and I..." Searching for the right words to describe the jumble of things going on in my head was less than easy. Nothing seemed to make sense. "... I don't really want to talk about it."

"And that's why you ended up in a rage, Alana, because you won't talk to me. You keep thinking that you can do this alone, but you can't. Am I wasting my time here? Is any of this doing you any good? The warden wants to cancel our sessions. She thinks you speaking with me is causing more harm than good. I have very little time to convince her that it is working, and you have less time to remember everything. Why can't you just talk to me?"

I heard the barest hint of desperation in his voice and argued with myself about the benefits of keeping things to myself.

"I'm scared," I admitted. My voice trembled as the words left my mouth.

"Scared of what, Alana?"

Averting my eyes from his, I took a deep breath. "I

have glimpses, feelings of déjà vu. I'm afraid that the really good bits are not real. That leaves me with all the bad."

"Would you please tell me about them?" he asked. The warmth was back in his voice.

I opened my mouth to speak but froze as the image of Daniel kissing me popped into my head. The heat of his lips on mine intensified my fear, and the feel of his hands on my hips made my body ignite under his touch and enjoy the hunger in his eyes. I sensed my face burning and covered it with my hands.

"What just went through your mind, Alana?"

Shaking my head for the love of all that was holy, a giggle escaped. Oh yeah, I could really tell him that I had been having false memories of him being my boyfriend. Delusional was not the word he would use, but I thought it was appropriate. I heard his chair screech and his light footsteps came closer to me. The couch dipped as he sat down beside me, and I knew I had nowhere to run.

His hands dwarfed mine as he pulled them away from my scorching face. He was still holding my hands. Without thinking, I linked my fingers through his, and Daniel didn't pull away. He smiled then, and I thought it might be the first time I'd actually seen a real Daniel smile from him.

"Alana, I wish you would trust me. You did once before. It would mean everything if you did again."

I listened carefully to his words and gasped. "So I did know you … We met before? I haven't imagined it?"

The shake of his head dislodged his glasses, but he didn't take his hand from mine to fix them. I softly took my hand from his and used my index finger to inch his glasses back in place. He watched my actions calmly and took my hand back, placing it on my knee. Still holding my other hand, Daniel sank back into the couch, slouching down so we were at the same eye level, legs stretched out in front of him. He let out a deep sigh.

"You've started to remember." It was a statement rather than a question.

"I don't know what's real and what isn't."

"Us, here and now… that's what's real. Can you not hear the truth in my voice when I tell you that?"

It was if my mind had no control over my body as I leaned into him and relaxed my head on his shoulder. He no longer felt like my shrink. I knew him before all this. He confirmed it, and I ached with the need to remember him. Daniel had said to trust him. I had once before, so I took a giant leap of faith and told him about one of my very first dreams, where I'd heard the word Treatment for the first time.

"I had a dream about my parents arguing. It had happened before I left for the training centre. They were shouting at each other about Theresa and about my dad's work with Treatment. My parents never fought, but I had realized for months before I went away, they had been distant. Dad's longer hours and Mom pretending she was happy, when deep down she was miserable, had taken a toll on them both.

Even Sophia noticed, but I think she was too young to understand. She probably thought it was like when she broke my old music player. You know, one that played discs inside of the players. Dad had given it to me with a heap of CDs, and I loved it. Sophia knocked it over, and I yelled at her and refused to speak to her for a week. Stupid now, thinking back, but it was something that could not be replaced at the time. But then again, neither could Sophia."

I sniffled, holding back my emotions. It all seemed so petty now, and I dealt with the fact that even had I known what would happen, I could not change it. I really wanted to dig deeper and ask Daniel where we met before and if my glimpses were real. Instead, I chose not to spoil the moment. You would think that I was not scheduled to die in less than two months, but I was content to enjoy our time together with that feeling of utter safeness while I leaned against Daniel.

"Your father and Theresa worked on some top secret projects together. I know very little about that, but I am trying to find out more. I came here for one reason, Alana, and that was to get you to remember. I can help you, but I need you to be completely honest with me and listen when I tell you that your memories have started to unlock. I hope they will all resurface with some gentle prodding."

I stared at him with glassy eyes as if making an important decision.

"We will work on it. I have a few more things up my sleeve. Trust me, please. That's all I ask. I won't rest until you remember, Alana. I promise you."

"I have had other dreams as well… about you."

He stiffened and held in a breath before saying, "And that is why you were embarrassed? What happened in those dreams?"

I couldn't say it. How was I supposed to tell him that it was my mind playing tricks on me? "I can't tell you, it's more than likely some Stockholm syndrome thing or something like that. My feelings for you are confusing enough, and I'm not ready for you to dismiss them just yet."

"You have feelings for me?" he asked. His hand tightened around mine.

I remained quiet and hoped he would drop it because I wasn't ready to deal with it. Last night was draining enough and right now I needed… I didn't know what I needed. Daniel respected my privacy when I didn't answer and let me sit there, pressed against him for a while. His body seemed tense, yet mine became more relaxed than ever.

After far too little time, Daniel pulled his hand away and gave me a quick hug before getting up and returning to his desk. I missed the warmth of him immediately. Hugging my knees to my chest once more, it didn't feel the same. The room was so silent that I heard footsteps coming down the hall and realized Daniel had gotten up so as not to get caught sitting close to me. At least I hoped he hadn't thought we had done anything wrong.

"Alana, you okay?" I snapped to attention at the sound of his voice calling my name, and I gave him a smile. "Yeah, I think so… Sorry if I weirded you out telling you I have feelings for you."

Daniel acted as if he were ready to speak, but the door opened and his lips clamped shut. Connors greeted Daniel and then turned to me. "Come on, McCarthy, let's go… your little band of followers has been asking for you."

Extending my legs and stretching, I stood, feeling stiff from sitting too long. "Followers?" I asked, perplexed.

Connors laughed. "You know, Jay and the gang. He says you owe him a game of cards and refuses to play unless your ass is in the chair… his words, not mine."

He stepped outside, and I followed, glancing at Daniel as I put one foot in front of the other. The sound of my name made me turn, and I was captivated by ice-blue eyes and the hunger I saw from the dream in those eyes.

"Alana, about those feelings you have for me?"

I held my breath, my heart beating like a drum against my chest. I nodded silently, not trusting myself to speak.

"I feel the same… about you, that is. I'll see you tomorrow."

And for the first time, I wished that I remembered him more than how my parents died. Guilt washed over me. I was in a life and death situation, but all I cared about was hearing a boy tell me he liked me. I retreated out the door and twisted around, feeling the weight of Daniel's gaze on me before the door closed.

Had I just imagined that? Daniel said he had feelings for me? Could it be that my dream was actually a memory, and Daniel had come here to help me? If I could forget him, then what else was my mind suppressing?

I stayed a step behind Connors as we made our way back to the mess hall. Soon after, I joined Jayson and the others but felt I was going through the motions of being there. My thoughts and most of my concentration were elsewhere. I tried to clear my mind and not think back to what had happened, but I couldn't help replaying his words over and over in my head. That was when I resolved to remember. Someone like Daniel would not have come to help me if I were really a cold-blooded killer.

When lights out signalled, I sought refuge in my cell and welcomed the quiet that greeted me. All along I had thought I was ready to know what happened, but maybe I was in denial. Maybe I needed to forget some things in order to remember others. Did that make sense? I had always been strong and outgoing, but in prison I had become quiet and withdrawn. But I felt stronger now and would not go down without a fight.

Something had been going on at home because my dad was involved in an event or plan at work that had caused my parents to argue. When I actually thought about it, certain details slotted into place. Theresa worked closely with my dad, and her name had been dragged into arguments a few times... could I ask her outright? She would laugh in my face at my conspiracy theories, but I had stopped thinking about my life and began to dwell on how I was going to die. Truthfully, I was not ready to die yet.

Okay, mind, I'm ready, so get your ass in gear, and let me remember. No more cryptic BS… get to it already so I can move on. You've done your job well, but now it's time for me to be in charge again. I choose to remember. Give me the good and the bad, I'm ready. Let's do this.

ALANA

SO MY RESOLVE TO ASSURE MY MIND THAT IT WAS OKAY TO
let me remember didn't go so well. In fact, I slept soundly
that night, only waking when the door to my cell whirred
to life and opened. But I suppose since it had kept me in
the dark for this long, it might have trouble kick starting
itself. It would be similar to leaving a car or a motorbike
idle for too long and would take a few attempts to start it.
My mind had no better motivation—it died when I did.

But then again, talking about your mind in the third
person was a little on the crazy side.

I got up, went to breakfast and chatted with Jayson,
Marshall, and Afsana while Emily and Darren sat with us
but stayed mainly out of the conversation. Marshall and
Jayson were having a debate about which of the guards
were involved with each other and what not. Jayson was
certain the female guard with the buzz cut was gay, but
according to Marshall's gaydar, she was interested in one
of the straight guards who was on the warden's personal
security detail. I laughed along with them as they put
forward their points until Marshall brought up Connors,
and I listened with interest.

"So, come on, man… you cannot tell me that you
think ole Connors is cuter than me? I am utterly devas-
tated." Jayson joked, a broad smile eclipsing his face as

Marshall shrugged, although I could make out the faint tinge of red on his cheeks. Those of us who blush recognize our own.

"What can I say, dude. We Americans always had a thing for the Irish," Marshall said in a low voice.

"Shush man, you know that word is contraband. The Islanders like to forget where they came from." Jayson looked at me, and I shrugged, so he continued, "Hey, Alana, you spend most of your time with Connors, toing and froing to see Dr Costello. Put in a good word for our boy Marshall, will you?"

"I'm pretty sure that Connors likes girls from the many times he has attempted to charm me, but I can sound him out if Marshall wants me to."

Marshall shook his head, but Jayson whooped and grinned. "Please do, Alana. Ignore Marshall... I bet he uses that charm to deflect his gayness... only a gay man would spend so much time on his hair to make it look like he barely touched it."

I sneaked a glance at his hair and laughed. Catching Marshall's eye, he spotted what I was giggling about and started to laugh, as well. Soon we were both doubled over in fits of laughter with Jayson just staring at us before he ran a hand over his own head and sent us into more hysterics.

Afsana seemed appalled at our behaviour, and I immediately saw the hero worship in her eyes for Jayson. He had taken her under his wing, protected her and helped her make friends because in another year she would be alone, and we would be dead. Or in Marshall's case, he would be let out to find his place in the world. Afsana was thirteen or fourteen, and it would be a long wait for her to die if she had no one around her. Damn, that was a bleak thought.

It sobered me up, drying up the tears of laughter

that had slipped free of my defences. The boys continued with their banter, and I sat back in my chair. We had about ten minutes until those not on death row would head off for their daily dose of socially acceptable education.

Without notice, amidst the noise of chatter and banter, I heard a loud clank as a metal tray hit the ground, and then the sound of a plate smashing on the concrete floor. I swivelled in my chair to get a better look and saw that some poor boy had dropped his tray at the feet of Veronika's boyfriend. The kid was trembling from head to toe.

"I didn't mean it. I didn't mean it. I didn't mean it," he shouted and a panicked feeling washed over me as he screamed out loud. "I didn't mean it!"

His words overcame me, cold and familiar as I listened. A different voice penetrated my senses. Lost in the grip of a flashback, I became powerless to stop the memory from grabbing hold of me and submerging me back to a place so dark and full of death that I felt suffocated by it.

I immediately had portions of a flashback with voices and fear overtaking my thoughts, but I struggled to stay in the present.

I heard the raised voices below, a frequent occurrence between my parents lately, but this time another voice was added to the fray. It was one I recognised but for some reason, I couldn't put a name to the voice. Pulling the pillow over my head to block out the screams and shouts, I still heard the sound of plates smashing on the ground and my father yelling for the other person to get out of his house.

Sheer terror overcame me and I was unable to move even to check and see if Sophia was okay. I had hoped my leaving to go to the training centre would ease some tension in the house, but I now knew those hopes were dashed. Tomorrow would be better, tomor-

row I would...

The sound of a gunshot ripped through the air, followed by two more and my mom's sobbing. Sophia shrieked as another shot echoed through the air... and another. My heart pounded, and I scrambled into the crawl space, my secret passageway that I shared with Sophia, connecting her room with mine.

Time zipped forward, and I listened to the sickening sound of another shot in the dark. The sound of sirens, loud and wailing in the distance, drew nearer and nearer and then the front door crashed as it closed. I was alone in the stagnate silence.

Plucking what little courage I had left, I exited the crawl space and cautiously made my way across my room, opened my bedroom door and waited. I heard nothing but the ticking of the clock, so I ventured down the stairs, each step in sync with the hammering of my heart. The front door was closed, but the living room door was ajar.

My hands shook uncontrollably as I eased the door gently and slowly, unsure of what to expect. Nothing could have prepared me for the horrors that met my eyes when I spotted the carnage before me.

Dad lay slumped down on the ground beside his chair, his head resting on the seat of it, his arms cast down by his sides. Empty brown eyes stared back at me, so like my own, and I clasped a hand over my mouth to keep from screaming. A single gunshot had marred his forehead, the faintest dash of blood on his face. It was the blood that soaked his shirt that caused bile to rush up my throat. His blue shirt was drenched in the liquid and I let a muffled sob escape me.

Dragging my gaze from my dad's cold stare, I braved a look at my mom. She lay on the ground with her back to me, and I was grateful for not having to see the same expression on her face as my dad's. I had to step over her feet to get a closer look. My stomach rolled as I caught sight of the tangled mess of hair and blood and whatever else oozed from the wound at the back of her head.

I swallowed hard, panic gripping me as I focused on the last body in the room. A cold chill crept up my spine and my throat became constricted, suffocating me as my eyes fell on Sophia. I could not escape the pure and utter devastation.

My baby sister was dressed in her princess sleepwear, her skin pale and her eyes wide open in shock. Her pink pyjamas were stained with blood, the disgusting colour almost covering the happy images of smiling princesses. She just lay there, looking up at me. I broke. My knees hit the ground, and I dragged myself closer to her, pulling her into my arms and letting her head sag against my chest. I placed my hands over her blood-soaked chest with a fleeting hope that maybe her heart still beat under all the gore.

"Come on, Soph, please wake up… please don't leave me." I sobbed, knowing my pleas were useless. The sirens wailed, closer now, and I heard the sound of trucks screeching to a halt outside. "You hear that Sophia… help is here. Please open your eyes. Don't leave me."

The front door burst open, and a tactical team flooded the room. They pointed their guns at me. Their mouths moved, but I heard nothing. Two of the team splintered off, and I assumed they went to check on my parents, but I could not leave Sophia. Letting go would mean that I was alone… it was not an option.

I heard the mumble of voices and then felt an arm grab hold of me, Sophia's body slipping from my hands and collapsing on the ground. The harder they pulled, the more I struggled to hang onto my sister.

The team stepped aside, and a familiar face entered the room. She didn't look at me but quickly surveyed the carnage. Her lips pursed as she turned back to me. I lifted my head to meet the eyes of Theresa Lane… the woman my parents had been fighting over. She shook her head, and as her gaze narrowed, she opened her mouth. "Alana McCarthy, you are charged with the murder of Warden Cormac McCarthy, Sorcha McCarthy, and Sophia McCarthy. You will be taken to the Underage unit of the Department of Corrections where you will await your eighteenth birthday to be punished for your crimes. Do you have anything to say?"

"Yes. Wait… I didn't do this… I heard it happen… what are you saying?" The words left me in a rush, my mind trying to

process everything that had happened in such quick succession.

"We found your father's gun, Alana, right next to you when we arrived, and we will find all the evidence to retrace your actions. As a Grand Master of Justice, I am within my rights to charge you with the murders of your family even without the evidence." Her lips curled up in a sneer.

"Someone else was here... Please, I didn't do it... I didn't do this. There was someone else here. I. Did. Not. Do. It!" My shouts went on deaf ears because she just waved me away and motioned for the guard to take me into custody. I struggled in the guard's grasp and begged him to let me go while my screams echoed through the death-filled room. My words were jumbled and incoherent, even to me, as I hysterically pled my innocence.

Theresa snapped at the guard, "Jesus, will you shut her up already... can't you just knock her out?"

I wiggled even more in his grasp and used my voice in a last ditch attempt to get my point across. "I swear I didn't do this. Please, you have to list—"My words were cut off as something sharp hit the back of my head, and my world of blood plunged into darkness.

Slamming back to the present, I let out a strangled scream, and my eyes darted around wildly. Jayson was kneeling down in front of me, and Marshall was holding my hand. I jerked it free of his hold and noticed the welt marks where I must have dug my nails into his palms. My face was clammy and damp, and I raised my fingers to it, frightened that it might be blood. Thankfully, only tears. I tried to ignore people as they watched and hung my head.

"You okay, Alana? What happened?"

I swallowed hard, searching for the right words to say. I knew it was a memory. It vibrated in my bones and in my heart. The joy of discovering that I did not kill my parents was snuffed out by the flashing image of Sophia's dead eyes. I shook my head, unable to speak.

"Did you remember something? Should I call the doc?" Jayson asked. I was frozen in silence, lost to the horrors in my mind.

"McCarthy?" A familiar voice called, and I timidly glanced up at the sound of his voice. Connors' face came into focus, and I blinked away tears. Struggling to my feet, I assumed he'd come to take me to see Daniel. Putting one foot in front of the other, I began walking away, not even caring if the earlier conflict that caused my flashback had been resolved.

As if on automatic, I headed for the far end of the hall. A hand on my elbow stopped me in my tracks. Connors' face was marred with pity as he opened his mouth and said, "I'm sorry to do this to you, Alana. Something obviously has you spooked, but your appointment with Dr Costello is cancelled today. The warden wants to see you."

The image of Theresa from my memory surfaced, and my chest constricted as if there was not enough oxygen to let them function. Staring at my hands, I half expected to see them covered in blood, but they were clean. I nodded as Connors steered me towards the stairs leading to the control room. Surprisingly, we didn't go to her office, but then again, I couldn't help but wonder why she wanted to see me at all.

I barely had time to return to a functioning human again before we stopped outside the glass room. Connors knocked before swiping his card at the door and double doors swung open. Theresa Lane was sitting amongst an array of monitors, some displaying images of the prison, others filled with statistics and numbers that made no sense to me. After a quick, reassuring squeeze on my hand, Connors was gone. I stood face to face with Theresa.

As always, she was neatly dressed, her navy blue suit

oozed power and sophistication, her makeup applied to perfection and not an unruly stray hair in sight. Her eyes trailed over me, and I resisted the urge to shudder, feeling dirty under her scrutiny. She beckoned me forward, and I complied because what other choice did I have? She crossed one foot behind the other, and I watched a camera light blink red and knew we were being watched.

"Alana, I just wanted to check in with you since our last encounter and see how you were doing." Her words and tone conflicted, and I sensed she was no more concerned with how I was than I was with her. I had to be careful; my gut was warning me to be careful.

"I'm fine, Warden. Thank you for asking."

She had acknowledged my politeness with a dip of her head before she went on. "I feel responsible for you in some ways, Alana. Your father was one of my closest friends, and he would turn in his grave if he could see you now." I refrained from speaking, and she took my silence as her queue to continue. "As I said before, your father was a good man, an honest man. Honourable people like him are few and far between. Take Dr Costello, for example. He is one of the brightest, most intelligent people I have met, and he works into the small hours researching your condition."

The word *condition* came out of her mouth as if she were saying something horrid and dirty that might stain her in some way. I remained quiet. "Do tell me, Alana... do you think that Dr Costello is wasting his efforts on you since you will die regardless of your memory returning?"

I bristled at her words and couldn't stop myself or my response, regardless of her position. Thinking the words through before I spoke, I wished we could just get on with it. "I think Dr Costello has been a great help in recovering my memories. I have had glimpses of the past year. Nothing significant, but enough for me to hope that I can die with the knowledge that I did not kill my parents."

It was Theresa's time to look uncomfortable.

"I wish I could remember because there is no logic or reason behind my charges. I have always known that I couldn't kill them, but with Dr Costello's help, I'm sure I can unlock my memories. Even with the precious little time I have left."

She uncrossed and then re-crossed her legs before answering, "And I am sincerely sorry that I could not extend the period of time to allow you the time to… as you said… find peace. But it is not within the parameters of our laws to grant you a stay of execution when you have already been found guilty. Unfortunately, Alana, there is nothing else that can be done."

I folded my arms across my chest, defensively, protecting myself. "I will just have to hold onto the hope that I can remember in time. But you are right. Dr Costello is an intelligent man and should not be blamed for my inadequacy for not being able to remember. As you said, given more time who knows what I might have remembered."

We stared at each other, neither of us willing to look away first. Theresa pushed a button on the desk and said, "Send Connors in to collect the prisoner." I waited in stony silence until he appeared at the door.

"I really do hope you are successful, Alana, if only to give you peace of mind. I'm sure I will see you again before your execution." She turned her back to me, shifting her seat around to fiddle with the keyboard in front of her, dismissing me.

Rising and without another glance at her, I headed out the door. I followed Connors down the stairs and thanked him. His face appeared troubled, unusual for the ever smiling guard. I watched, my eyes following him as he exited the mess hall and disappeared into the corridor leading to Daniel's office.

Disappointment welled up in my chest as I would have to wait another twenty-four hours to see Daniel, but I had time to contemplate my memories and the meeting with the warden. Not wanting to be alone, I re-joined Jayson and Afsana. Having reassured them that I was fine, I sat back and closed my eyes, listening to their conversations but trying to rid myself of the blood-soaked images that haunted me whenever I closed my eyes.

DANIEL

"It's been awhile but I still feel the same,
Maybe I should let you go."
(ED SHEERAN: GIVE ME LOVE)

THE ANTICIPATION WAS KILLING ME AS I WAITED FOR ALANA to arrive. My thoughts never strayed far from the closeness and almost normality that our last few sessions had brought us. Despite the urgency that weighed heavy on me, I longed to be able to hold her again. The last time I had was the night before she had left me. Every day in prison was a painful reminder of a fate that should not have been ours.

My office door opened, and I glanced up from my messy collection of papers. Connors entered. The door closed behind him, and I could tell by the look on his face that something was wrong.

"Where is she? Is she okay?"

He put his hands up, but I couldn't calm down. Dread filled up my stomach, and it became painful. Connors sat in front of me at my desk and let out a long breath, as if he was deliberately trying to prolong my agony. I let my hand grip the edges of the desk, so much so that I saw the whites of my knuckles under the strain. My foot tapped impatiently as Connors chewed on the inside of his mouth before he broke the silence.

"No Alana today, Danny-boy. The warden wanted to see her."

Alarm bells rang in my head. "Do you think she suspects something? Are we in trouble?"

Connors shook his head, and the vice grip on my insides loosened but did not vanish. "I don't think she suspects anything about our little rebellion, Danny, but we may need to bring your grand scheme forward sooner than later. I've been hearing rumours that more guards are being brought in next week… but for what I have no clue."

A week, we had a week, not two months. Could I pull it off? Well, I either would… or I would die trying. Connors looked tired as if the stress of working as a double agent had finally taken its toll on my young friend. He was beginning to look older than his twenty-four years.

"You can still back out, Connors. You have done enough for us. We still have time to work on it if you want to bow out."

A weak, forced, one-sided smile turned up his lips. "I promised you that I would help you and her in any way possible, and I will not go back on my word. Jayson knows what he is supposed to do, right… and his little pal… has he asked her yet?"

I shook my head. "Jayson is working up to it. She will do it though—as will the others. Is there anything else I need to know?"

Worry danced in my friend's eyes, and he slumped lower in his chair. "I think she remembered something. There was an incident at breakfast and in all of the mess, I stole a look at Alana. She had this expression on her face, you know, like she had seen a ghost or something.

While everyone else watched what was going on, her eyes glazed over, and she didn't move even when she whimpered. Jayson tried to snap her out of it. The American flinched as she gripped hold of his hand, but I've never seen anyone in a trance like that. Her hand muffled her scream when she came back to us, and I don't think I will ever erase that terrified look from my memory. Do you think she remembered that night?"

Leaning my head back against the chair, I sighed. "It is possible. Over the last few days, she has been more open to memories. She told me she had feelings for me, and I suspect that she is confused about that too. Damn it! I wish I could see her today and try and get her to talk to me."

"I know, Danny, but if I had questioned it more, it might have brought closer attention to us. Our only hope is to stay undetected until zero hour. You still have everything on your end squared?"

"Yes, everything is in place. Connors, I can never repay you for this, you know that right? You can never go back after this. Are you okay with that?"

"I made peace with my choices when I dialled your number and told you what had happened to your girl. No going back now, Danny-boy. You've always had my back, and now I've got yours and hers."

We did that awkward man thing where neither of us knew whether we should hug or shake hands. I laughed, elevating some of the unease. Contemplating what to say next when I heard the buzz of Connors' pager, I lost my train of thought anyway. He reached for the phone, keyed in a code, listened, and hung up.

"Seems the warden is done with your girl. If I get anything from Alana, I'll come back and let you know." He got up and stepped away from the chair, knocking twice on the table and leaving me alone with my thoughts.

I worried why the warden wanted to see Alana. Did she suspect something? Was Alana safe for the moment while I finalised our details? The knot in my stomach hardened and I had to admit that I was scared. Scared that I had taken on too much trying to help Alana and risking the lives of so many for the love of one girl. Nerves wracked me, and I tried to remember when I last felt this

165

anxious. I closed my eyes and thought of that Thursday, the day I lost her.

I had the whole day planned out. We would have a picnic in our favourite spot in the green and chill out before Alana left to go home. I had a lecture scheduled for the next day so I would make my way there by myself early on Saturday morning. I was a tangled bag of nerves.

It had all started a week earlier when she'd asked me to come down. Her parents wanted to meet me, and I agreed without hesitation because I had something that I needed to ask her dad. It may have been old-fashioned, but with Alana's age, I had to get it right or things might turn sour. Throughout the day, I had practiced what I would say over and over in my head, telling him it would be a long engagement. I wanted Alana to know I was committed to her despite the fact our careers would separate us for maybe months at a time.

Without her dad's approval, Alana would not be happy, and neither would I. She had a special bond with her dad, and I envied her that since my own dad didn't give a monkey's butt about me. When I had a family, I wanted to have the type of relationship with my children that Alana had with her dad. They were friends as well as being father and daughter.

So we had a lovely afternoon, relaxing and kissing until the sun set and we said our goodbyes under the stars. I watched her dance away from me and smiled because in a few days she might say "yes" and I would be hers forever. Sappy, but true.

During my long day of lectures and meetings, my mind was elsewhere. I fumbled through the day, my only comfort being a few texts from Alana as she made her way by bus from the top of the Island down to the very bottom. She commented about her companions on the bus. One text informed me that she had arrived home safely.

I heard nothing again until around ten, my nerves keeping me awake as I tossed and turned in bed, anxious for my travels the next day. A beep on my phone alerted me to the text, and I put on my glasses so I could read the message.

CAN'T WAIT TO CU 2MORO... LUV YOU XX

I texted her back telling her that I loved her too and somehow was able to drift into a heavy sleep. I'd been sleeping so soundly that when I heard an annoying buzz early the next morning, it took me a few minutes to realize it was my phone. The irritating noise stopped, but I was awake by that time.

I picked it up and checked who the caller was. Ten missed calls from Connors. I looked at the time. Five minutes after five in the morning. Damn it. If he had drunk dialled me when I had a long day ahead of me, I would kick his ass when I saw him. Being down south meant I could meet up with him and finally introduce him to Alana.

The phone buzzed again in my hand, and I pressed it to answer it. Holding it up to my ear, I lay back down in bed. "Connors, have you any idea what time it is?"

"Danny-boy, I need you to listen to me... it's about your girl."
I sat up ramrod straight in the bed. "Connors. Is she okay?"

My heart crumbled while I listened to the words as my best friend spoke them, not fully understanding. "Something happened at her folks place, Danny. They say she killed her whole family. Shot 'em all in cold blood. I saw the pictures... it was horrific."

"She didn't do it, Connors... she couldn't have."

"I hear you, Danny, but they brought her in last night, knocked out cold. I was in the room when she woke up, and when they told her what she supposedly did, and it was like nothing I had ever seen before. The girl broke down in tears and said she didn't remember."

"What didn't she remember? Can I see her?"

Connors sighed, and I held my breath. "Danny, she just doesn't remember what happened. She claims to not remember anything. Alana says she went off to the training centre, and the rest is gone."

"What are you saying, Connors?"

"I'm saying she doesn't remember you, Danny... the past six

months are gone. One of the guards knocked her unconscious with the butt of his gun, and they think it affected her memory somehow. I dunno… you're the expert … is that possible?"

Sure, it was possible. I had read reports from criminals who claimed not to remember their actions, saying they blacked out during a vicious rage and used that defence. But I had to see her… how could she forget me?

"I'm getting in my car now, Connors. Tell me where to meet you."

"Danny, don't come here. Not yet. I have to go, but will ring you when I have more news… gotta go… they are moving her to the wing."

It was only then that I was reminded of where exactly Connors worked. "What wing is she in, Connors? What wing?"

There was no sound at the end of the line. "Connors, what wing is she in?" I growled. I knew, God help me, I already knew, but I had to hear him say it or I wouldn't believe it.

"Danny, she is in the Underage Department of Corrections, and she has been assigned to me. Danny… she's on death row."

My world shattered. How had plans for the future turned sour in a matter of hours? I clutched the phone so hard I was afraid it would snap. Connors was speaking, but all I could hear was a rush of blood to my head.

"Danny I gotta go… I promise you I will watch over her. I'll be in touch."

The phone clicked, and he was gone. And I was lost.

I had completely gone to pieces waiting for the phone to ring again, trashing my room. Pictures were flung across the room, books ripped from their shelves and crumpled down into a battered heap on the ground, and I cried. I despised the distance between us and fought the urge to go to her… not understanding how she could forget me, forget all about us. I knew it was a possibility but did not want to believe it. After a few hours of pacing my destroyed room, I opened the bedside table and pocketed the small ring box. I went to speak to the head of the psychology department and told him I had heard about the events down south and asked for a transfer in order to study the case.

At first he seemed surprised, considering I was posed for a new position within the department that assessed prisoners. I lied, telling him memory loss had always fascinated me, and I would love to study the girl further, assess her and see if she really had lost her memory. It had taken four months of red tape and bureaucratic BS before I got the transfer, with my department head deferring placement for a year.

I packed up my belongings and got straight in a car and drove all night to the prison. After a quick tour, I was shown to my office and asked to have Alana brought to me straight away. Hope flooded my veins thinking that when Alana saw me it would spark some sort of recognition, but I got the opposite.

Connors had brought her to me and winked before leaving us alone. My heart beat so loud that I was afraid she would hear it in my voice while I searched for some little hint in her eyes. Instead, the fragile, broken girl in front of me paled in comparison to the fiery one that had insisted I take her out for coffee.

She had lost weight. Her eyes were sad, and her body language was defensive. She sat on one of the armchairs in front of my desk clutching her knees to her chest. God, I wished I could take her in my arms and tell her she would be safe, but the girl I was looking at was a stranger.

I knew then that it would take more than the time we had to gain her trust and try and bring my Alana back to me. No matter what, I would try until the last breath left my lungs.

My office door opened again and Connors was already back. I looked up at him, but he shook his head. I sighed and got up. Walking over to the cupboard, I opened the doors and pulled two glasses and a bottle of whiskey from the shelf. Connors' grin widened as he took the weight off his legs and sat, his boots resting on the edge of my desk. I joined him, putting the glasses down and poured out the liquid. Passing a glass to him, I rested into the chair and mimicked his way of resting shoes on the opposite edge of the desk.

"Things must be nearing an end if you take out the good stuff, Danny-boy. I could arrest you for having illegal brew, you know."

"Then you would have to arrest yourself for partaking in illegal activities, my friend."

"Touché." And he grinned, lifting the glass to his lips, savouring a gulp. I sipped mine and ran things over in my head.

"Can you get your hands on those blueprints, do you think?"

Connors took another slug and grinned. "Yeah, the girl in records has a thing for me, so I should be able to get my hands on them."

I chuckled and said, "Only you would use a life and death situation to chat up girls."

He grinned back at me. "Keeps me young."

We drank the rest in silence, each of us lost in our own thoughts. I guessed we had sat there for about ten minutes before Connors' voice penetrated the quiet.

"So, Danny-boy, do you think your ole man will come through?"

"I hope so, Connors. I think he was happier about my rebelling against the parliament than anything else. His exact words, 'I knew you would turn out to be a chip off the ole block, Son.' My dad is not searching for redemption, just another excuse to stick it to the powers that be."

Connors raised his glass and winked. "And we will take the bastard's help no matter how much of an asshat he is, Danny. To freedom."

I raised my glass and clicked it with his. "To freedom."

Connors laughed, and I joined him, but soon it was time for him to leave, and I had some things to sort out. With Connors gone, I unlocked my desk drawer and took out the photo of me and Alana and placed it on the desk. I needed her company for a while and set the tiny box on the desk in front of her photo before I pulled out a folder that held my master plan.

I flicked through the documents until I came to the notes I had jotted down during my phone calls with my dad. Finding the number I was looking for, I picked up the phone and dialled the number.

The phone answered immediately, clicking to answering machine with no greeting. I left a message as my dad had instructed and waited. Minutes ticked by and finally the phone on my desk rang.

"Hello. Dr Costello speaking."

"You Jimmy's boy?" A gruff voice asked.

"I am."

"How can I help ya?"

I laid out my plan for him and waited for him to speak.

"That can be done. Did Jimmy tell ya how much?"

"He did. I have it in cash for you once the package has been delivered."

He paused for a second. "Half up front."

"My dad said to tell you to remember how he kept his mouth shut about Dundalk." My dad had given me that little snippet if his friend argued but didn't tell me what he meant by it.

171

The voice at the end of the line grunted and said, "Fine, but Jimmy and me are square after this... you tell him that."

"I will."

"I'll be on to ya." The line disconnected, and I replaced the receiver. Another piece was now in place... or was I just tightening the noose around my own neck as well as Alana's? I hoped for the former.

Deep down, in the pit of my stomach, my gut told me that nothing would ever be the same again.

ALANA

"I'm waking up; I feel it in my bones,
Enough to make my systems blow."
(IMAGINE DRAGONS: RADIOACTIVE)

I EXPECTED TO BE HAUNTED BY YESTERDAY'S FLASHBACK AS soon as I closed my eyes. I expected to wake up screaming and checking to see if my hands were bloodstained. I expected to open my eyes and still see their bodies littering the floor. I expected to be ready to resist the urge to vomit as my sister's lifeless eyes stared back at me. I expected to bolt upright in a cold sweat, horrified by images that would scar me for the rest of my short life. But none of that happened. I was wrong; my mind unleashed another memory on me. This time the emphasis edged towards my dad and seemed more like a gentle reminder than the harsh images I had dealt with up until now.

The bus had dropped me off at the edge of our tiny town, and I enjoyed the breath of air after being cramped on the coach. After about an hour, the bus began to reek of sweat and cheap perfume. I hoisted my duffle bag over my shoulder, waiting until the weight was steady and then set off on the short walk to my childhood home.

Not much had changed in the last six months. The blacktop road still stuck to the soles of my shoes when I walked. Humidity in the air made it seem heavy, and the trees blocked the setting sun from my vision, covering the path as I walked, casting dancing shadows at my feet.

I stopped at the checkpoint into the village, glad there wasn't a line because that late in the afternoon everyone was still at work or home for the evening. After flashing my badge at the guard, I exchanged pleasantries and was on my way again. The village contained no more than a hundred houses, each street designated depending on the family status within the Island. We had one little square that was home to a range of shops and bakeries and the one public house. I passed the school I had attended and did not even cast a glance in its direction. That place held no happy memories for me... no friends to keep in touch with.

As expected, I returned polite gestures to others while continuing on my journey, eager to pass through the streets and spy the familiar house far back in a prestigious part of the village designated to the officers of the Parliament. I tried to ignore the inquisitive looks as I strolled through the streets, but I knew the past six months had done wonders for me, physically and emotionally.

I was no longer the smallest girl in the room... actually that should be rephrased... even though I was still the smallest girl in the room, the physical training I had undertaken had added muscle to my body, defined strong arms that I didn't bother to hide under my vest top. As I rounded the corner to my street, I held my head high. I had a lot to be proud of... success when people had expected me to fail. Besides, I had the love of a good man.

Tomorrow would be an interesting day when my dad and my boyfriend came face to face for the first time.

The row of houses on my street came into view and I spotted a ball of excitement rushing towards me. Sophia's smile was an ocean wide as she raced up the street to greet me. Her hair had grown longer and she had too. She'd gained a full inch or two since I last saw her. I let my bag drop to the ground and held out my arms to her, engulfing her in a hug as soon as her body was within reaching distance.

"I've missed you so much, Soph," I murmured into her hair. Ruffling her hair as she skipped alongside me, she tried to fit in as much news as her little mouth could possibly say before she ran out of steam. I heard all about school and her music lessons and about the boy in her class who pulled her hair. She burst into enthusiastic

giggles when I threatened to kick his ass for her.

I spotted the silhouette of my mom standing in the doorway of our house. Sophia bounded off to her. Mom's smile widened as I drew nearer. Never has a hug felt as good as when my mom wrapped her arms around me. I breathed in the smell of her perfume mixed with flour. She took my face in her hands and said, "Let me look at my beautiful daughter." I laughed and kissed her on the cheek.

We went inside and all revelled in the home comforts I had come to miss. The house smelled of the makings of a stew, my favourite dish ever. Also, I could make out the unmistakable odour of something baking in the oven, and my mouth began to water. I would make up for this on Tuesday when I went back to training.

Mom asked how I was and if they were treating me well at the centre. I relayed the hardships of being a warden's daughter but told her that I was tough. She squeezed my shoulder and an expression passed over her face, far too quickly for me to make anything from it. We chatted some more while she made coffee and it seemed as though I had never left.

When the coffee was brewed, Mom asked if I'd take a cup to my dad. Of course, he would be in his office. Their first born was returning home after six months away, but with my dad, work still came first. Nothing new there, I supposed. I sneaked a peek at my mom, but she was already watching me. An easy smile overtook me as I accepted the warm cup from her hand, and I left her to her cooking while I went in search of my dad.

It wasn't that I didn't know exactly where he was… his office. Leaving the kitchen, I went as if heading to the garden but took a right at the door leading to a section of the house where dad had built an office when he had become warden a couple of years earlier. His voice was muted and grumpy, and I knew there and then that the weekend would be a disaster.

I stood outside the door and raised my free hand to knock, abruptly stopping when his voice rose, and I listened to one side of the conversation. Assuming he was on the phone wasn't a stretch because Mom was the perfect hostess and would have sent me with two cups instead of one if we had company. From the growl in his voice, I knew Dad was angry, so I hesitated outside the door and listened.

"Damn it, Theresa. I told you that the experiments would not continue."

"Because it's unethical… we are not God."

"I am your boss—do not forget that—do not threaten me."

My father laughed, but it sounded cold and serious. "Theresa, The Grand Masters, will side with me… if Treatment were designed to help those far too damaged to help themselves, then I would be all for it. But your ideas, what you want to do… it's perverse. We are not such a higher power that we get to decide this for them."

A pause followed, much longer than the ones before and then Dad snorted and said, "You have my decision, Theresa. I am sending my report in the morning. No, woman, do not come here….we have nothing to discuss."

The phone slammed down and my dad cursed. I had waited barely a second before I knocked on the door, and my dad called, "Come in."

Cautiously pushing the door open, I entered, trying to keep my face neutral so dad would not know I had listened in. He looked up from his papers and blinked in surprise, glancing at the clock over my head. "Is it that time already?"

I smiled. "Yeah, I've been here for a while. Mom asked me to bring you a coffee. You work too hard, Dad." I placed the cup on his overflowing desk when he cleared some space for me, and I turned to leave again, a bit disappointed that he had not been counting down the hours until I returned.

"Alana, wait. Sit with me for a bit… I want to hear all your news."

That brought a smile back to my face, and I sat down on the windowsill. Honestly, it was the only free spot in the office. We exchanged a few remarks about life in the training centre, and he told me that he was speaking there in a couple of weeks and asked if I would like to spend some time together. Maybe we could get together for a meal. Although he would probably be too busy... I appreciated the sentiment.

The phone on his desk rang again and Dad swore, glancing from me to the phone. Uneasy about the situation, I got up to leave, but he let it ring. Turning from me, he said, "I promise we will have the whole day tomorrow, Alana. I just have a few things I need to tie up tonight."

Forcing a smile, I left his office, closing the door behind me. I sighed as he snarled a greeting into the phone. After that, I was happy to return to Mom and her cheerful kitchen where she poured me a fresh cup of coffee and gave me a knowing smile.

Theresa again. It seemed that she haunted my memories as much as my past. Angry arguments with my mom and Theresa's name came up. Hushed, disturbing phone calls and my dad uttered her name. All roads led to Theresa Lane, but where did they end?

Determined to get some answers, I spent the morning preparing for my session with Daniel. I thought back to the most recent dream, remembering that I had been seeing someone special on that last day. Could that person have been Daniel? If that was so, why didn't he just come out and tell me? Why all the secrets? I was sick of secrets and wanted the truth. At this point in my life, I deserved it.

Yesterday's flashback had been incomplete, as if there were a few links missing, and I wasn't allowed to see the full picture. Now I know I wasn't responsible for my family's deaths, but if I didn't do it, then who did? Was there time? Would I ever find out?

After I had showered, eaten and changed my clothes, I was ready to interrogate the good doctor. I should have been relaxed, as I had resolved to be but had so many questions. Frustration crept up on me, spreading like wildfire. The more I thought about everything over the past few months, and even the last two days, the more that remained hidden from me.

Connors must have sensed my tension because he kept unusually quiet as we walked the corridor to Daniel's office, letting me in without a word. He quickly retreated, but not before I caught a look pass between him and Daniel. What was their deal anyway? They seemed pretty friendly for people from opposite ends of the spectrum.

I wasn't the only one who seemed on edge today. Daniel sat behind his desk, but I heard the sound of his foot tapping against the floor. He tidied up some papers on his desk as I eased down into the chair and settled into uncomfortable silence. After a few minutes, I leaned my elbows on the desk and tapped the desk in rhythm with his feet. His leg stopped moving, and he looked up at me with those blue eyes boring into my soul. He raised an eyebrow as if I were a naughty schoolgirl. My fingers continued dancing on the desk.

"Are you trying to annoy me, Alana?"

"How does that make you feel?" I said, throwing his favourite phrase right back at him. He ignored me, finally closing a folder and sitting back in his chair. While he ran his hand over his chin, I noticed a thin line of stubble starting on his jawline. It suited him.

"I understand you had a meeting with the warden yesterday. How did that go?" Those beautiful eyes watched me with caution.

A shrug was all I could manage. "I can't shake the feeling she was fishing for something, trying to trip me up somehow."

"Did she ask about our sessions?"

"Yes, and I told her you were doing a fantastic job, and I had started to remember." The words came out angrier than I meant them to. Daniel blinked at the venom in them.

"And why does that make you angry? I am trying to help you, remember?"

That was all I could handle of the games and deceit. I threw my hands up in the air. "But you won't tell me anything. How can I know what is real and not if you don't give me a hint."

Daniel folded his arms across his chest. "Okay, so ask me questions, and I will answer them."

Hesitating, waiting for the punch line or the trick, I stalled. Why else would he change his melody after all these months when he could have just told me straight out.

"Okay... if you're sure." He didn't say a word. I wasn't sure he was even breathing, and I swallowed hard. "I remember bits of the night my family was killed and know I didn't do it." A long pause hung in the air while I waited for him to speak.

"Is that what happened in the mess hall yesterday? You had a flashback?"

I nodded in agreement, my mouth suddenly dry. "Yeah, but I didn't get the full memory back. It was patchy, like a video skipping certain parts. I heard a noise downstairs and that's... that's when I found them."

'"But that is not all you remember, is it?" He pushed as if he needed to hear the answer as much as I needed to say it.

"I think I've had glimpses although I know I'm forgetting something important. I can feel it in here." I pointed to my chest with my finger, right where my heart should be. "Are my feelings for you real? Are those memories real? Are you the one I forgot about?"

Again the silence and he didn't answer me. I slammed my open palm down on the desk hard enough for it to sting and suddenly enough for him to jump. This was

like drowning, lost in a sea of confusion, frantically trying to hold onto something real. In my heart of hearts, I
wanted more than anything for Daniel to be my *something
real*. He opened his mouth to speak, and I knew by his
expression that I wasn't going to like his answer.

"Don't... just don't... if you are going to feed me
more psychobabble about me remembering by myself, I swear to God I will punch you in the face." His
lip twitched and I was amazed that he had the nerve to
laugh right in my face. "And you're laughing at me... is
my life that funny to you? Just tell me something real for
the love of God. Are you *my someone... the someone* I'm
forgetting?" The last sentence came out in a shout and I
was on my feet so suddenly that I knocked over the chair.
I stood there watching it crash to the ground with a loud
bang.

By that time, I was panting, and my fists were balled
up, ready and willing to unleash my fury. Daniel sighed,
a deep and mournful sound as he got to his feet. Walking
slowly around the desk, he put his hands on my shoulders and turned me to face him. Tears welled up and
fell, and I let them. Daniel cupped my cheek. Using his
thumb, he brushed away a single tear.

I watched him, really studied him and knew right
then that I was in love with him. It was me, the person
I was and would be, regardless of anything else. Here I
was, the Alana who forgot six months of her life, and I
was in love with the blue eyed boy touching me with a
tenderness that I craved. But I needed more answers before I did anything else. Was what I believed in my heart
and soul true?

"Are you who I am forgetting?" I begged, needing
him to say the words. He had already admitted that he
had feelings for me, but was that all? So I asked him again,
once more. "*Please*, Daniel have I really forgotten you?"

He bent his head closer to mine, and my breath caught in my throat. In one hushed word, I got my answer as the sweetest word in the world crossed his lips. "Yes."

An uncontrolled cry escaped, and I rid myself of the mournful feelings. I rose up on my toes so the distance between us was gone. Without regard to anything else, I crushed my lips to his before he had a chance to retreat.

He reacted immediately, not pulling away but tangling his fingers in my hair as if he was afraid I would try and run. I had no intention of that. It was heated, familiar, and amazing. His lips fit mine perfectly and as his tongue slipped past my bottom lip, I inhaled the scent of him, the images I so desperately needed came back to me in a rush.

At that moment, I understood how powerful our memories could be. As Daniel kissed me relentlessly, all my memories of him flooded back to me, each one a devastating reminder of what I had almost lost. When I looked back at it, I couldn't help but be reminded of a quote I once heard. It was about how the pieces of who you were and the ones who make you what you are now, mold into one. I understood the full meaning at that moment. Memories are bullets. Some whiz by and only spook you. Others tear you open and leave you in pieces. I felt as if I had been torn open and exposed for all to see, my memories laid bare.

Our first meeting, our coffee date, stolen moments in between classes... it all came back. Like a slap in the face, each piece of the puzzle snugly fit into place. I could not hold back the sob that had built up in my throat.

Daniel pulled back immediately, his expression awash with concern. I traced the contours of his face with my fingertips, remembering the feel of him. As I stared into his eyes, I was reminded of how much I'd always loved him.

"Daniel? Oh God, Daniel..." I cried into his shoulder. He shushed me and began to apologize, but I stopped him. When I lifted my head and held his gaze, I said, "I'm so sorry, Daniel... I'm so sorry... I don't know how I could ever have forgotten you."

DANIEL

"And I'm not breaking down, I'm breaking out,
Last chance to lose control."
(MUSE: HYSTERIA)

"I'M SORRY."

I wasn't apologizing for anything in particular, just uncertain if I heard her right. But I knew with one look in those dazzling brown eyes that Alana was back. Her mouth curved into a lopsided smile, and I stole a kiss. Part of me still believed that she hadn't remembered me and that her words are nothing but regret at the relationship she had lost somewhere in the corner of her mind.

She came up for air but stayed close, her arms now wrapped around my waist. When she cuddled into me, it caused a wave of elation and crashed over me, pushing aside the nagging thoughts of our impending fates.

"What was so bad that I wiped you from my memory, Daniel? I'm so sorry to have done this to you. I love you."

I steered us towards the couch and sat down. She immediately snuggled into me. "You remember everything, right? About us, I mean? Has everything come back?"

She shook her head. "No, just us ... When we first met, our first date, and the first time you held my hand and kissed me."

"As I remember it, Alana, it was you who kissed me." I was amazed that she was in my arms once again, like I always hoped she would be.

Her smile was one of the most beautiful things I had ever seen, then and now, and it was all mine. I drank her in as she continued to speak. "I remember you lying

183

next to me, me watching you sleep… I remember every-thing… even you talking about your best friend, Chris. Oh, that's Connors, I take it?"

"Yup. I asked to be sent here to help you. Alana, be-ing so close to you but being so far away has been torture. I love you, babe, you know that, right?"

She swept her hair from her eyes and blinked back tears. I kissed her again because I couldn't help myself. I had been starved for her for so long and greedily took what she offered. Adrenaline raced through my veins and as her fingers brushed the hem of my shirt, I restrained myself and pulled back from her embrace.

"If we don't stop now, I will forget that I'm a gentle-man." I swallowed hard at the heat in her eyes and sat back. She sighed and cuddled into me, raising my hand to check my watch before she spoke. "How did you find out?"

"Connors called me on the morning I was due to drive down to see you and meet your family. He told me what had happened. I tried to get here sooner, but for some reason the warden did not want me here."

"But what about the program? You were so excited."

"None of it mattered without you." Alana sniffled, so I continued. "When I finally got assigned here and you walked into my office, I waited for any sign that you recognized me, but you didn't. I have waited every day since then for some hint."

"I didn't mean to," she whispered. I kissed the top of her head.

"I know that, babe. None of this is your fault, but I do have a theory."

She sat up straight and waited. "What? Tell me…"

Inhaling a deep breath, I entwined her fingers with mine. "Your memories seem to come back when your senses trigger something you've locked away. Jayson tell-

ing you a story, the incident in the mess hall, our kiss…"
I paused, unsure how she would handle my next words.
"I think if we take you back, back to your house, then we
may finally get the result we all want."

The cogs turning in her head were almost visible
as she thought about what I said. Her nose wrinkled up,
and she began to curl the ends of her hair, turning them
over with her index finger. I placed my other hand, the
one not holding hers, on her thigh to steady her, let her
know that I was there for her.

"What if I can't go back? I've seen the aftermath,
what if what I don't remember is worse?"

"If this is your last chance to finally get answers, are
you willing to let your fear stop you?"

She shook her head and allowed a bitter laugh to
taint the moment. "One problem with your plan, Daniel.
I'm in prison for murder. They aren't exactly going to say
'Oh, hey, sure, no problems. Of course, you can go on a
day trip with your boyfriend. By the way, how do they
not know we know each other?'"

I traced circles on her thigh and smiled. "Neither
of us were really social butterflies. A small number of
people knew we were seeing each other and thankfully
most of them are overseas on assignment. Not many requested to be sent to this wing of the prison and luckily
no new positions have come up that need to be filled with
graduates."

She was about to say something when the door
opened suddenly, but we couldn't shift positions in time.
Chris Connors stepped in, the door closing and his
mouth forming an O. He laughed and threw his hands
up in the air.

"Finally! Please tell me your girl has got some of her
noodles back in the box because the sexual tension between you two was starting to drive me crazy!"

We both stared at each other and all three of us laughed. "Yes, Connors, Alana got her memories of us back. We are still working on the rest."

"Well, praise Jesus. McCarthy, your boy has been a pain in my ass for months now. Trying to keep this a secret has been a bitch."

Alana beamed at him. "Thanks, Connors—for keeping us both safe. I don't think we can ever repay you."

His grin widened. "Don't mention it, McCarthy. I'd do anything for Danny-boy and now you too. But as much as I hate to break up the lovebirds, you still have to play inmate, and Danny-boy here must pretend to be a real doctor."

I shook my head as I reluctantly rose, pulling Alana with me. Taking her face in my hands, I gave her a quick kiss. Connors whistled. "Come on, Romeo. You waited six months for her to remember, one more day 'til you see her again won't kill you."

Before I could sneak another kiss, Connors pulled her away, and she blew one back at me before they were out the door. Alone again. Did that just happen? *I have her back. I really have her back.* When they were gone, I went to the cupboard and pulled out the almost empty bottle of whiskey and took a slug from the bottle. It seemed like a whiskey type of moment.

Sitting back down at my desk, bottle in hand, my mind started planning the next move on the chessboard. I needed Alana away from here, and if that meant making a phone call that would either work in our favour or not, I was willing to try. It was a long shot, but if the last few months had taught me anything, it was that I could be persuasive when I wanted to be.

Taking another swig from the whiskey bottle, Dutch courage I suppose, I picked up the phone and dialled the extension to speak with the warden.

I waited for the call to connect and asked to speak with her. Apparently, she was not taking calls that day, and I was asked to leave a message. I said that it was important that I speak with her because it was in regard to the welfare of an inmate. A click sounded on the line and then another as the secretary, who most likely spoke to the warden, came back to me. She asked me to hold the line, which I did. Waiting an anxiety filled five minutes was torture until my call was picked up.

"Dr Costello, what is so important that you could not wait?"

"Forgive me, Warden, but as time is of the essence, I felt a sense of urgency was called for in this case." My fingers tightened on the bottle as I continued. "Miss McCarthy has recovered a lot of her memory from the night in question, and I believe I may have the solution to ensure we all gain the truth about that night."

"And what might that solution be?" Her tone was clipped and short, but she gave no inclination of her feelings about Alana remembering.

"Alana's memories have returned due to her mind's reaction to certain sensorial triggers. She has the flashbacks of the aftermath back but has described having holes, gaps in them. I believe if I were allowed to bring her back to the scene of the crime, it might trigger the last of those memories that her mind has locked away."

Silence and static greeted me on the line, and I waited. My pulse raced and my heart did its best impression of a bass drum.

"Are you serious, Doctor? Are you honestly asking me to allow a convicted murderer a day pass on the off chance she decides to tell the truth?" Her voice wavered, and I made out the barest hint of anger in it.

"I am, Warden. I take my research very seriously. If taking her back to where it all started will uncover who really killed her family, then is it not worth that? You and Cormac McCarthy were friends. Don't you want to know what actually happened?"

More static, and I inhaled and held my breath.

"I have always wondered why you were so interested in this girl, Doctor? What caused you to give up your life and other research to come here and study her?" I caught the hidden meaning behind her words. She was trying to intimidate me, force me to reveal something that I wouldn't and couldn't. I swallowed hard and began to reply, almost choking on the words.

"It has nothing to do with the girl. It is all about the research. Do you know how much money I will get in grants and awards if my report on this is published? I can pay off the debts my father saddled me and my aunt with. Unlocking Alana's past has more to do with what it will do for my career than proving her innocent. This little project of mine could make my career." The line went dead for a long moment, but I heard her breathing. "I may be young, Warden, but I am ambitious. I would not have studied hard to become the youngest in my field if I weren't. I want to make a name for myself and am grateful to anyone who helps me get there."

The lies made me feel dirty as my stomach twisted, and I tried to remind myself that although the words were not true, that everything I said and did was for Alana. I heard the sigh in my ear and shifted the phone to the other side.

"And when would you like to organize this outing, Dr Costello? You cannot take a dangerous prisoner out alone. These things take time to arrange."

"While I appreciate that, Warden, in Miss McCarthy's case, time is not a luxury we have. I have a vehicle we can use and was hoping to go as soon as possible, tomorrow maybe. Once you have signed off on it, then all I need is for you to assign a guard. I don't wish for it to be a disruption, Warden, but we are pressed for time."

"I cannot let you go off on a whim because you think the girl will remember."

Taking a gulp of whiskey to take the dryness out of my mouth, I found comfort in the way it burned the back of my throat. "In my professional opinion, Warden, I think the expedition would be beneficial to Miss McCarthy. If she does remember, then it may grant her some much-needed closure before her death day."

I heard her fingers drum against something while she mulled over what I'd said. She took her time, keeping me waiting, each second stretching out as if it were hours. Closing my eyes, I prepared for her to reject my proposal and dash all hope of helping Alana. In agony at the delay, I bit back the urge to say, "Well?" It would have gotten me nowhere with her. Instead, she beat me to it with a sigh.

"Fine, I will allow you to take her tomorrow. Although I cannot let you go with just one guard, Dr Costello. Her supervising officer is Christopher Connors. He is reliable. Officer Connors will drive you both. I will send him to you with the release forms, and he can choose another guard to accompany you. That will ensure everyone's safety. Should Miss McCarthy step out of line, then Connors or his counterpart will use force if necessary, behaviour chip or not."

The excitement overwhelmed me, and I gave her my thanks. "I understand. Thank you, Warden. Your assistance will be noted in my report."

That must have pleased her because she made a *hmm* sound as if agreeing with something unsaid. Perhaps she thought I would praise her work here in the UADC, when, in fact, the report I was putting together would only discredit her. If only I could uncover the secrets that lurked in the cage. For now, I had higher priorities.

"I want to know what comes of your little outing, Dr Costello. Should you learn something new, don't hesitate to let me know. It would be frightful to think that poor Alana might meet her death for crimes she has not committed."

She tested me again, and I heard her questioning Alana's innocence to provoke me. I saw through the unspoken words and the tone of her voice and remained calm despite my rapid pulse and beating heart. We had come too far to stumble now.

"I can assure you now that she hasn't. Her memory indicates a detail that another person was in her house that night, long after she had gone to bed. She heard voices downstairs and gunshots and remained alive because we can only imagine the murderer did not know she had arrived home for the weekend. It was the only reason she was not killed along with Cormac, Sorcha, and Sophia. Alana did not kill her family, and we are very close to discovering the real perpetrator."

The sharp, gasping intake of breath brought a smile to my face.

"I hope so, Doctor. Good day." The phone clicked in my ear, and I stared at it. How in the hell did I pull that off? I set the receiver down and drained the last of the bottle with one swig. Suddenly, I had no energy. The emotional highs and lows of the conversation were excruciating, and I sat back in my chair and closed my eyes. I had waited for this day for so long, and now that it was here, I shut down. The whole resolution was anticlimactic.

I must have drifted off because the next thing I knew I was being shaken awake by a grinning Connors. Rubbing my face, I tried to wake up while Connors plopped a folder on my desk. I reached to open it. Release papers. Flipping through them, I still couldn't believe it. We would get out of there for only a few hours, but it was an important achievement.

"So, we're going on a road trip," Connors said. It was more of a statement than a question, but his voice reflected doubt. He pulled a bag of peanuts from his pocket and tossed one into his mouth. "Danny-boy, you have a way with words, my man. How did you manage it?"

"By pretending to be a cruel bastard and saying that my career was more important than the truth. She lapped it up."

Connors popped another peanut into his mouth. "By any means necessary, my friend. Success any way we can get it."

"She also believes that you are reliable, and she can depend on you to protect me."

"Ha! I do like my reputation for helping damsels in distress. Does that make you a damsel? Oh, Danny, does this mean I get to drive your car?" The Cheshire cat had nothing on him.

"You break it, you buy it. Any idea who you will get to come with us? We need someone trustworthy, not a spy for Theresa."

"Megan will come. I'm sure I can keep her distracted for a couple of hours." He beamed his cheeky smile, and I shook my head at him.

"We are supposed to be saving the love of my life, not feeding your ego."

"I am willing to take one for the team, Danny-boy. Let me be a hero."

I snickered and found the tension that had built up in my gut was tying me in knots. Tomorrow would make or break us. It would be the last chance to get Alana to remember. I hoped she was up for the challenge. A single hurdle was left to clear before I could signal for everything to begin. One way or another, she would be free.

ALANA

"Secrets don't sleep 'til they're took to the grave."
(BRING ME THE HORIZON: SHADOW MOSES)

I SPENT THE NIGHT TOSSING AND TURNING, CONFLICTED IN my emotions. While I felt elated that I had finally remembered Daniel, the guilt and sadness at having lost him in the first place was like a boulder on my chest. How could you forget someone you loved with every fibre of your being? Why in God's name would your mind do such a horrible thing to you? Thinking about my feelings for Daniel since I first saw him, when my memories were gone, was all that brought hope for me. If that beacon could lead me to the truth, how could I forget him?

But as much as I longed to bask in the warm, fluttering feeling that I had thinking of Daniel, I was worried about him. If word got out about us, he would be arrested and an immediate death sentence awaited him. Connors would pay the price too. My gut feeling was that Jayson was also in on their plan, but I hadn't confronted him yet. Daniel had brought all of them together to protect me. I hoped his efforts would not be in vain.

Night turned into day, the black of night slowly faded to allow a small sliver of light to penetrate the grey clouds and let sun rays dance on my walls. The door to my cell slid open, and I listened to the sounds in the hallway as inmates made their way down to breakfast. The idea of eating was repulsive to me at the time because of the tension throughout my body. Eating might make me sick. Missing a session with Daniel was not an option.

So I lay there, stressing, and even though I tried to play the new memories over in my mind, I couldn't help but fret about going back home. If Daniel were successful, then I would have to go back to the house and try and picture their bodies and get myself to remember who killed them. Panic rose in my chest, and I tried to quash it down, bury it under images of my lips on his, the feel of my hands on his skin and breathe in the scent of him. I hadn't noticed until then, until I actually fully remembered him, that Daniel smelled of soap and apple. The scent was from shampoo he had used when we were in training together.

I was so caught up in my thoughts that, at first, I didn't notice a presence standing in the doorway. Hoping the guard would leave me in peace to count down the minutes until I was safe and loved in Daniel's arms, I ignored him. He cleared his throat, but I still didn't move until he spoke. "Hey."

The familiar voice jerked me to attention. Swinging my legs free of the blanket, I sat up to look at him. Daniel leaned in the archway, a smug look on his face. Dressed in dark jeans and a snug, plain blue T-shirt, his brown hair was slicked back to reveal the full shape of his face. His startling blue eyes, the way his cheeks dimpled when he smiled, and even the smallness of his nose amazed me. And he was mine.

"Hi," I replied, unsure of what else we could say with so many eyes watching.

"You okay after yesterday?"

I nodded and smiled, a bit embarrassed that all I wanted to do was kiss him again. A voice inside told me to do that so I wouldn't forget him again.

"Do you know how hard it is for me not to just go over there and kiss you?"

I blinked in surprise, scanning outside my cell to make sure no one could hear. "Daniel, you have to be careful."

"It was worth the chance to see the look on your face."

"Not that I'm not grateful to see you first thing in the morning when I look like a hot mess, but why are you here?" By that time, I was shaking my head and laughing.

He remained where he was, and his smile widened. "You always look beautiful first thing in the morning. Plus, we have a long day ahead of us. You up for a day trip?"

Daniel might not be every girl's first choice, but when he said charming things like that, I would agree to anything, no matter what it was.

"You got permission to go?"

"I did."

I swallowed hard and chewed on my bottom lip. That was it. I was going back there. Oh, God, what if I freaked out? What if the memories didn't come back to me? In a few weeks, I would be eighteen and dead. At that point, everything Daniel, Connors, and whoever else was in on this did, would be for nothing.

The world spun. I could not fill my lungs with enough air for them to function. My palms began to sweat and hot tears rolled off my cheeks. I feared I was dying and the panic would take me down with it.

And then a soft hand slipped into mine, warm and comforting. I tried to focus on him, elevate the vice grip on my insides and suck it up. But as I closed my eyes while Daniel tried to soothe me, I could not grasp what he was saying. Instead, I focused on a happy memory of me and him alone, wrapped in each other's arms as the sun descended before us. I pictured myself back there, safe and sound. Slowly, the panic lessened, and I could breathe again.

I peered sideways at Daniel as he lingered on the

edge of the bed. As patient as ever, he said nothing while he watched me with concern until I calmed enough to speak. "Sorry… I'm a mess."

He brushed a loose bit of hair from my eyes, and when his fingertips grazed my forehead, I shivered, a good shiver under his touch.

"Don't ever apologize to me for being scared. I'd have fallen to pieces if I were in your shoes. But we can do this—together—we can do this."

He took his hand from mine and stood. I did the same. Once I had put my shoes on, Daniel gestured me to follow him. Certain that everyone's eyes were on me as we walked side by side, I tried to act normal. My suspicions about Jayson were confirmed when I caught sight of his brilliant smile and a cheeky wink when he spotted us together. I fought not to laugh.

When we came to the door, Connors was standing there with one of the female guards. She was extremely pretty, her gorgeous red hair pulled into a side braid. From the way she looked at her redheaded counterpart, she had a crush on Connors. I watched as she pulled a pair of handcuffs from her pocket. Daniel put out a hand to stop her.

"Is that necessary? Alana is not coming under duress."

"It is protocol," she grumbled.

Connors cracked his neck from side to side. "C'mon, Meg. McCarthy here won't try anything. You have my word." He grinned at her and she returned the cuffs to her pocket.

"Fine, but try anything and we will have some serious trouble." She spun on her heels and sashayed away, with Connors' eyes trailing her. He looked up and spotted me laughing and simply chuckled, a deep and resonating, familiar sound.

We followed the guards through the labyrinth of corridors, passing the exit for the yard and walked for what seemed like forever. When we arrived at a security desk, Connors handed over a bunch of papers and flashed his ID. The plump desk guard looked me up and down before grunting and pushed a button that opened a heavy door. I studied the door out of sheer amazement. Our cell doors were so high-tech that it was sometimes easy to forget that the outside of the prison was surrounded by stone walls spanning the entire country. Its entrances were heavily guarded by metal doors, in case technology failed.

I stepped out into the air and got blasted by a whoosh of wind. As I stumbled on the gravel, Daniel caught me by the elbow to stop me from eating the dirt. The wind tousled his hair, but he just grinned at me, letting go of my elbow when he had determined I could actually be trusted to walk in a straight line. Thankfully, he didn't make any comments about ninety-pound weaklings.

Daniel threw a set of keys at Connors and jogged towards the vehicle. While we waited for him to return, I took in my surroundings. Miles of brick encircled us. The only other thing visible from our viewpoint was the overpowering building that had been my home for months.

From outside, the prison appeared bleak and barren, showing no signs of the technology or state of the art gadgetry that was flaunted on the inside. I watched the faint glint of the sun bouncing off the glass roof and wondered which window wall enclosed my cell. Strangely, I did not have the sense of freedom I'd expected when I stepped outside. Instead, I experienced an overwhelming sense of exposure. Nowhere to run or hide, out in the open for all to see.

Screeching tires brought me out of my thoughts, and I heard Daniel groan as Connors pulled up in a long, sleek, black car. When it came to a sudden stop in front of us, a pile of dust was left in its wake. The passenger door opened, and I laughed. That earned a stern look from Meg. The driver's grin spanned from ear to ear. Daniel just shook his head and said nothing, opening the rear door for me. I climbed in the car, sliding across the leather seats to make room for Daniel, and he slammed the door behind him with a bang.

"Connors, try to keep my tires in one piece if you don't mind. I recently had them replaced." Connors looked over his shoulder into the back seat and just wiggled his eyebrows, grinning like an idiot.

Megan slipped into the passenger seat, and I heard a click as she pressed something on the dash that locked us in. This was not the car I remembered Daniel driving. His old car had been a beat-up, blue square of a thing that he had christened *Smurf*. I think it was a Ford Fiesta, and it made more noise than the volume of the radio could cover.

But this car was luxury and elegance all in one. It screamed newness, from the polish on the dash to the scent of air freshener mixed with leather. Daniel had always been careful with his money. He'd earned quite a lot lecturing and consulting, but I wondered what had made him decide to splurge.

Connors drove slowly towards the main gate, and we waited as the gigantic metal door slide sideways. The gate moaned and groaned as if opening was an inconvenience. I waited, my nerves starting to grip hold again. The emotions didn't ease up even as Connors put his foot on the accelerator, and we peeled out of the prison with another squeal of the tires.

I wanted to speak with Daniel, use his voice to talk my mind off the feeling of dread in the pit of my stomach. Megan's beady eyes focused on me, so I turned and gazed out the window. Outside the car, the scenery whizzed by, and I did not get the chance to enjoy my first, and most likely last, trip to the outside world.

The journey from the prison to my village was short, about half an hour the way Connors drove. We all sat in silence until Connors turned on the radio. Music was a welcome distraction. Between the prison and my house, there was nothing but road and green trees and fields. Every now and then, when Connors had to slow at a crossing or for another car, I spotted cattle or sheep on farms. Soon the road narrowed, the green disappeared, and I knew we had arrived.

Connors rolled down the window, and I sank down as low as possible in my seat. The guard on duty, a boy who lived up the road from me, peered through the open window and stared at me. His face went white in shock, and for a second he could not speak.

"Officer Connors and Flynn. We are here under orders from Warden Lane. I have the paperwork here for you." Connors spoke in an authoritative voice and held the papers out for the boy to take. On hearing Connors, the boy jerked his attention from me and took the folder. As he squinted through the papers, Daniel brushed his hand against mine, and I exhaled.

"I take it you know where you are going?" the boy asked, looking back at me.

"Yeah, we do," Connors said. Without another word, the barrier lifted, and Connors rolled the window up. I smiled when he said *asshole* under his breath. Our progress was much slower in the town, and I watched as we passed familiar buildings, ones I had barely looked at the last day I'd come home. Today, I studied each brick, every oddly painted house, all the gates and every person, not because I would never see this place again, but because a part of me longed for a glimpse of my parents or

sister in the crowd. If that happened, maybe my nightmare would end.

We rounded the corner and turned onto my street.
In Daniel's car, we looked important, maybe like special
dignitaries or something, and I could make out neigh-
bours pulling curtains aside to gawk. Thankfully, it was
early morning and most of the children were in school.
None of Sophia's friends would watch me with frightened eyes. I had enough to deal with today without the
pain of that.

Connors and Megan opened their doors and got out.
When the doors closed behind them, Daniel squeezed
my hand, and as he exited the vehicle, I closed my eyes
and inhaled the scent of leather and newness. *I can do
this... I can do this.* I repeated the mantra over and over
in my head trying to reassure myself that I could, in fact,
do it.

It was now or never. Twisting in my seat, I placed my
feet on solid ground. I eased out of the car and tried to
ignore the small crowd that had gathered. It was difficult
blocking out the shocked whispers and hushed conversations, but the word *murderer* lingered in the air like a bad
smell.

I swallowed hard, walked forward, stopping at the
gate of my house. All I could do was stare at it. The
house seemed the same, from its sunshine yellow paint to
the wooden frame around the windows. Even the wind-
mill in the garden turned in the wind. But even if the
house appeared the same, the inside would always be tar-
nished, stained by bloodshed and stolen innocence.

A hand on the small of my back snapped me to attention. Daniel was standing beside me, reliant and reassuring. Connors and Megan stood at each side of the
front yard gate, feet apart, shoulders squared, a soldier's
stance. Megan's fingers touched the gun at her belt. Con-

nors stood, arms folded across his chest.

"Are you ready?" Daniel asked in his softest voice.

"No," I said, but my feet moved instinctively and followed the path to the front door. I waited for the guards to follow us, but they didn't. Connors called over his shoulder. "You owe me one, Danny-boy. You have about two hours."

Daniel bobbed his head in thanks and wrapped his hand around the door handle. I sucked in a breath and held it as he turned the knob, opening the door. He nudged me forward with gentle pressure on my back, and I stepped over the threshold, waiting until Daniel closed the door behind us before I felt safe enough to breathe.

Alone with Daniel, he slipped his fingers into mine, and we held hands. He led me towards the kitchen, bypassing the closed door that contained the stuff of my nightmares. Gone was the smell of baked goods, the sound of my mom whistling along with the radio. No more childish laughter lighting up the house. Silence. This house was silent. It smelled of chemicals and bleach and other disinfectants.

"It didn't happen here," I said in a small voice.

He pulled me in for a hug. "I know, I just wanted to give you time to process. We can take as long as you need."

"You would have liked them, and I know they would have loved you."

"I wish I had met them too… and had the opportunity to thank them for giving me the chance to know you." He kissed the top of my head. If I hadn't been so stressed, I might have swooned.

"Smooth talker." I nudged him gently in the ribs.

The abandoned swing set in back caught my attention. This place was no longer my home. It was a fact I had to accept and understand. No matter what happened, I would not return to this place, a place that housed nothing but pain, sorrow, and nightmares.

Slipping free of Daniel's hold, I walked across the kitchen, my hands trembling as I slid the door that separated the kitchen and living room. I took a deep breath and stepped in. The smell of bleach burned and tickled my nostrils. Nothing seemed out of place. My dad's chair still occupied the space beside the fireplace. A discarded copy of *Alice in Wonderland* lay on the coffee table. I looked around, but nothing triggered my memory.

I spun to face Daniel. "It didn't work."

His fingers brushed my cheek. "Give it a chance, Alana. You can do it. Do you trust me?"

"Always," I replied without skipping a beat.

"Then let me try something. Do you remember where you were standing when you found them?"

I nodded. "I came in the other door and saw my dad first."

"Okay. We can use that. Come with me." He held my hand and pulled me back into the kitchen and through the hall. We stopped outside the room door, and he wrapped his arms around me from behind. "Alana, I want you to close your eyes. Go back to that night but know I am here if you get scared." When I complied, he continued, "Good, now listen to the sounds of that night. Hear the raised voices; listen to the gunshots. You have just come down the stairs and opened the door. What do you see?"

I did as he asked, jumping slightly as the gunshots echoed in my head. Remembering the fear from that night, I thought I was going to die. The weight of Daniel's embrace left me. With eyes closed, I opened the door and stepped into the past.

A rush of images battered my fragile mind, and I gasped for air as the last piece of the puzzle fit into place.

Eyes brimming with tears, my knees buckled, and I hit the floor. Darkness overcame me, and I heard my name, but the empty feeling of stillness and nothingness was far too alluring.

ALANA

"Breathe deeply in the silence, no sudden moves
This isn't everything you are."
(SNOW PATROL: THIS ISN'T EVERYTHING YOU ARE)

LOUD POUNDING ON THE DOOR WOKE ME FROM A SOUND SLEEP. *Through tired eyes, I glanced at the clock. My eyes quickly adjusted to the darkness, and I spotted the red light on the clock as it blinked 12:04 a.m. Who would be knocking on the door this late at night?*

Sitting up in my bed, I clutched the covers to my chest, listening as my dad's footsteps moved from his office at the back of the house to the front door. The banging continued as the key turned, unlocking the door. Then my dad's voice drifted upstairs, angry and loud.

"Theresa, I told you not to come here. My mind is made up. I am emailing my report to Grand Master Johnson in the morning."

"Please, Cormac. Can you just hear me out?"

My dad must have agreed because I caught the sound of the door closing, and then I could make out the voices that wafted through the ceiling into my room.

"Get on with it, Theresa." I had never heard that tone in my dad's voice before, and if I had been on the receiving end, I am sure that I would have shivered.

"Cormac, all the tests prove that the ability to shape minds must be done before the subject reaches adult maturity. You've read the reports, listened to the scientists. What reason could you possibly have for not taking the next step with Treatment?"

"We are not God, Theresa!" He shouted at her, and I cringed. I saw a light come on as my mom stepped out onto the landing to check on Sophia. She opened the door to my room and said, "No matter what you hear, Alana, stay in this room. You hear me?" She

didn't wait for an answer but closed the door. From the lack of creaks on the staircase, I'm sure she waited at the top of the stairs, listening.

"You said it yourself, Cormac, that it was barbaric to sentence children to death for crimes that could be rectified. Why, if it is not possible to change the laws, can we not use those who would have died anyway to perfect our serum?"

"Have you listened to yourself, Theresa? I can't believe that if you actually said, out loud, what it is that you want to do, that you wouldn't change your own mind. You want to use children, children, Theresa, as guinea pigs for a serum that will fundamentally alter who they are. It was one thing to experiment with the vilest and most violent, but you're talking about children. They can be redeemed."

She sighed. "Cormac, they would die from execution anyway... what harm is it to make something useful of it and create a functioning member of society? Instead of sending soldiers into a war zone, we could send out our own personal troops of super soldiers, ready and willing to die for us. If we need to take out a threat, send in one unsuspecting looking girl to blow up a gang of rebel leaders. We'd have the power to save those who are deserving of our effort. These... these creatures have already killed or done horrific things. Let this be their redemption."

"Are you listening to yourself? Who are we to choose one life over another? Theresa, I am telling you... I will not sign off on it. I am shutting it down. Dear God, what monsters have we become that we are standing here debating using children as pawns to create a better world. I cannot live in a world where children as young as Sophia are subjected to Treatment, making them mindless robots to do our bidding... all in the name of science."

"Things would have been different, Cormac, if you had chosen me over that woman. She made you soft. Your children have made you soft. You used to be a man of worth. Look at you now." The words came out in a hiss.

My dad and Theresa?

"That's where you are wrong, Theresa. Sorcha does not make

me soft, she makes me strong, strong enough to stand my ground and do what is right. Maybe if you weren't stuck in the past, you would have compassion for others and not be blinded by greed and power."

I pulled the pillow over my head not wanting to hear any more, too scared to go check on Sophia. The pillow muffled some of the sounds, and my heart pounded inside my chest. My mother entered the living room and even with the pillow, I heard her voice yelling at Theresa to leave.

The kettle whistled and cupboards clanged as my mom made as much noise as possible in the kitchen. Theresa and my dad were still shouting, and I shook as dad's voice grew louder. Finally, I heard a yell. "Get out. Get out of my house, Theresa, or I will have you escorted out."

"I cannot let you do this, Cormac. Everything we worked for. All that we planned. It will be for nothing if we do not proceed with Treatment. I will not let you drag me down because of your conscience."

And then my dad's laugh sounded cruel and vicious. "And what are you going to do with that, Theresa... shoot me with my own gun?"

"I can make it look like a murder-suicide. Pretty simple to do if you know how. I've wanted to put a bullet in Sorcha's head since the first day you looked at her across the room. I lost you to her then, and now you can watch while I smear the carpet with her brains."

"Theresa, put down the gun before you hurt yourself. I have put up with you for far too long, like a wasp buzzing around my ear with your jealousy and insecurities. Give me the gun."

That's when the roar of a gunshot echoed throughout the house, followed by two more pops of the gun. I cried silent tears while my mom begged for mercy for Sophia, but as my sister whimpered, a shot whistled through the air and then another.

Afraid that my heart was beating so loud that Theresa would find me, I hurried to the secret passage that connected Sophia's room with mine.

I didn't dare try and make a getaway or go to Sophia out in

the open. So I crawled along in the pitch black, my hands feeling around the walls until I felt the familiar crack in the cupboard and let myself into Sophia's closet.

As I opened the door, I froze at the sound of someone coming up the stairs. Peeking out through the gaps in the wood, I watched Sophia's bedroom door open, and she screamed a high pitched, terrifying sound that caused the hair on the back of my neck to stand up.

"Come now, Sophia." Theresa's voice was bitter, and I tried to move my body, command it to burst free of the closet and tackle her, but it refused to move. I stifled a cry as Sophia cringed away from Theresa when she grabbed her hair.

"You could have been our Sophia, mine and Cormac's, and then maybe things would have been different. Close your eyes now, and I will make it all better."

She covered Sophia's chest with a cushion and I heard the sickening sound of another shot in the dark. Scrambling back out of the closet and through the crawl space not wanting to see anymore, I stayed cramped in the dark passage while Theresa left my sister's room. Sirens, loud and wailing in the distance, drew near. The front door slammed shut, and I was alone in the stagnate silence.

My eyes opened and I was lying in Daniel's arms, eyes drenched in tears and my entire body shaking. When I opened my mouth to speak, all that came out was a squeak. I was lost.

I had known for a few days that I had not killed my parents, but thinking back to what Jayson had said, it might have been better not knowing. He was right. I could have helped Sophia. Instead, I froze, and now she was dead. I could have saved her or possibly died that night alongside them. At the moment, either option would be better than the ache in my chest.

Daniel pulled me closer, kissing my forehead and whispering reassuring words to me as I let the warm floods of tears come. I finally began to grieve for my family. That woman had killed them all for no good reason. Jealousy? Power? Because my dad had said *no* to her experiment?

Anger flooded in. I would kill her for this. Before I followed them to the grave, I would avenge my family. I had to make sure that someone knew what she did and what she planned to do for those like me who were convicted and sentenced to die. I had forgotten who I was once before—I would never allow her to take that away from me again.

As I rose to my knees, Daniel cupped my face with his hands. Worry creased his brow, and I let him wipe my tears with his thumb.

"Are you okay? Did you remember?"

I nodded slowly but had to swallow hard before I could speak. My mouth was dry, and the words cut like a knife against my throat. When I stared into his sparkling eyes, I knew I was safe.

"It was Theresa…" My voice squeaked the words.

He looked at me, puzzled. "What was Theresa, Alana?"

Swallowing hard again, I cleared my throat. "Theresa Lane murdered my family. I saw it all happen. She came to argue with my dad about him shutting Treatment down. They had worked on a serum to use against violent offenders, but she wanted to use it on young death row inmates to see if it worked. Dad refused and was putting it in a report the next day."

Daniel knelt there in front of me open-mouthed, so I continued, afraid that if I stopped I wouldn't get the whole story out. "She used my dad's gun on him when he refused to change his mind, and then she shot my mom. I watched her shoot Sophia and couldn't move. She must have carried her downstairs and positioned them."

"And how come she didn't see you."

"I hid in the crawl space. She... she didn't know I was home... never looked in my room, just Sophia's... when she walked back in after the crime, she had the perfect person to pin it on."

Anger danced in his eyes and he swore, "We will get her, Alana. She won't get away with it."

"I deserve to die. It's my fault Sophia's dead." I was numb. Guilt overtook me as the image of Theresa shooting my sister replayed in my mind.

"Alana. Theresa Lane killed your sister. None of this is your fault. You know that, right?"

Shaking myself free of his hands, I bowed my head. "I froze. I did nothing. I am a coward who couldn't even move and stayed hidden like a frightened little girl in the shadows. Sophia's death is on me, and I will accept my fate for that. I know the truth now. I could have saved her."

My stomach churned and the bile that had threatened to creep up my throat all day finally did. Rising to my feet, I turned quickly. Taking the stairs two at a time, before I emptied my stomach on the floor, I left a speechless Daniel behind me.

DANIEL

"I think I've already lost you, I think you're already
gone."
(Matchbox Twenty: If you're gone)

As soon as Alana hit the ground I knew something
was wrong. I wasn't quick enough to catch her but had to
make do with cradling her in my lap. She twitched and
muttered, and all I could do was hold her. The last time I
felt this helpless was the day I realized she had forgotten
me. I could do nothing but watch her eyes moving behind
closed lids and whisper words of reassurance, whether
she could hear me or not.

Words became more audible, her breathing and
pulse quickened. Tears trickled down her cheek. I resisted the urge to wake her. The conflict in me was obvious—
the boy who loved her and the doctor—wanting to pull
her from whatever nightmare had its tendrils wrapped
around her. She had been plunged into memories so
dark and twisted that her mind had let her forget.

"Sophia, please wake up… please don't leave me."
Alana whimpered and I hugged her closer. I would have
to wait for her to ride the emotional rollercoaster on her
own, but I'd be ready to catch her if she fell.

She screamed, struggling in my arms as I tried to hold
her. This was going on too long, and I wasn't ashamed
to admit that I was frightened of what this would do to
her and curious to know who was there… had she seen
who had killed her parents? Was that who she spoke to?
A range of emotions rolled over her face. Grief. Anger.

Guilt. The last one surprised me. She rose to her knees, untangling herself from me, and as we faced each other I placed my hands on either side of her face, supporting her. Her face was pale, and she seemed hardened, as if the knowledge had changed her.

"Are you okay?"

She bobbed her head slowly, and I waited patiently for her to speak. She stared at me again. "It was Theresa…"

"What was Theresa?" I was confused but remained quiet, although horrified, while she replayed that night for me.

"I can't believe it was Theresa Lane who murdered my family. I saw it all happen.

"Yes, I know. We'll get to the bottom of this, I promise, Alana." It was all I could say because my own mind was still in shock at the revelation.

When Alana explained more details about how she'd hidden in a crawl space and that Theresa probably didn't know she had been home, she cried again. Alana was the perfect scapegoat for Theresa's vile actions. And she would bleed for it.

I assured Alana that we would make sure Theresa didn't get away with it, but Alana was too far from me, lost in unnecessary guilt.

She kept repeating, "I deserve to die. It's my fault Sophia's dead." Her eyes told the story. She wholeheartedly believed it.

I repeated that it wasn't her fault, but I got the sense my words weren't getting through.

She shook herself free of my hands and bowed her head as if she was ashamed.

Theresa and Cormac McCarthy had worked in secret to create a serum that could cause a person to forget who they were, and act on orders given to them by those in power. That must have been what happened to Veronika. Another failed attempt to use Veronika to prove her point.

And it begged another question. Did all those poor inmates who went off to their deaths actually die or were they used and tested for Theresa's own personal gain until their minds crumbled like pastry under the stress of the serum? Now, I wanted to be sick. I couldn't let Alana or Jayson or any other human being be subjected to that.

The toilet flushed, and I prepared to engage Alana again, wanting to convince her that none of this was her fault. In her heart, she had to know that Theresa Lane would be held accountable for her actions—one way or another.

Alana didn't come downstairs, so I left the living room behind and climbed the stairs two at a time. The bathroom door was open, but Alana was nowhere to be found. I glanced around the landing. Two doors remained closed. One was slightly ajar. I eased it open and stepped into what I could only assume was Alana's bedroom.

No surprises that her room at the house and her room at the training centre were strikingly similar. Where the training centre walls had been painted a rich honey colour—each room, no matter what dorm you resided in, was painted the same—Alana's were black. The depressing dark walls became almost hidden under an array of posters hung in an almost reckless manner. Photos of her and her family occupied areas along with some music and film posters.

Her room at the centre had been decorated in much the same way. Photos had littered the walls there too. When we had gotten together, she added ours to the jumble. I had stripped those walls of any evidence of our relationship and kept them in a box in my room. It only added to the many times I became thankful that neither of us shared a room. Alana's dad had been so prestigious that his daughter occupied a coveted single room.

Here in her house, furniture was sparse. A compact desk and a cupboard filled one wall. A bed and bookcase took over the other. In between those two walls, a built-in wardrobe completed the gap. When I finished studying the layout of the room, I looked over at Alana, curled up on her bed clutching an old stuffed bear to her chest. Her head lay on the pillow, but her eyes remained open, frightened, as if closing them might lock her in with the horror and torment.

She didn't acknowledge me, but I sat on the edge of the bed anyway. The silence hung over us and after ten minutes, I couldn't hold my tongue any longer.

"Alana, please, babe, talk to me."

She tucked her knees up to her chest, but when I reached out to touch her, she pulled away. My hands returned to my lap. "I know you're confused and you blame yourself, but, Alana, if you had not have stayed safe, you would be dead too. Theresa would have gotten away with it. There wasn't anything you could have done that would change the outcome. You lived to seek vengeance for what happened here.

I know it hurts now. Nothing I can say or do will take it away or make you feel better. Trust me, I hate that fact. None of this is your fault."

She sniffled. "She was in love with my dad and did it out of lust for power and jealousy. If you love someone that much, how could you hurt them?"

Rubbing my face with my hands, I tried unsuccessfully to think up something profound to say. "People do strange things in the name of love."

"I will kill her for this. I will." The resolve in her voice was serious, deadly. It would be easier for her to accept what had happened if she could focus her anger on one person. Actually, that might keep her alive while I tied up some loose ends.

"You are not a killer, Alana."

"I can be … I will be."

Silence filled the room again. I'd seen it many times before. I knew the signs, when Alana had made up her mind to do something and would single-handedly fight tooth and nail to do it. It was one of the reasons I loved her, that determination, the grit, but it might also be one of the reasons I lost her. I couldn't go through that again.

"Please, don't do anything that could take you away from me, Alana. I only just got you back… if you go down this time, I'll be right with you."

We glanced into each other's eyes, and there was a moment of acceptance in her eyes. She knew I would give my life for hers, and she understood. It would be us or nothing. I chose us.

She uncoiled herself and reached for me. I knelt on the bed, and she joined me. I kissed her as if it would be our last kiss. I needed to brand her to me, breathe in her skin and feel her against my skin. An urgency existed between us, and we were willing captives of it. Her fingertips grazed my hip as she yanked my T-shirt over my head, careful not to dislodge the glasses.

Her fingers danced along my ribcage, and I bit my lip as she pressed a gentle kiss along my jawline. My fingers trembled, my whole body ablaze as I lifted her jumper over her head and tossed it aside. My patience ran thin, and I lowered her to the bed while my lips travelled the familiar path from her lips, then her jaw, and to that place on her neck that made her happy.

She gasped and her grip tightened around my waist as her hand fumbled with the buttons on my jeans. If she went any further, I wouldn't be able to stop. Months of pent-up need and lust blurred my focus so all I saw was her beneath me.

Catching hold of her hands as she was about to open the last button on my jeans, I said in a broken voice, "Alana, are you sure you want this? Tell me *no*. Tell me to stop and I will... we don't have to do this now."

I swallowed hard. Alana grinned up at me, and I knew she was my Alana again, full of mischief. She looped her fingers at the waist of her pants and shimmied out of them. The woman had me right where she wanted me, and I was going crazy looking at her. I crushed her mouth with mine, tasting her, letting my tongue explore the heaven that was her mouth. I groaned as she undid the last button on my jeans and helped guide them over my hips.

We lost ourselves in each other, stripping away the horror, the pain, the loss, the guilt of the last year. Skin against skin, my lips on hers, we began to heal. Each familiar taste and comfortable contact brought us closer to who we had been and who we could be again.

When it was over, I cradled her to my chest, and we lay together for a while before either of us spoke.

"I never remember it being that intense." She teased and I kissed the top of her head.

"You know, I never thought I'd lose you."

She snuggled into me, and I felt as though I could catch a bullet, or walk on water or something more poetic than I could ever contemplate. I wished we could stay there forever, locked in each other's embrace, never to spend another night apart. She never even knew that I had wanted to marry her six months ago. Nothing had changed for me. One day I would call her my wife.

The banging at the front door made Alana freeze. Heavy feet stomped around downstairs, and for just a minute I forgot that Connors and Megan waited for us outside. I was off the bed and shoving my legs into my jeans in a hurry, much to Alana's amusement.

"Hey, Danny-boy, where are ya?" I had only heard one set of feet, so I growled.

"Connors, don't you dare come up here or so help me—"

My words were met with hysterical laughter as I dressed. I turned and glimpsed at Alana as she slipped back into her black prison clothing. Alana must have sensed my glance because she winked at me over her shoulder and smiled. I stepped in her direction and her in mine.

"Danny-boy, get your skinny ass down here, or I will come up and douse you both with cold water!"

I shook my head smiling. "I guess we better go."

"I wish we didn't have to."

"Me either."

Hand in hand, we left the room, pausing as Alana gave one last look around and closed the door behind her. I let my hand drop from hers as we descended the stairs, single file, a beaming Connors waiting for us. He opened his mouth, another quip no doubt on his lips, but he stopped as I glared at him over Alana's head.

She kept on walking straight out the front door without so much as a twitch of her eyes in the direction of the living room. I followed a step behind, proud that she held her head up high, ignoring the even bigger crowd that had gathered outside. By God, there had to be hundreds of people across the street and in the general area. Maybe the entire town had come to watch their old neighbour return to the scene of her supposed crimes.

Alana walked around the back of the car, opened the door and vanished inside. Megan climbed into the passenger side again, and I felt the first drops of rain on my skin. I jumped as Connors put a hand on my shoulder.

"Did she find what she was looking for? Do we know who killed her parents?"

I nodded. "Yes, we do and you're not going to believe it," I whispered one name in his ear and his return stare said it all. He must have thought I'd gone mad.

"Seriously?"

I acknowledged with a simple head bob.

"We are going to get that bitch."

All I could do was nod again like an idiot as we headed to the car to join Alana and Megan. Once inside, Connors started the car but turned the radio volume way down as if realizing Alana needed time to get things straight in her head.

As we found our way out of the city, Alana laid her head back against the seat, closing her eyes. I watched her out of the corner of my eye. She breathed in and out in controlled steps. I could almost hear her counting to ten in her head until somewhere between her thoughts she drifted off to sleep. Instinctively, her head lolled in my direction, and I slid slightly closer so she could rest her head on my shoulder.

Megan's eyes in the mirror had spoken before I heard the words. "Do you need help moving her?"

"No, leave her be... after what she has just seen I'm inclined to let the girl rest any way she can."

She narrowed her gaze and scowled, but a swift nudge from Connors pulled her eyes from mine, and we continued on the journey in silence. Alana slept through it all, barely stirring. I was grateful that she was not haunted by nightmares as she breathed heavily in her sleep.

Only when we were within the confines of the prison did I sweep her hair from her face. Her eyes fluttered open. She smiled and leaned forward, but something in my face must have stopped her. Rubbing her eyes, she glanced around and said, "We're back?"

"We are."

As we exited the car and waited while Connors parked the car, I noticed the clouds had turned from grey to black, and the little drizzle of rain had now become more persistent. Alana rubbed her arms with her hands, and I wished I could wrap mine around her to keep her warm.

Connors returned, and we headed back through security, along the maze of corridors until we entered the mess hall. It was late afternoon, so only a few of the death row inmates were around. Jayson caught my eye, an eyebrow raised in question. I tilted my head slightly, letting him know she had remembered.

Alana put her hand on the railings unconsciously, heading up the stairs. I whispered her name. She hesitated. I walked around her so the railing was between us. Connors led Megan away by the arm, and I heard her giggle. Sometimes it really was great to have a best friend who was a Casanova.

Alana avoided my gaze. She wanted to confront the warden, I could tell, but I had to make her wait. Our plan wasn't in place yet.

"Alana, please don't do anything stupid. Do not confront Theresa. Please, babe…think with your head. Trust me, I have a plan, but we need to move cautiously."

She grunted, and I tapped her hand, forcing her to look at me. "Don't shut me out, Alana, not now. Give me another two days… two days—that's all I ask."

She sighed. "Okay… two days, Daniel, and then I act. With or without you."

"With me." I growled and she smiled. She took another step, and I stopped her again.

"I love you," I said quietly.

"I love you too."

She jogged up the steps and disappeared. I hoped

she could rein in that fiery temper of hers long enough for me to arrange a few more things. Vengeance tended to be a powerful emotion. No reasoning would separate her from getting it even if she became consumed with the notion.

I loved her, and she loved me in return. In the end, would it be enough?

ALANA

"See I'm just trying to find my place but it might
not be here where I feel safe."
(PARAMORE: MISGUIDED GHOSTS)

YESTERDAY HAD PASSED IN SUCH A BLUR THAT I COULDN'T
help but feel that I didn't have enough time to process
everything. Despite the fact that I had gotten my
memories back, I still felt adrift. I seemed lost in a tidal
wave of conflicted emotions that crashed over me, sudden
and dangerous, using its sheer strength to pull me under
and out to sea with the current.

When I thought of what Theresa had done, the hot
rage that had threatened to scald me quickly manifested
into guilt. It was an ice-cold slap in the face as I thought
of all the things I could have done to save Sophia. Of
course, regret came as part of the package. I replayed
scenarios, wishing I could pause the incessant video in
my mind and change the outcome. But the end scene
always completed the tragedy with no encore, no second
act, no way to alter the past.

And then there was Daniel. The very thought of him
made my insides flutter. When I closed my eyes, I could
feel his lips on mine, taste him. My entire body ached for
him. Being with him again had been so perfect, and it
was nice to have something so beautiful amidst the blood
and lies. The gentleness of it, and the urgency, combined
as we moulded our bodies together. Thinking of it made
the hairs on my arms stand at attention. I tried to convince myself that it was okay to be happy. Certainly, I

needed to focus on the fact that I had found Daniel again, and he had a plan for us to be together. I had to believe we could live out our lives together.

But then the vicious cycle overcame me and allowed my thoughts to darken. It smothered me in guilt for thinking of happy things when I needed to latch onto revenge and seek vengeance for my dad, my mom, and Sophia.

Somewhere in the midst of all the darkness, I must have fallen asleep. I did not dream nor was I haunted by my memories. It was as if someone had switched off a light, and I slept. When the light was turned on again, I was awake. My cell door was open, and I desperately needed a shower. Not the least bit hungry, I asked one of the female guards if she could take me to the shower rooms. She left the area to ask permission, and I gathered up some clean clothes, ready to go when she returned.

Once there, I went in alone. Empty and silent, I stripped off my clothes and adjusted the dial, not bothering to wait for it to become lukewarm. The ice cold waters cascaded down on me while the water belted down on my skin, and I flinched. I was grateful that it could hurt me… I needed to feel something different, something real.

When the shower temperature was warmer, I washed my hair and scrubbed my skin to redness. Once I had cleaned off, I remained there until my skin wrinkled and my fingers and toes began to tremble. Who was I kidding? No amount of water would wash it all away, drench me in its pureness and soak up all the dirt and darkness. Oh, if it would only disappear down the drain. The darkness was part of me now… I would have to live with it until the day I died—no matter how soon that was.

Turning off the current of water, I wrapped myself in a towel and sat on the bench. Time ticked by, and I sat staring at the walls until the guard hammered on the door and told me I had five minutes to get dressed or she would drag me out and parade me around naked. I quickly dressed in my black pants, vest, jumper... it matched my mood.

The guard escorted me back to my room and I couldn't do anything but wait for Connors to come get me and take me to Daniel. I pulled my knees to my chest as I perched on the bed and leaned my head back against the wall. What was Daniel's plan? Why could he not be straight with me? Great. Now I was getting angry at Daniel for no reason other than the fact I wanted to know his plan... some girlfriend I turned out to be.

"Alana, where were you yesterday? I was looking for you all day." Jayson's voice penetrated the bubble of self-pity, and I smiled as he propped himself on the bed and swung his legs back and forth near the floor like a child at the playground.

"Yeah, I uh... Dr Costello got me a pass to go home... to see if I remembered anything." I spoke quietly and his brows wiggled in excitement.

"Aaaannnnd?" He drawled.

"I didn't kill my parents."

"Well, duh... knew that already, sweetheart... stop stalling and spill... you tell me your secret, and I will tell you mine."

"What secret?" I asked, curiosity getting the better of me.

He shook his finger. "No, uh. You first."

"I know who killed them. I remembered but promised I wouldn't say anything yet... Dani— eh... Dr Costello advised me not to until after I saw him today." My cheeks no doubt reddened at having almost said Daniel, but Jayson just laughed.

"Puh-lease... I know all about you and the good doctor, Alana."

"How?" I said and looked sideways at him.

Jayson smirked. "Another story for another day."

At that point, I knew he wouldn't say any more either, and we lapsed into a comfortable silence. I guess we stayed that way awhile, and then he reached over and tapped me on my shoulder.

"Aren't you the least bit curious what you might have missed while you were trippin' yesterday?" I knew by the gleam in his eyes that he was dying to tell me, but I was in no mood for games.

"Is it something major?"

"You could say that..."

"Either tell me or get out... You're giving me a headache."

"Well, miss I got out of the wrong side of bed this morning... I don't have to tell you." His grin only widened, and I couldn't help but laugh and push his shoulder hard.

"Just tell me already."

"William Johnson is coming here on Friday."

I knew the name, but it took me a second for two things to happen: One—I remembered that William Johnson was the man responsible for creating the Court of Justice system and launching it worldwide. Not only that, but this prison was his concept. Two—my mind registered hearing my dad tell Theresa he would send his report regarding Treatment to Grand Master Johnson. Could it be that this was the Grand Master of Justice my dad meant?

"Did you hear me, Alana? The man who birthed this fine establishment is coming here Friday to give a talk. The place is buzzing with excitement. We get to have a party and everything."

If my dad had intended to tell him about the effects of Treatment and Theresa's plans to use it on teens, then

I had to speak to him. One way or another, I had to get close enough to speak with him.

"Uh oh… you have that look in your eyes, Alana… I don't like it."

"What look in my eyes?"

"The look that says you are about to dive into a nest full of bees and hope not to get stung." Huh, what a fitting description.

I ignored his statement. "Why is he coming? Is it an anniversary or something?"

Jayson shrugged. "He is making his way around every section of the prison system. Some think it's because he is getting on in age and won't make the trip again. He's coming in a helicopter and all… man, I haven't seen one of those since I was a kid."

"And will we all be going to his talk?"

With a nod, Jayson replied. "Yup, according to one of the guards, he wants to see how things have settled since your dad died."

I didn't get a chance to respond because Connors appeared in the doorway. He looked from me to Jayson and all but dragged Jayson out of the room. I heard Jayson chuckle, so I knew he wasn't in much trouble, but Connors looked pissed when he came back.

"What's got your knickers in a knot?" I teased as we followed the daily path down the stairs and across the mess hall before exiting through the door.

"Jayson's a flirt. Danny's done a lot for him. He needs to not look at you like that."

"Like what?"

"As if he wants a quick tumble between the sheets with you. Danny doesn't deserve that."

"Hey!" I caught his elbow, forcing him to look at me. "I love him, Daniel, I mean. I would never do that to him, ever."

His face relaxed and his cheek twitched. "Okay, sorry... I'm just on edge today."

"I heard about Grand Master Johnson..."

"Yeah. Security is going to get amped up, and we have too many fingers in hot water at the moment. A lot could go wrong."

My eyes met his, and I knew Connors was scared. "Is this about me? Are you guys in trouble?"

Connors nudged me forward. "Not my place to say, McCarthy. Ask Danny."

"Ha—I'll do just that."

Connors let us in Daniel's office. He was standing with his back to us, hands clasped behind his back, staring out the window. He swivelled towards us and gave me a knee-weakening smile. I crossed the room and forgot that Connors was in the room with us. As I wrapped my arms around his neck, I shuddered when he put his hands on my hips and we kissed.

Connors cleared his throat. "Um, still here people... don't we have stuff to discuss."

So I wasn't going to have time alone with Daniel. We separated and Daniel eased himself into his desk chair. I yelped in surprise when he pulled me into his lap. Connors paced the room. I had never seen the man so on edge and restless.

"Connors, sit down... you will wear a hole in my floor." Daniel tried to make a joke, but Connors kept pacing.

"We are running out of time, Danny-boy ... we need to bring things forward."

"When?" Daniel asked, his tone flat.

"Friday... it has to happen Friday. They will be putting Theresa's new security system in place over the weekend. While Johnson is here on Friday, the equipment will be brought in, quietly and under the radar, while everyone is concentrating on Johnson's visit."

I had no idea what they were talking about but kept my mouth shut and listened.

"Do you have an exit plan?"

"I do... I just need to sort one thing out, and we are set. Is all your stuff in place?"

I leaned my head on Daniel's shoulder and felt him nod. "All I have to do is make the call."

"Can someone fill me in here? I'm lost." I interrupted.

Daniel caressed my cheek. "You're better off not knowing. If things go wrong, then you can tell the truth. You don't need to know anything at this point, please just trust us."

I grabbed his chin with my hand and yanked his face, forcing him to look at me. "If you are planning something that might end up hurting you or Connors... don't... don't do it for me. At least tell me that."

"Just promise me that when I tell you to go, if I tell you to run, you will."

"Daniel I—" My words cut off as he fixed me with his eyes.

"Promise me." Daniel all but growled.

"I promise." What else could I do?

"So Friday... got it... should I inform the other fella as well?"

"Please. Jayson needs to know and be ready."

"Hey!" I shrieked. "How come Jayson gets to know and I don't?"

"I care about your safety. Jayson can hold his own."

I snorted while thinking back to my own plan and cast my eyes towards Connors.

"Hey, Connors, can I ask you a question?"

He stopped pacing and returned my gaze. Even though he said nothing, I saw his eyes flicker to Daniel and then back to me.

"Can you get me close enough on Friday to talk to Grand Master Johnson? Before whatever you both have planned happens."

Both men looked at me quizzically, but it was Daniel who asked me why.

"I need to get close enough to him to tell him that Theresa killed my family and that she wanted to make mindless super soldiers from inmates."

I didn't think I had ever seen or felt the anger that radiated from Daniel. Connors quickly excused himself, and when I was alone with him, Daniel almost blew a fuse. I jumped off his lap as he slammed a hand down on the table.

"Are you serious? Are you *really serious*? If you do that, you will jeopardize everything that we have worked hard all these months to set in place."

My hands on hips, I spat back at him. "And you expect me to just sit back, wait and see if you can pull off whatever scheme you and Connors have cooked up? That bitch killed my family and deliberately let me take the blame for it. I can't let her get away with it."

"She will not get away with it, Alana. Trust me. I have everything in place. Theresa Lane will get what she deserves, but you cannot be a part of it. I will not let you blindly put yourself in danger. And what's to say he will believe you? You have no evidence, only the frantic words of a girl desperately clinging to a life that is slipping through her fingers."

Talk about a punch in the gut. Anger radiated from me like a fire. "Is that what you really think of me? You ask me to trust you, but do you trust me? No. If you can't trust me and tell me what the hell you guys are neck deep into, then why did you bother? Why risk it at all?"

"Because I love you!" Daniel bellowed and the words

echoed throughout the room. Connors returned, and we clamped our mouths shut.

"Can I suggest we all just cool down because I could hear you out in the hallway, Danny-boy. What if the warden had passed by? C'mon guys, don't fall apart on me now."

I turned and faced the window, looking out as the leaves fell from the trees, drifting slowly until they blanketed the ground. I was like the leaves, breaking away from the tree and falling slowly into nothingness.

The guys muttered behind me, but I didn't care. How could Daniel not think that I would want to be part of what brought that bitch to her knees?

I waited until Daniel came to me and wrapped his arms around me from behind, kissing my neck before speaking. "I'm sorry. We are all on thin ice, Alana, and we need to think with clear heads."

Part of me knew he was right and part of me wanted to ignore him and move forward with my own plan. But I would need Connors on board for that.

A beep sounded, and Connors said, "What now?" A short pause later he answered his own phone, "Her session with Dr Costello is not over... will it not wait till after?"

We both turned and watched as his brow creased. "Yes, sir." Connors hung up the phone and looked at us grimly. "The warden wants to see you right now, Alana."

My heart skipped a beat and then proceeded to pound against my chest like a jackhammer. I not only had to go face-to-face with the woman who'd murdered my family and put the blame on me, but pretend I knew nothing. I couldn't tell her that I'd remembered anything. My temper flared. It was obvious that everyone else was worried that the crazy girl would do something to put us all in danger.

Daniel took my face in his hands and pinned me with his stare. "Alana, you promised me two days. Do not give Theresa anything. If she suspects that you remember, then we will all die. Hold your tongue and be patient. Trust in us, and we will have our revenge."

"Okay." I spoke the words, but they were bitter on my tongue. Could I really sit across from her and keep quiet?

Daniel brushed his lips against mine. "I love you."

"Love you too."

Connors and I left Daniel to his own devices, and we turned right instead of left. I watched as the elevator doors opened, and we stepped inside. The whirl of the gears was strange, and slowly we moved upwards. Before we come to a stop, Connors glanced down at me and said, "Don't fuck this up, McCarthy. I enjoy breathing."

And then the doors clanged open, and we stepped out. I hoped I didn't fuck it up either.

ALANA

"I wanna hate every part of you in me,
But I can't hate the ones that made me"
(YOUMEATSIX: BITE MY TONGUE)

SOMETIMES A STARTLING SENSE OF CALM COMES BEFORE A
vicious rage. I did not tremble nor did my eyes give away
anything. To anyone on the outside, I was the epitome
of cool, calm, and collected. But inside, buried beneath
promises and love, lay a blanket of unbridled rage and
resentment. It was a force of rage that bubbled up waiting
for one word, one action to unleash it and project the
tornado that gathered inside me.

When we entered her office at the end of a long
walkway, Theresa Lane was seated behind a desk. In her
presence, the room seemed too small and uncomfortable.
She indicated for me to take a seat, and I complied because I had promised Daniel that I would be the perfect
inmate. I would pretend that I didn't know that the mur-
derous bitch sitting across from me was responsible for
ruining my life.

Connors hesitated, his hands on the back of the
chair as if he too were afraid that I couldn't hold my temper… that I would spill everything out on the table. But
Theresa dismissed him, saying he wasn't needed because
she just wanted a friendly chat with me.

When Connors reluctantly left us alone, I scanned
the office, looking for something to focus on. Theresa
liked to show off, and I guessed that from the abundance
of diplomas, awards, and trophies that covered the walls

and cabinets, she did it often. On the cabinets sat an array of pictures, but I was far too short to see them from my current position. From the ones I could see, it affirmed my belief that she valued work over other aspects of her life. In every photo, Theresa wore different types of uniforms. Most were familiar to me because my dad had had several similar ones hanging in his closet.

Finally, I turned and faced her. Part of me delighted in the flash of dismay that crossed her face before she masked it with that of the warden, a woman in charge, one who demanded respect. But not from me. I felt the anger slip through my shield of calm and tried to squash it back down by thinking about Daniel and all he had done to get us here. I could bite my tongue. For now. It might hurt, and I might do it literally, but it was important to keep my promise.

Theresa Lane watched me as if she did not know how to start the conversation. Maybe she was trying to figure out if I knew something that my face obviously did not give away. We had known each other for years. Theresa hadn't changed much. Not a dark blonde hair out of place, pulled back into a severe bun, her appearance had remained the same too. While I studied her in this setting, knowing what I knew, the lines on the sides of her eyes only added to the bitter appearance. Her lips were pressed into a continuous scowl, and she cast her eyes over me, looking me up and down like I had her before she opened her mouth and began to speak.

"Thank you for coming to speak with me, Alana." *Yeah, like I had much choice.* "I sincerely apologize for cutting your session with Dr Costello short, but unfortunately with the Grand Master arriving in two days, I do not have a spare moment to myself."

Theresa paused. I said nothing. Theresa blew out a breath.

"I had not wished this for you, Alana. Losing your memories and your family in such a manner." Theresa shook her head and shuddered. My grip tightened on the arms of the chair. "Your father had such hopes for you, and now all that promise is to be no more."

"I hope that wherever my dad is, he is proud of me, no matter what I do or have done."

She cocked her head to the left. "Have you remembered, dear?"

Swallowing, I readied myself to lie. "Bits and pieces... nothing in full."

"Care to elaborate?" Her voice had gone dangerously steady.

I looked her dead in the eyes. "I did not kill them. There was someone else there that night. I heard raised voices and gunshots, and when I came out of the crawlspace in my room..." Her eyes widened, but I could hold back the smile inside. *Ha, one point to me for surprise.* "... I went downstairs and found them all dead. I tried to get Sophia to wake up, but she was already gone."

"And you have no idea who this other person was?"

"No," I answered through gritted teeth.

She smiled, then a slow evil grin lit up her face and darkened her eyes. "Well, now that is such a shame. I really do wish that things had been different, Alana, that you had more of your father in you so you would be honest and tell the truth. Projecting blame onto an invisible assailant is cowardly. I did not take you for a coward."

Breathe in and out. Breathe in and out. Do not leap across the table and strangle her. Think about Daniel. Do not let your fate become his. I repeated the mantra over and over and bit the inside of my mouth so hard the coppery taste of blood almost made me choke. *I can do this, I can stay calm.*

Frustration caused a tiny bead of sweat on Theresa's forehead, and she dabbed it daintily with a handkerchief that she pulled from the pocket of her blazer. I knew that handkerchief. I had been the one who had bought it and had my dad's initials embroidered on the blue piece of material one year for Christmas. He always carried it when he went to work.

She was baiting me, trying to make me lose control and snap, but I would work hard not to let her win. I was stubborn and hated to lose.

When she had finished and pocketed the hanky again, she said, "Can I speak freely, Alana? Woman to woman?"

I shrugged, giving the impression that I wasn't bothered either way. She might think I'd fall for the friends act, but I didn't want to hear her speak about my dad as if she knew him better than me. Regardless, I had to sit there and listen, faking interest.

"I'm sure you're aware that I used to be your father's girlfriend. We grew up together and dated as teenagers and then at the training centre. Cormac... he had always been a good looking boy and was an even more handsome man. I loved him so much. We could have been happy together."

Her voice trailed off while thinking about my dad. I wanted to be sick. She had a look of pure adoration on her face as she spoke of him, and I felt the urge to slap it right off her face. But then she snapped out of whatever thoughts she had and smiled at me.

"It was not to be, Alana. True love does not conquer all. We had many years of happiness, your father and me, but during our final two years of study, I became pregnant. Your father wanted me to leave my studies and raise our baby. He believed it was far too dangerous for me to be pregnant and out in the field. We argued about it, and I told him I would not put my career on hold for a child. It was to be the final nail in our coffin."

Holding my breath, I knew what was coming… because Dad would have told us if there was a brother or sister out there.

"I went against your father's wishes and joined the field expedition. We were tasked with bringing in a man who had raped and murdered seventeen women across America. He, like most criminals, did not want to be apprehended, and we gave chase. I had always loved to run and was fast. I caught up with him alone about a block from his home. We fought, and I tried to disarm him. He stabbed me in the stomach, and your father shot him.

I lay in your father's arms bleeding, and Cormac knew that I had lost the baby. It broke us. Cormac never forgave me for going against his wishes. He had been right. Truth be told, I never wanted children because my career was everything. They would have been in the way. But Cormac wanted a big family. At the hospital, I had surgery and nearly died, but they had to remove the one thing that could have saved my relationship with your father. My ability to have children."

She described the loss of her child in such a cold, clinical manner that the hairs on the back of my neck stood up. I tried to feel sorry for her, but I was not that good of a person. She smoothed her hair and continued. "Cormac distanced himself from me after that. In his eyes, I was damaged. I loved him so deeply, but he disposed of me like garbage. And then he met Sorcha, and she put a spell on him so he would fall in love with her. She was everything I was not. All she wanted was Cormac, marriage, children… and she gave him everything I couldn't."

She spoke of my mom with a lot of hatred. Mom had been the kindest, gentlest, most loving person I had ever known. When I had asked her years ago why she didn't have a career first… wait to have children… she simply told me that there was no more rewarding job than being a mother.

Theresa stood and stared out the window again. "I hated your mother, Alana. And I hated your father for discarding me with such ease. But I still loved him. To this day, I still do."

"My parents loved each other. They were happy. If I'd ever had the chance to have that, then I could have died happy."

"Unfortunately, for both of us, Alana, life is a cruel mistress who rejoices in the misery of people. You and I are a lot alike, you know. We are both trapped by choices that others made that brought us here and now."

"I'm sorry, Theresa, but you and I are nothing alike because I still have hope and love, and I don't blame others when the blame is all my own. I am sorry that you lost your baby, and that my dad acted the way he did, but my mom never did anything to you."

Theresa spun around and slammed her hands down on the table. "Sorcha took him from me with her curves and constant fluttering of her eyelashes. If she hadn't had crossed paths with Cormac, then we could have worked things out and been happy."

I snorted... couldn't help myself. The woman was delusional. Seriously? At least Veronika had embraced her madness, but Theresa really believed that my mom had been the reason she and my dad had split.

She sneered at me. "Enough of story time, my dear. There is another reason I asked to speak to you. Since your little trip yesterday did not achieve any results, I regret to tell you your execution has been moved forward."

My mouth dropped open as my heart raced. "You can't do that ... I have another few weeks until my birthday!"

Oh God, I was never going to see Daniel again.

Theresa smiled, delighted by my surprise. "With special circumstances I can ask for an inmate's death to be brought forward. You should thank me, Alana. It's not every day that someone is put to death by the man who made all this possible. Grand Master Johnson is looking forward to killing the girl who took his dear friend from him."

I jerked upright and the chair jumped off the ground. "You bitch... you planned this all along, didn't you? It wouldn't surprise me if you asked the Grand Master to come especially for the execution." From the look on her face, I knew I was right. "You won't get away with this."

She rounded the table and stopped in front of me. "I have already gotten away with it, Alana. You will die very publicly for your crimes on Friday. No one can stop it."

"I will... I'll expose you... I'll tell the Grand Master about your plans for Treatment. Your super soldiers."

Her laugh soaked up the air in the room. "So you do know more than you let on. Interesting. Tell me, Alana, what else are you pretending not to remember?"

I leaned in and whispered. "I know you killed them... I remember everything, and you will not get away with it."

Theresa stepped back and blinked. "How long have you known?"

"It all came back to me yesterday... thanks for that. If you had not given Dr Costello permission for me to go back, I might never have recalled who I had seen that night."

"That boy is far too good at his job for his own good. Well, at least that is out in the open."

"Why... why did you do it? You claim that you loved my dad, but you still shot him? Why? Try and make me understand." I begged her in a small voice.

"I had nothing without my career. Cormac was lost

to me, and I could not lose what I had worked for my entire life because of your father and his *conscience.* Progress must be made. Your father would have ruined it."

"And what was Sophia?"

"Collateral damage." She showed no emotion, as if taking the life of my sister was nothing but a means to the advancement in her lust for power.

"She didn't deserve to die. I heard what you said to her. You could have walked out of my house and left her alive. If you had shown some compassion, then all this might be more acceptable. But you murdered my family out of jealousy."

She swiped her hand out and cleared the cabinet of its picture frames. Snarling at me she hissed through her teeth. "I could not leave any witnesses who might identify me. Had I known that you were home, I would have put the gun to your head and watched it explode and smear the walls. Do you know what it's been like, watching you day in, day out and have this weight over me, smothering me, waiting to see if you remembered? You stupid little girl, you should have kept your mouth shut."

I edged closer to her, my hands trembling. "And now I know... I'm going to shout it from the rooftops for everyone to know what a vindictive, jealous, and bloodthirsty bitch you really are. You will pay for what you did."

"Try it, little girl, and we shall see who gets caught in the crossfire." Her lips curled up into a sadistic smile as my eyes widened.

"I don't have anything left to lose, Theresa... give it your best shot."

She chuckled. "Are you sure about that, Alana? Do you seriously not think that I know all about your boyfriend and all those strings he pulled to get himself here?"

I froze and saw a look of pure pleasure in her eyes.

She knew about Daniel. I had to warn him and make sure he got out okay.

She leaned into me, and I smelled her breath, felt the heat of it against my face. Her voice was low as she said, "I am going to enjoy letting him watch you be executed. Or should I let you watch me put a gun to his temple and blow his very knowledgeable brains all over the place?"

And with that image at the forefront of my mind, the layer of calm evaporated, leaving me in an undiluted rage that I could no longer hold back. The palm of my hand connected with her face before I could stop it and left a nice red welt on her face. She staggered back from the force of it before lashing out.

I ducked, using my youth and speed to dodge as she tried to land another blow. I balled up my fist and punched her in the stomach. She cried out, and I kicked her knee. That's when she buckled, her knees hitting the ground. I pushed the chairs aside and knew I had to kill her. It was now my job to protect Daniel.

Raising my fist, I was ready to hit her again when she glared up at me and screamed, "Someone, please help me... she's trying to kill me." And then she grinned as the door smashed open. Theresa balled herself up in the corner like a victim. I was tackled into the desk by a guard. Struggling against the weight of him, I tried to buck out, kicking backwards so he would let me go.

The guard was too strong. I was caught. As another guard helped Theresa to her feet, I could only listen as she lied, telling them I attacked her without cause or reason.

"She's lying! She killed my parents," I screamed, and my heart stopped as the guard leaned in and whispered, "We know and we don't care."

I let a battle cry echo throughout the office and into

the hallways, but it was wasted because I couldn't break free. I had broken my promise. They would all die because of me. I had to warn them—somehow—I had to warn them.

Theresa straightened herself, stepped forward and backhanded me across the face. It burned, but I would not let her see me cry. Never would I let her have that satisfaction. As soon as I got back to my cell, I would get Jayson to pass a message to Daniel.

"It seems, Miss McCarthy, that you are too much of a problem for me. Take her to Treatment and wait for me before you begin. I want to watch her become a shell before I take her life on Friday. Not a word to the doctor... I will handle him."

I screamed in frustration, and Theresa said something so familiar that it was as if I were back there on that night. That's when I realized the man holding me was there too.

"Jesus, will you just shut her up already... can't you just knock her out?"

The guard laughed in my ear. "With pleasure."

I braced myself, waiting to feel the brunt of his gun on the back of my head. Instead, a hand suddenly clasped over my nose and mouth, a foul smelling cloth made me feel dizzy and nauseous. My last thought, before I sank into darkness, was a plea for Daniel to forgive me.

ALANA

"The policy is set and we are never turning back.
It's time for execution; time to execute."
(30 SECONDS TO MARS: R-EVOLVE.)

REGAINING CONSCIOUSNESS SLOWLY, MY MIND WAS FOGGY,
my throat dry. Uncontrolled coughing distracted my
thought process for a minute as I tried to sit up. My hands
and feet were shackled to the chair. Not unlike a dentist's
chair, it reclined at an angle so I was looking at the ceiling,
but only when I tilted my head could I look from side to
side. If I raised my head, I could see in front, but the view
was restricted. I tried to squirm against the cold bite of
metal that enclosed my hands and feet. Instead, I turned
my head to take in my surroundings.

I was trapped inside a glass-like box secured in the
centre of the floor. All around me, people in white coats
moved quickly and avoided glances at me in my glass
cage. Scientific equipment was everywhere, but I didn't
know all the names. Some people had blank stares into
monitors and were typing so fast I can barely see their
fingers move on the keys. I presumed they were some sort
of data input staff.

My arm hurt as I stretched, spotting a tube attached
to it in the crease of my elbow. A monitor beeped to my
left, but I didn't understand anything displayed on it. A
number of wires were hidden beneath my vest, and I
followed them as they snaked out from my body and into
the end of the beeping machine.

Instinctively, I swallowed and licked my lips while

calling out to a group who passed by the cube. "Can someone help me, please?" My voice echoed in the cube bouncing back to my own ears.

The people scattered as I twisted in the seat, relentlessly trying to escape. I froze as one side of the cube slid open and Theresa Lane stepped inside with me, the door sliding shut behind her with a clicking sound. Wearing a white coat over her uniform, she looked like any other lab tech. I squirmed again as the restraints chaffed against my skin.

"You have no way to escape, Alana. If I were you, I'd enjoy the last few minutes you have as yourself. In a while, you will be a mindless slave who will gnaw off her own arm to please me."

"You won't get away with this… if not me, someone else will expose you."

She dismissed me with the wave of her hand. "Darling, there won't be anyone around left to tell your story. Once I get rid of you, I will deal with your precious Daniel. He is quite attractive, and it's a shame to destroy someone so intelligent and good looking, but he has deceived me and has written his own fate."

I struggled to think… to try and come up with something, anything that would make her stop, even for a short time. "I wrote everything down. If anything happens to me, I have given instructions for that information to be forwarded to your superiors. If you do this, you will be caught one way or another."

Theresa scowled at me. "You're bluffing."

I let a smirk curl my lips. "Are you willing to take that chance?"

"Tell me who has the documents or where they are, and I may let you live as yourself for your last twenty-four hours."

My head shook side to side. She had no way to know

240

that I was bluffing, and it was more important than ever that I keep my cards close to my chest until I was out of options. "No chance, Theresa. You would just kill them. They already know every single gory detail and sin you have committed. You better keep an eagle eye out for whoever might decide to slip the information into Grand Master Johnson's pocket tomorrow."

I couldn't be certain of the time of day, but from the shadows that leapt along the walls, I suspected I'd been knocked out for some time. More than likely, it was early morning, and I really was running out of time.

"Tell me something, Theresa. Was it all worth it? Killing my parents? Shooting my baby sister in the chest? Veronika's death? All those who died before and will die for your chance to play God?"

She dragged a metal chair along the floor, the legs screeching against it. I wished I could cover my ears. Setting the chair down next to mine, she faced me and sat, crossing her right leg over her knee and resting her hands in her lap.

"Well, I'll tell you a story, Alana, so you might understand why the Treatment is so very important."

I nodded, just wanting to prolong things and pray that someone came to my rescue.

"Cormac and I, and a few of our other students, who are now all wardens throughout the prison, came up with the idea during one of our study sessions. If we could create a serum, a drug that could control those primitive and primal actions of those most likely to reoffend, or those far too dangerous to be let loose on society, we could help the world by wiping them out altogether.

We planned it out, using scientists to assist and measure what would be needed to take the violent urges from offenders and make them comply, allowing us to adapt them for useful purposes.

Much as antidepressant medication raises the levels of Serotonin and Noradrenaline in the brain, our own serum would decrease the parts of the brain more inclined to cause a violent outburst and so on.

But after we tested the serum on animals, we found that it had an amazing side effect. We injected a rabid dog with the serum. Overnight his behaviour modified. He became docile and obedient. When instructed to attack, the animal did so, and when he was commanded to stop, the dog halted his attack."

My dad had been part of this? That's disgusting and vile. How could my dad have been part of this? Did I ever know him at all?

"You see," Theresa continued, ignoring the look of disgust on my face, "the next logical step was to test the serum on humans. So we offered some of the violent death row inmates a chance to live. They gave us permission to test them in exchange. Should the serum work on them, they would be given new identities and allowed back into society."

"They signed their own death warrants."

Theresa uncrossed her leg and then crossed her left leg this time. "They all knew the risks, Alana. They would have been executed regardless. We presented them with an opportunity for redemption."

"How many survived?" I asked.

"None. We tried repeatedly to figure out why the tests had been successful on animals but would not work on human subjects. Finally, one of the scientists suggested it was because the brain and its thought patterns had already been carved out and could not be changed. He informed us that if we performed the experiment on children or teenagers whose brains were still learning, they could be changed.

Cormac was appalled and refused to continue any

further. We had invested a lot of time and research money, and I was not about to fall short at the final hurdle. Cormac refused to listen to reason and his life was forfeited because of it."

She really was a psycho, believing that she had a right to mess with people's heads for the greater good. Dear God, how far would she go to prove a point?

"It would be so much better, don't you think? You wanted to be a soldier all along. Can you not see the benefits of having something replaced and disposable at your beck and call? Instead of sending a young man with a wife and children in to diffuse a bomb, send in a convicted criminal. No one cares if they live or die."

"Their families care. They are somebody's daughter, son, sister or brother. No matter what you say, nothing will convince me that what you are doing is just. You are nothing but a killer with more blood on your hands than most of the inmates in here."

She rose to her feet. "That may be true, but in years to come I will be remembered for my brilliance and resilience. You will fade from memory as the last of the people you knew either die or forget you."

I frowned but refrained from adding to her rant.

"Veronika's brain was too damaged for the serum to work. I've seen the experiments on her brain after her death. She was flawed. Her brain had already latched onto her psychotic nature, unwilling to change. But you, dear, may be the answer. I am witness to how strong your mind is. It shielded you until you were strong enough to accept what had happened. You will be my greatest achievement. Even in death, Cormac is helping the program's development, and I will see that he is held in reverence for it."

With her back to me, Theresa strutted over to the door, and it automatically slid open. She beckoned a scientist forward, and I eyed the woman, my eyes pleading with her not to do this.

"Theresa, please don't do this."

She shot me a sarcastic look over her shoulder, and I witnessed the madness in her eyes. "Last chance to save those who have helped you, Alana. Give me the names, and I will spare their lives."

I shook my head and clamped my mouth shut in exaggerated defiance. She might take me down, but I would not take the others with me. Theresa sighed and waved the woman forward.

"Goodbye, Alana. It was quite an experience knowing you." And with that, she vanished. A feral scream ripped from deep inside me. The woman entered the cube, and the door closed behind her, sealing us in.

My life was almost gone, and I was about to lose everything. At that moment, I realized what I had: Daniel, Connors, Jayson, even Afsana, the people who had tried to help me. They'd tried to make me see that losing my family didn't mean I had lost everything. They had all sacrificed so much for me, and now I could not repay them for it.

I would never hold Daniel again or feel my body heat under his gaze as those blue eyes drank me in. The thought of never kissing those lips, hearing his laugh or basking in the safety of his arms almost brought me to tears.

In frustration, I cried out again and squeezed my insides. Bucking against the restraints was useless. During the past year, I'd experienced a lot of emotions... grief, loss, guilt, anger, love, but through it all, I'd never felt as hopeless as now while I awaited my fate. I prayed for the first time in my life, that if there were a God, he would spare me, vowing I would never ask anything of him again.

The woman in the lab coat reached my chair and remained standing, blocking Theresa from my line of sight as she surveyed from outside. My eyes searched for an ounce of compassion in the woman, but most of her face was concealed by a mask, and her eyes were devoid of any emotion. All my hopes of dignity were dashed as I pleaded with her and begged her to let me go, to stop whatever she was doing. I could only watch as she filled a syringe and tapped my vein.

Closing my eyes, I saw Daniel, my Daniel, with eyes the colour of clear skies and a smile to drive me insane. I held onto the image of him for dear life. If I had to die, then I would do so thinking of him.

"Alana, whatever I say, do not indicate that I am speaking to you, understand? Blink once for yes, twice for no."

I hesitated when she spoke and opened my eyes... blinking once and staring at the woman. She was fairly normal looking, someone who would not stand out in the crowd. Most people would skim over her in a crowd unless they were looking for her in particular. Round face and small eyes with dark hair that framed her face. She had a slightly crooked nose, and her lips were pursed in a serious line.

"When I push the syringe into your arm, I need you count to fifteen, then convulse. Make it look good or Theresa will be suspicious. I'm putting my ass on the line here, so do not mess it up. I need you to convulse for about thirty seconds and then let your eyes roll back in your head and pretend you are unconscious. Do you understand?"

I blinked once and the woman kept talking softly through the mask. "Then I will inject you with a sedative that will pass their tests to make sure you really are out of it. They will take you back to your cell and wait to see if the serum has taken hold. You remember how Veronika was, right?" I blinked. "Good, they will expect that of you too... having tried to use suggestion while you sleep to induce a walking, talking zombie. Knowing Theresa, it will be the same thing she used on Veronika. You will have to pretend not to know any of your friends. Don't be friendly with the guards. You have to act as if the serum has worked, at least until Grand Master Johnson's lecture."

"Why?" I exhaled, needing to know why she would take such a big risk for me.

"You mean why am I helping you?" I blinked once. "Your father was a good man, an honest man. When I advised against using Treatment on children, he listened and ended up dead. Are you ready for this?" I blinked once again, and she gave me a weak smile.

"While you're asleep, I will be removing the be-haviour chip. You won't feel a thing when I'm doing it 'cause you'll be out cold. But you might have a little dis-comfort when you wake. Try not to let it show. And I'm afraid you'll have a scar... unnecessary if I had more time to remove it, but I don't. I hope you're a good ac-tress, Alana, for all our sakes."

Why would she be taking out my chip? I watched as she stuck the needle in my arm and the plunger emptied whatever she put into my system. Counting to fifteen in my head, I bucked against the restraints. The metal cuffs scratched my skin and burned as I pretended to convulse. But the pain only made me feel more alive. My desire to live was strong. I concentrated so hard on convulsing that I almost forgot to count to thirty before I let my eyes roll back in my head and closed them, lying still in the chair.

"Good girl... I'm going to put you under now, Alana. It's up to you now, honey. By the way, Daniel sends his love."

My saviour had whispered in my ear before I felt the prick of the needle in my arm. The grogginess washed over me, and I struggled to remain awake. I needed to make sure that the woman told the truth, that I wasn't being set up. My eyes remained closed, but I heard the slide of the door and then Theresa's voice.

"Is it done? Did it work?" Theresa's voice was frantic and strained.

"When she wakes, we will know. Right now, we can only observe to see if she reacts in the same way as Veronika." The woman was still talking, but I was slipping fast and couldn't hold on as sounds became gargled. Soon, I lost myself to the drug, letting it pull me under.

DANIEL

"Now that I know what I'm without, you can't just
leave me.
Breathe into me and make me real."
(EVANESCENCE: BRING ME TO LIFE)

SHE REALLY WAS AMAZING. I HAD BEEN OBSERVING HER SINCE
she had woken up yesterday. Alana had portrayed
Theresa's perfect zombie soldier. She walked around
pretending not to know anyone or anything. At first I
was afraid that my helper had gone back on her promise
to aid us because Alana was doing such a good job. She
even had me fooled.

Admittedly, I had flown into a panic when Connors
told me that Theresa had baited Alana, and she had
snapped. I had been ready to march in on my white
horse and try and save the day, but Connors reminded
me that my Alana was not some damsel in distress who
needed saving. From the way she was handling things, I
knew she wasn't, and the tragedy that followed her like a
shadow would not break her. She wouldn't let it.

Today was the day, the one we had been working
up to since Alana first ended up here. My plan had slotted into place, and once Grand Master Johnson gave his
speech, it would begin, and we would be free. I had bar-
gained with the devil, but he had come through.

You see the thing with my dad was that Jameson
Costello could not back down from sticking it to the Parliament. They were the people who had sent him to the
Free Islands of Australia. With his contacts, Alana and I
had a second chance there. And maybe, just maybe, so

248

did me and my dad.

The morning had arrived. Inmates were forced to get up early. Breakfast was a quick rush of jamming as much food as possible down your throat before the guards shifted you from your seat. They ordered you to help them move all the tables from the floor of the mess hall. A wooden stage had been erected underneath the viewing room where Theresa Lane surveyed her kingdom from above.

Neither Connors nor I could get Alana on her own. Since her confrontation with the warden, she had been closely monitored for signs of degradation. But like a trooper, Alana carried on, and Theresa watched. The inmates cleared away the tables and spread out the chairs, all lined up in neat little rows.

Prisoners would all sit in sections by their colours, death row inmates in front. Jayson knew his job. Our business arrangement was a strange one. I had learned that his sister's foster family had left England for the Free Islands months ago and had promised to take him with us when we went so he could find his sister. I knew where she was but would guard that secret until he held up his end of the deal and we were out of here.

Yes, I was indeed plotting a prison break. But how could we escape one of the most secure facilities in the world? With a lot of help, that's how.

Around midday, all the inmates had gathered together in the mess hall, taking their places. The staff was to be seated next to the stage along a line that would face the inmates directly. That way we could watch out for potential threats to the warden's image of administrating the most secure section of the prison.

I pushed away from the archway where I'd been leaning and stepped forward until I paused long enough to slip an envelope in Connors' pocket and move on. We didn't look at each other and had said only what was necessary last night when he had come to my office to discuss our final plans. The phone calls and the final plans were made with Connors there to witness it. He knew all that I knew... just in case anything went wrong.

When I was about to take my seat, suddenly the warden appeared in front of me. We stared at each other for a brief moment. Alana had been right, that smug expression on her face really did need to be smacked off.

"I am sorry that your experiment had to be cut short, Dr Costello. Although Miss McCarthy has indeed taken well to Treatment, it remains to be seen whether the need for execution is necessary now. Perhaps the Grand Master will study my work and approve Treatment to replace the death penalty. It would be a glorious thing, would it not, to have a hand in the creation of a better world?"

I smiled. "It is such a shame, Warden, and I now have no reason to remain here. My professor has requested that I take my internship in America. I will be leaving as soon as the Grand Master's visit is done."

"It is a shame to see you go, but we must do what is best for our careers. I'm glad you understand that." And then she turned and sauntered off, disappearing outside the door. I let out a sigh of relief while taking my seat. My eyes wandered throughout the inmates who were already seated until they found the inmate I sought.

Alana sat ramrod straight, her eyes staring dead ahead, empty and void of emotion. She must have felt my gaze because her eyes drifted slightly in my direction. For only a second, we held a glimpse of each other. It held so much promise, love, and trust. In an instant, she became the perfect zombie again. I looked at my watch and began to count down the minutes.

The door that Theresa had vanished through burst

open, and she entered, walking next to an aging man. He sported a full head of greying hair, the same as his moustache, and he wore the Parliament's navy colours, an array of medals decorating his snugly fit jacket. He was slightly smaller than he appeared in pictures, but his height might have been compromised by the round belly. He nodded as the warden spoke to him, her fingers lightly touching his arm. A full-scale team of bodyguards followed him, dressed in navy suits and earpieces.

The Grand Master took the stage while the inmates sat like perfect angels. Theresa found her seat a few people away from me, and I caught her peering at Alana to see if her prized possession still functioned.

The Grand Master tapped the microphone twice, then cleared his throat and began to speak. *Here we go... zero hour.*

"Warden, staff, and inmates, thank you for greeting me with such enthusiasm and respect." Clueless eyes blinked back at him, so he continued. "When I first conceived the idea of using a stricken country for something so unique and redeeming, I never thought that it would be such a success. But every time I hear the story of how an inmate was educated and returned into society to become part of the people they may have hurt before, I am filled with an overwhelming joy. This prison and the inmates are all part of a unique family dynamic."

A loud snort sounded with a few snickers of laughter, but William Johnson seemed unfazed.

"Despite the hardships of your past, most of you young men and women will eventually be released. I, like any educator, want to see you succeed in life and become who you were meant to be, not what circumstances forced you to be."

Still no response from the crowd, guards, or inmates.

"We must also acknowledge those who have made

the most impact on your life and remember those who worked tirelessly so you would indeed have futures. Cormac McCarthy had been a strong advocate to dissolve the Death Penalty for children, especially for those who may have been redeemed."

Alana didn't as much as flinch when Johnson mentioned her dad's name, so I did it for her.

"But the Parliament and the Court of Justice would not set out these policies if it were not necessary and—"

"I have a question?" Jayson raised his hand, his face full of mischief... he was going to enjoy himself.

Johnson's expression remained stoic, but he nodded for Jayson to continue.

Jayson rose to his feet. "How do you decide who is redeemable and who isn't?"

"A very good question, young man. We have very clear guidelines on how to determine if a candidate for execution truly deserves it."

"And do you look at individual cases and review them or just let your wardens decide who should live or die?"

The noise in the room was beginning to elevate, and Jayson fed off it, attention seeking prat that he was.

"Take me, for example. I stole meds for my sick sister because our mom died, and I had no money to feed us... so I stole. I then accidently ran into an old man who fell, hit his head and died. I didn't mean for him to die. How could I have even known he'd be there? But he did, so do I deserve to die for an accident?"

The Grand Master was flummoxed. "Well, I... I..."

But Jayson wasn't done. "And take my little friend here." He pointed at Afsana, who wore a horrified, pale face. "Take this girl... her crime was deciding to stop off at a market on her way home and pick up some supplies for a school project. A bomb went off and instead of actually doing what they were trained to do, your members of the United Army chose to make her a scapegoat. The real killers got away. Have you even seen her case?"

The warden paled as shouts from the inmates supported Jayson. She beckoned for guards to go to Jayson, but The Grand Master held up his hand.

"Are you trying to tell me that you feel unjustly wronged?" he asked.

Jayson flashed his most charming smile. "Hell, yeah. You claim that the Court of Justice works in our favour, but who listens to us? Who actually sits there with us and goes through the facts? I don't deserve to die for what I did, even though I have to live with what happened for the rest of my life. In here, I feel it every day." Jayson pointed to his head and his heart. "How can you say that your vision has paved the way for a better world when sixty percent of us in here are victims of your corrupt perceptions?"

The din in the hall rose and the Grand Master lost control of the crowd. Jayson jumped up on his chair and started to shout. "We demand to be counted… we demand to be heard." It was a tad melodramatic, but it seemed to rally the troops. The inmates joined in with Jayson's chant, and I delighted in seeing the warden's face turn purple with rage.

The Grand Master bent down and whispered in the ear of one of his security team and tried to speak into the microphone once more. "Young man… if you all would just quiet down for a moment, I am willing to hear you all out. Please, there is no need for this."

Theresa barked orders to the guards, and Connors moved into place, going to stand in front of Jayson and Alana and to block Jayson from her. But that was all part of the plan. Alana suddenly burst into action, giving Connors an elbow in the gut and pulling his gun free. None of the guards knew how to react because they all assumed Alana had been neutralized by Treatment.

She leapt up on the stage, shielded herself with the body of the Grand Master and raised the gun in the air. The sound of gunfire ripped through the room and stilled everyone... Theresa Lane scrambled to get to the stage, but her own security team held her back. The entire room quieted and watched as the audible sound of a gun being cocked echoed throughout the room. My girl pressed the gun to the back of the man's neck. She said something, and he leaned in. His own security team inched forward, but the Grand Master held up his palm to stop them.

He leaned in closer as Alana again whispered in his ear. His eyes widened in surprise and narrowed in suspicion. It appeared that the Grand Master listened to Alana's story. She'd summed it up in five minutes before Theresa Lane screamed for someone to help him.

When she finished, Alana stepped back, and I saw an expression of relief wash over her. She had her revenge; the Grand Master knew our story. Theresa Lane would suffer. Alana didn't have to become a monster like Theresa.

Grand Master Johnson stared open-mouthed at Theresa. She forced a smile while saying, "William, I can explain."

He yelled for someone to detain Theresa, but the noise rose up again in the room, and his words became garbled. Alana remained on the stage, and I moved closer to her, eager to follow the plan and get her to safety.

The inmates began to riot and many fought against the guards. Connors dragged Jayson down from his chair and pushed him and Afsana forward. The girl was vital for our plan to succeed. Alana made to move away from the stage as I inched nearer her, dodging inmates and guards while prisoners scrambled to get hold of the devices that could set off their behaviour chips. I grinned in glee when Theresa yanked out her computer as she pushed free of her bodyguards, trying relentlessly to key in Alana's code and screaming in frustration when it would not work. I had covered all the bases.

Connors managed to free Jayson and Afsana, and they waited only yards away for me and Alana to join them. Once Alana was with us, the plan was to go to my office and Afsana would set off a small explosive, knocking out the office wall. It was our escape route. Most of the perimeter guards would have left their posts and come to help out with the riot. They were probably on their way now. Our outside helpers would take care of the rest.

We were inches apart, me and Alana, so much so that I could almost reach out and touch her fingers as she moved to the end of the stage ready to step off and into my arms. I guess some things are just never meant to be.

Alana's eyes showed terror as they become huge before I had a chance to react. The cold metal of a gun pressed against the side of my head while people rushed around me. All I could see was her, my Alana.

I knew all along that a plan this in-depth would have its variables. That was why I had contingency plans. Theresa Lane stood there, holding the gun to my head. Since Alana had taken everything from her, she planned to do the same to Alana.

"You and your little bitch have ruined it all. I should have put a bullet in her when I had the chance, but you can die knowing she will have to watch me pull the trigger."

I smiled and held Alana's stare. In that brief moment, I saw the life I had lived with her and the life we could have had. Our time together had been cut short... like all those other great love stories. We'd known true love, and our sacrifices were made so we could be free. It was epic love, filled with everything needed for a grand love story—drama, lust, loss, bravery, and a villain. We had it all. Unfortunately, all the really special love stories have a tragic end.

"She will survive, Warden. You can believe that. You cannot kill that much strength and beauty. I'll see you in hell, Theresa."

My lips moved, and I mouthed *I love you* to Alana while Theresa cocked the gun, pushing the barrel deeper into my skull. Pain exploded in my head before a moment of quiet and then...

ALANA

"I tried so hard and got so far, but in the end, it
doesn't even matter
I had to fall to lose it all but in the end it doesn't
even matter."
(LINKIN PARK: IN THE END)

I PRESSED THE GUN INTO THE BASE OF WILLIAM JOHNSON'S
neck and angled my body so I was protected from
anybody who might want to take a shot at me. Sweat
broke out on the Grand Master's neck and dripped down
below his shirt collar.

"Sir, I mean you no harm. My name is Alana McCarthy, Cormac's daughter. He wanted you to know something."

Grand Master Johnson held up a hand, halting his
bodyguards who were inching forward. They poised
themselves to strike, but this was my last chance, and I
had to take it.

"I need you to know I did not kill my family. Theresa Lane did. She killed my dad because he was about
to send you documentation regarding Theresa's experiments. She called it Treatment.

She wanted to use it on children and teens and see if
she could manipulate their brains into becoming soldiers,
mindless disposable soldiers. My dad was an honourable
man and would not do that to children, so she murdered
my whole family to cover up her crime. Please do not let
her tarnish your vision. My dad believed in rehabilita-
tion, that most people could be redeemed. If you don't
act, my family will have died in vain."

Theresa screamed out for someone to save the Grand Master, and I took a step back. I had done it... my part was complete... and I scanned the crowd for Daniel so I could follow him. When I finally found him, he was making his way towards me. My heart skipped a beat. We did it. Freedom was possible.

I stood there in disbelief as Theresa slipped out from behind her guard. Daniel froze when Theresa held a gun to the side of his head. He didn't appear frightened, only calm. I saw her mouth move as Theresa sneered at him, but Daniel focused on me.

My heart raced, and despite the noise and chaos raging on around me, I could not hear a sound. It was as if my head had been submerged in water and all noise ceased. Daniel said something to Theresa and her eyes flared with anger. That's when I read Daniel's lips. He said *I love you* to me. The gun boomed, and the bullet ripped through Daniel's head, and I watched him crumple to the ground in a bloody mess.

"Daniel!" I screamed and dived off the stage and shortened the distance between Theresa and me. I would kill her. She had taken everything from me and deserved to rot in hell for it. I raised the gun in my hands and took aim, fury overtaking me. Blinded by a red mist of grief and loss, I set my sights on Theresa Lane.

She pointed her gun at me, and I braced myself the inevitable. My feet were still moving, my heart pounding. Jayson stepped into my line of vision and stopped me. He raised a gun and fired. I wailed in agony, more for Jayson than at Theresa's death as her lifeless body hit the ground next to Daniel's. Jayson had taken away my chance for vengeance. I could no longer make her suffer. Her death had been too quick, too easy, and now I had nothing to hold onto.

"You're not a killer, Alana. I had to do it."

I heard the words, understanding the sound of his voice, but I wanted to be free of it. My eyes drifted down to look at the boy who had fought so hard for me to remember him. He'd given me love and friends and a chance at a second life. Where sparkling blue eyes used to be, now lifeless ones stared at nothing in particular.

Having lost so much, how could I lose more? This feeling, this emptiness, this numbness, I couldn't live with it for the rest of my life. It would haunt me. My past would follow me like a disappearing ghost. Then, just when I felt the slight pang of happiness, the ghost would reappear and bring with it all the nightmares of my past.

Without notice, I was knocked to the ground. I hadn't even realized I had done it, but while absorbed in my own dark thoughts, I had slowly brought the gun to my own temple and readied it to fire. There I was... looking up into the tear-stained face of Chris Connors. He shook me hard, and I started to cry.

"Don't you dare... don't you fucking dare. Danny did not die so you could wallow in grief and take the coward's way out. We stick to the plan, McCarthy. It's what Danny would have wanted."

Connors got up, pulling me with him. One hand wrapped around my arm, and he dragged me through the throngs of people who'd scattered, moving out of our way. I peeked over my shoulder and saw the Grand Master being escorted through a door at the opposite end of the room. He vanished without another glance.

The door closed behind us as Jayson led a sniffling Afsana towards Daniel's office. Connors refused to let me go. I couldn't think and didn't want to. None of this was worth it without him.

Connors barred the door behind us and eased off me. He took long strides over to Daniel's desk and used his other gun to break the lock. I watched in a daze as he grabbed some things from the desk drawer and put some of them in his pocket. He tossed a bag to Afsana.

"Come on, girl. You know what to do."

Afsana nodded and knelt on the ground. She had containers and tubes with solutions in her hand and mixed it all together. I stared in silence as she did it, then she told everyone to stand back and cover their ears. We did and she pitched a tube at the window. It exploded in a tremendous orange blast. Even with my ears covered, they still rang.

We edged towards the ledge and peered out. I glanced at the wall and noticed a gate had been left unattended. Our escape. Daniel really had thought of everything. It was a short drop down, but still a drop. Connors said it wouldn't hurt if we landed right.

Jayson grinned and said, "See all you suckers below." And he simply walked out into the air. I saw him hit the grass and roll. He got up and brushed off his pants and shouted up to us. "It's not that high, trust me."

Connors motioned for me to go next and I did, stepping off the ledge as Jayson had done, landing with my feet on the ground easily. Once in the grass, I scanned around, half expecting for someone to catch us, but no one came. Jayson held out his arms and caught Afsana, who, with a gentle nudge from Connors, was next. My tall friend followed and fell much like Jayson had, rolling in the grass until the momentum ceased.

Once on his feet again, we all ran for the gate, nobody looking back. A shot rang out, and Jayson cried out as Afsana hit the ground, but we didn't stop. The rest of us slipped through the open gate. A car idled just outside and a window rolled down. A man in a balaclava sat behind the wheel.

"You Jimmy's kid?" he asked Connors, who shook his head.

"He didn't make it," Connors replied before opening the back door and shoving me inside. Jayson slid to the other side, and Connors jumped in the front. The driver sped off, and I cast my gaze back and watched as the walls of the prison slowly blurred in the distance.

We were all sombre, and the driver never spoke until we went farther into the outskirts of the city border along a winding road. We finally came to a stop by a small pier where a massive container ship awaited us. Connors thanked the driver as we got out.

Connors stripped down to his boxers, right there, and cast his uniform aside. He pulled on jeans and a rust coloured jumper and ushered us towards the ship. After speaking to the captain, we were escorted to a small cabin to wait until the ship set sail.

"Where are we going?" I croaked, my voice hoarse.

"Danny got in contact with Jameson and secured us passage to the Frec Islands. It'll take a couple of weeks, but we will get there. Jameson is meeting us at the boat with new identities and a place to stay."

I blinked back tears, feeling very much alone and already missing Daniel. Connors dropped something into my hand and then handed me a letter.

"Danny said to give this to you if he didn't make it out."

Clutching the box and the letter to my chest, I stood in disbelief of the past few hours. Below us, the roar of an engine came to life, and the ship shuddered. I held my breath as it inched away from the pier, waiting, half expecting someone to come and drag us back for execution. But no one did.

After an hour of silence, my two companions drifted off to sleep. I poked my head out our cabin door and asked if I could go above deck. With permission, I climbed the ladder and was greeted by the smell of salt water and wind. The ship had a large open deck, and I walked to the stern and sat on one of the ledges.

Carefully, I opened the letter and clasped my hand over my mouth at the sight of Daniel's handwriting. Tears blurred my vision, but I blinked them away so I could read Daniel's last words to me.

Alana,

If you are reading this, then I'm sorry that I've left you alone. But know that I love you and that has never changed. We did our best, my love, but now you must carry on and live the life that I envisioned for you.

I know it hurts, but in time you will be able to think of me and not feel sad. Hopefully, you'll look back at the time we had together and smile. That's okay. It's fine to move on. All I ever wanted for you was to be happy.

So I need you to do something for me, my beautiful, fiery girl. Move on. Take advantage of your second chance. Don't be afraid to fall in love again because if you do, he is the luckiest damned man alive to be worthy of your love. Do not use my death as an excuse. You deserve to love and be loved in return.

Now I know you won't forget me, but I have left you something that I should have given you a long time ago. Had things gone as I had planned, I would be there now on bended knee asking you to be my wife. There was never anyone else for me, Alana. Never.

Do not live as if you are a widow. You are not. Our love may have been an epic love that ended in tragedy, but the love of your life still awaits you. Think of me when you read Tolkien or poetry that reminds you of how tragic the world can be. Remember me for all the good times we had, and try and leave the bad memories alone. They will only bring you darkness. You need to bask in the sunlight.

Look after Connors for me. He is the brother I always wanted. We had each other's backs growing up. Tell him I love him and miss him. Also, tell him I said that he can watch over you, but he must find his own happiness too.

There is another envelope in this letter and it contains all Jayson needs to find his sister. I have also wired all my savings to an account in Australia where Jameson has created new identities for you all.

Alana, my love, all I ask of you is to be happy. Promise me that much. No matter what it is, if it makes you happy, do it. Do not waste a minute of your life on something otherwise. Because in the end, life is far too short.

All my love,
Daniel

I carefully folded the letter and put it back in the envelope before opening the box. Inside was a stunning ring, with a sparkling gold band and a blue stone which shimmered under the evening sun. I took it out, my fingers trembling and slipped it onto my ring finger. It fit perfectly. My heart constricted, and I let the tears flow freely, finally allowing myself time to grieve for Daniel, for Sophia, and for my mom and dad.

When the sun had dipped below the shoreline, I was still sitting on the bench watching the stars twinkle in the sky. I shivered in the chilly air but also rejoiced in it because feeling the cold meant I was alive. Daniel's memory would live on inside me. Someday, I would tell the world of his bravery and love.

Connors found me up on deck and I went with him to the galley for some food. I handed Jayson his letter, and we exchanged smiles. Daniel had come through for us all.

I'm not saying I got over Daniel with the snap of my fingers. For weeks, while we were at sea I was haunted by dreams of him. The most horrible among the nightmares was that he was alive and we'd left him behind. During most of the time on board the ship, I barely spoke or ate. At other times, I screamed and cried until I had no more in me. The weeks dragged, but with every rolling wave, thinking of Daniel hurt a little less.

One day the captain announced we would dock soon. Jayson, Connors, and I stood watching as the ship was guided into port, the glorious sun shining down on us. We gathered our meagre belongings and disembarked.

When we reached the end of the pier, I looked up and froze as if a mirage were coming towards me. Connors kept walking but stopped to shake hands with the man, and I saw him nod. Jayson nudged me forward, and I followed Connors and greeted the man with a handshake.

Jameson Costello was an older version of his son. Tall like Daniel, but harsher, sterner even, Jameson had none of Daniel's warmth. He shook my hand with his strong, calloused ones.

"Alana, my son told me a lot about you," he said." Welcome to the Free Islands of Australia. Welcome to a second chance."

Everyone should be entitled to a second chance, right?

EPILOGUE

"What a shame, what a shame we all remain such
fragile broken things"
(PARAMORE: PART II)

ALMOST A YEAR HAD PASSED SINCE THE EVENTS AT THE
prison. A lot changed. Grand Master Johnson went back
to America and asked for an independent review of how
prisoners were convicted. He also set out legislation for
underage offenders to receive life sentences instead of
the death penalty. Parliament had yet to vote on it, but
it seemed like progress. He also spoke publicly about his
shock at Theresa Lane's actions and professed that he in
no way condoned the use of Treatment on any inmate.
That experiment had been shut down. Or so he said.

He also pardoned me and Jayson, but we still kept
to ourselves. Connors now worked for a private security company, and Jayson found his niche mentoring kids.
He also found that his sister and her foster family had
moved closer to our small village, so they saw each other
frequently.

And me, what about me? I had spent a lot of time
with Daniel's family, his brother, and sisters and their
families. They were really nice people. Having decided
that I had moped around for long enough, Jayson got me
a job where he worked, and I really loved it. Helping kids
was my destiny.

Connors also got himself a girlfriend, one of Daniel's sisters, and they were expecting their first child together. We each had our own cottages on an island with

glorious weather that brought out a faint glow to my skin. Regardless of our own happily ever afters, someone was always missing, my special Daniel, who should have been there to enjoy paradise with us.

I think of him every day and wear his ring around my neck. He was right. Eventually, I learned to think of him and remember the happiness we had brought each other.

A long time ago, I had promised him I would find my happiness. While I wasn't quite ready to date and leave memories of him behind, taking them with me made me a stronger person. An epic love can do that for you. Oh, what an epic love it had been.

ACKNOWLEDGEMENTS

FIRSTLY I HAVE TO THANK ALL THE GIRLS AT CTP! YOU girls are the best ...... Rebecca, Courtney, Marya and Dyan, I cannot thank you enough for allowing me to share Shattered Memories with the world. If Carlsberg made publishing companies, they would all be as awesome as CTP!

Kathleen Lapeyre, Thank you for taking Shattered Memories and making it so much better. I appreciate all I learned from you.

My Parents - For always having faith in me when I rarely had any myself.

LJ and Taylor- For always reminding me how to smile.

Melanie Newton ..... for simply being awesome!

A big thank you goes to the most intelligent man I know, Mr Kenneth Sheehy. Without you I would not have been able to make the background information believable. All the credit for that lies with you.

To my family and friends that stuck by me when my world crumbled down around me and encouraged me to continue writing. I don't need to name names, ye know who ye are.

To my fellow JD1's. You guys are all legends and I love ye all! Thanks for making the past year one of the best of my life.

To the real life Alana McCarthy who allowed me to borrow her name. My Alana came to life because of you and I will be forever grateful for it.

And to the readers, old and new, thank you for all of your support and letting me do what I love.

Author's Note

THE LYRICS USED IN THIS NOVEL ARE MEANT TO ALLOW THE reader to see how the songs inspired me and each chapter in Shattered Memories. I hold no rights for the use of these lyrics. They were simply a muse.

If you liked Shattered Memories and the music that inspired the book, go like their Facebook pages, buy their albums and buy tickets to see them live. And enjoy them, for "When words fail, music speaks."

CPSIA information can be obtained at www.ICGtesting.com
Printed in the USA
LVOW07s0329070515

437293LV00006B/8/P